# EDGAR AND
# THE FLYBOYS

LOUISE GORDAY

Pat,

Enjoy!

Louise Gorday

2021

Book Cover Design by Damonza.com
Formatting by Polgarus Studio

Printed in the United States of America

To John

He loved Poe, cars, and lemon meringue pie

# Also by Louise Gorday

The Pickle Boat House

Bayside Blues

The Clockwise Carousel

The Church at Parkers Wharf

Spirit of the Law

# Contents

# Chapter One
# Setting the Spiritual House in Order

The weather gauge read a steady 87 degrees with 75 percent humidity, and the breeze was rolling in off the river in great hot waves. Yellow jackets swarmed the empty carcasses of half a dozen steamed crabs. Halfway through his third beer and with not a cloud in sight, Ryan Thomas ran a fingernail along the bottle label, absently trying to scratch off Mr. Boh's mustache. Suddenly, he put down the bottle. "One-point-five for the house, all cash. That's five hundred K more than you'll get from anyone else."

Hamelin Russell looked at the somber expression on his neighbor's face. Why did he sense that Thomas was trying to get rid of him? They'd had good times together, although cracking crabs and an ice cold Natty Boh was not one of them. What had he missed? "Three-point-five and water privileges," he countered.

Ryan drained the Boh. "Please, Hamelin. I'm sure you'll agree this isn't working. You need to set out on your own, get out of Maryland and meet other people, have fresh experiences. Your life has to have *purpose*. When they booted you out of the afterlife, they wanted you to work on redemption, not your tan."

"'Booted,' sir?" Hamelin reached over, took the bottle from Ryan's hand and chucked it into the nearby trashcan. "I would hope that is the demon drink talking. Otherwise, I am deeply offended and will seriously consider your offer of four and a quarter plus the water access."

"Dream on, buddy," Ryan said, screwing the top off a new bottle. He stopped a moment, staring at the bottle cap. "Or do immortals not dream? Do you even *sleep,* Hamelin?"

"Of course I sleep. I do everything mortals do. Not that I have to, but keeping the rhythm of the universe makes things run so much more smoothly." Hamelin Russell dipped a club cracker in the plastic cup of vinegar and Old Bay seasoning and swallowed it whole. "See? Yum."

Ryan sighed and shook his head. "Try it with crab next time. What you need is tough love, Hamelin. It's not my responsibility to save you, but here goes. Starting right now, I'm instituting a thirty-day moratorium. Stay away from me and Marie."

Hamelin gave him a quick look. "Has she said something? We've been getting along splendidly at Nonni's. I'm still the only customer in the place who can hand-toss pizza dough."

"Yeah, she told me. Maybe that's because you're the only one she can't keep away from behind the counter. But listen, Hamelin," Ryan said, aiming the bottle cap at the garbage can and missing, "don't you think you have more to offer the world than standing in a pizzeria window and wowing the crowd with your tosser skills."

"*Tosser?*" Hamelin asked, bristling.

"You know what I mean. I'm fairly certain the Weigh Station elders sent you back among the living to perfect more than your pie-making skills."

After respectfully shooing away three wasps, Ryan began rolling up the empty crab shells in the brown paper covering the picnic table. "Like I said, no visits or conversations—not even a friendly shout over the fence. Got it? If you've made progress in expanding your circle of life, we might negotiate things. Your house is that way," he said, pointing at the yellow bungalow on the other side of the hedgerow. He tossed the wad of brown paper in the garbage and headed off with his beer.

"You'll cave," Hamelin called after him.

Ryan never broke stride. He pointed at the bungalow again, then disappeared inside his own house.

Hamelin sat alone with a few yellow jackets that had given up on the tightly sealed garbage can, and watched the blue dredger out on the water, sucking up oysters. How could a mortal understand that a few months, a year, even a decade, had so little meaning to one endowed with everlasting life? Ryan Thomas was hallucinating if he thought he could outwait an immortal. He'd cave. Still, who wanted to live next door to a party pooper?

As a soul runner, Hamelin had done his share of partying over the past seven centuries. The early years—when he was an energetic, I-already-know-everything newbie—were the best. He and his comrades cut a swath of foolishness through the universe as they dutifully transported the souls of the newly deceased into the afterlife. But over time, his friends received final judgment and moved on, leaving him essentially alone, bored, and somewhat depressed as he tried to fathom why he hadn't followed the same trajectory. From there on, he became something of a goof-off, never doing anything quite egregious enough to send him hurtling to a final judgment of perdition, but nothing to crow about, either. Were his sloth-like Nevis ways sending him down an unrighteous path?

He hadn't left Nevis since the Way Station elders had decided to return him to Earth to buff up his soul résumé: good works, kind thoughts, more godliness. He had the means to make it shine—money, time, and the ability to assimilate in both language and custom to any place he chose. Maybe Ryan was right. Perhaps he needed a short vacation to set his spiritual house in order. He ran through an inventory of the many places that had caught his eye at one point or another—not exactly a bucket list, but close enough. Why, he could be gone forever, never to irritate small-minded neighbors again. His gaze wandered to the dredger again, and memories of his and Ryan Thomas's trip to Saint Paul, on the Eastern Shore, came flooding back to him. Settled! He would go east, the direction of the rising sun and new beginnings—maybe say hello to his dear friend Edgar. Edgar had crossed his mind more than once in the past few days. He would have to be discreet, though. He couldn't risk anything that would smack of official business and invoke oversight from otherworldly superiors. In the case of Edgar, that wouldn't do, not at all. For Edgar, or Edgar Allan Poe for those who didn't know him well, was one of Hamelin's mulligans—a dying soul he had given a second life to. And if that were ever revealed to the Weigh Station management, Hamelin would be setting up shop in a place much hotter than the western shore of Maryland on a sweltering July day.

The Station had seeded Hamelin with a pile of cash, which sat in an account at the First National Bank of Nevis—a golden parachute, as his fickle friend Ryan Thomas called it. But that money didn't get him from *here* to *there*. A speedy set of wheels would, but he didn't have any—or a driver's license either. As far as he was concerned, he didn't need permission from anyone to do what he wanted to do. But the car—how did people do that?

He went inside and searched the web for *how to buy a car without visiting a dealership*, and located Jaguar Annapolis, and two hours later, a 1970 Jaguar XKE in British racing green over all-black leather interior was whizzing his way. Oh, modern convenience! Money and a computer could get you anything. In another hour, he hit the road.

Right before the Chesapeake Bay bridge crossing—after a brief breaking in period of stripping gears and drifting across solid yellow lines —Hamelin decided he had things under control. After centuries of slipping in and out of war-torn towns, noisy hospital rooms, and the quiet, comfy bedrooms of the dying, he found it exhilarating to whip in and out of traffic, turning heads and receiving congratulatory beeps.

Traffic congestion eased as he made his way onto the Maryland Eastern Shore. Flat expanses of farmland growing tall, lush corn, mom-and-pop produce stands, and a quick pass through the occasional small town, such as Easton or Trappe, sent a thrill through him. He felt an independence that he had coveted for eons but had never quite achieved. Maybe he should buy waterfront here and let bygones be bygones with his friends in Nevis.

He stopped once at a Maryland Visitors Center and picked up a few travel brochures. *Capture a Maryland Memory. The Old Line State. America in Miniature.* Why, he could be gone forever! Ocean City intrigued him. With one hand on the steering wheel, and an occasional glance up at the road, he skimmed the brochure. He could hit the seashore in an hour and then travel along the shore until he reached Chincoteague National Wildlife Refuge. Wild horses, descended from those aboard a shipwrecked Spanish galleon—now, that sparked his fancy! But the farther he drove, the more a little voice in his head pushed him to set aside any distractions and head straight to Edgar. So he shoved the Chincoteague map in the glove compartment for the return trip, and when he hit Salisbury, he peeled off Route 50 and headed south on Route 13. That would eventually put him on 413 to Crisfield, and the ferry that would bring him to Ewell, the largest island that made up the Smith Island community. Edgar didn't actually live on Ewell, but on a smaller island just to the south. Once Hamelin was on Ewell, he would negotiate through passage.

Much to his chagrin, when Hamelin reached Crisfield, he discovered that the ferries didn't transport cars to the island and that he would have to leave his precious Jaguar behind. He left it straddling two spaces at the back of the city dock parking lot and climbed aboard the ferry *Chelsea Lane Tyler*. With calm air, the water like glass, and the temperature a wonderful eighty-five degrees, he settled in for a peaceful forty-five-minute ride across the Tangier Sound at the southern tip of the Maryland peninsula.

Smith Island was the last of the inhabited Maryland islands in the Chesapeake Bay. If Hamelin applied the half-empty, half-full glass scenario, it could be described as either quaint or failing. The Ewell community that still held on by its fingertips sat clustered on one side of the island, facing out toward the bay. Behind it stretched a deserted islet barely holding its head above water. It was nature's divide-and-conquer strategy—a patch of land here, a bigger inlet of water there. Nature was slowly chopping the island into little bits, and a few more great storms might be all it took to submerge the island for good. Had it looked like this four hundred years earlier when John Smith first came upon it and named it the Russell Isles, the British settlers would no doubt have pushed on past for something more promising. A hundred years hence, it would be no more, taking its waterman's lifestyle, local cuisine, and peculiar Eastern Shore dialect with it.

Hamelin hopped off the boat with two other people. He surmised that the one with the deep tan and the leathery face was a local waterman. The other sported a briefcase and a bit of *GQ* beard scruff— a landlubber if Hamelin ever saw one. He nodded to each as they ended the momentary connection of fellow passengers and set out in search of transportation to Edgar's island.

Classic Chesapeake Bay fishing boats and modern pleasure craft berthed along piers piled high with crab pots and stretching out into the glistening water. Hamelin stopped a moment to watch the undulating water. There was something interesting and powerful about the way deep water moved. Then he took a quick walking tour so he could let Ryan Thomas know he had put his time away to good use. The tour was quicker than quick. He noted a mini-mart here, decks and small food establishments there, and many houses peeling paint and boarded up with plywood. Kayakers were out, and crab pickers at the island co-op were busy. Golf carts were everywhere, but apparently no bridge connected Ewell to Edgar's island. Hamelin arranged a reasonable fare with one of the local boat owners to ferry him across, and was out on the water again within the half hour.

Ryan James had been correct. The thought of surprising old Edgar made Hamelin giddy. Hamelin really did need to get out more. A dinner of island delicacies, and a grand view of this paradise would heal his wounds and soothe his soul. And then, by the waning light, he would sit down with Edgar and read the manuscript he had requested 170 years before. It would all be perfect.

## Chapter Two
# Dark, Foreboding, and Riveting

Number 12 on Haven Road stood by itself at the end of the street—mere feet away from bay water splashing its foundation. The residence connected to the rest of town by a sea of weeds that swept across vacant lots right up to the front steps of what had once been a grand old dame of columns, porch swings, and wisteria. Edgar's house had peeling white paint, missing shingles that suggested stained ceilings, and a decided list to starboard.

Hamelin supposed he should knock. Of course, when transporting souls into the afterlife, he didn't bother with such niceties. The job was a *wham, bam, save or damn* kind of thing—dump the transportee at heaven's gate or hell's doorstep, and then on to the next client. For a moment, he considered the impropriety of walking in unannounced. But the moment passed, and he let himself in.

The back bedroom on the main floor was substantial—a bed, nightstand, chifforobe, and a clothes butler as you walked in, and then room left over for an expansive writing desk under a double window that overlooked the water. An interior fireplace—with a roaring, crackling with fire despite the summer heat outside—shared a wall with the next room. Hamelin found Edgar at the desk, forehead firmly planted on the blotter, one hand gripping a pen, the other caressing a partially filled wineglass.

"Edgar Allan Poe," Hamelin said softly, trying not to startle him. "Good to see you again."

The head slowly lifted. The eyes, no longer clouded by liquor, immediately narrowed as he tried to focus them. Without a blink or a fidget, Edgar said, "I know you, and I rue the day we met. Take it back."

Hamelin pulled back in feigned indignation. "Is that any way to greet an old friend?" He picked a yellow tabby out of a stuffed chair near the fireplace and made himself comfortable, stifling heat be damned. Oh, how he loved the unbridled power of a good fire.

"I believe we've had this conversation before, Edgar, and my response remains unchanged. Doubly so. If ever there was a chance of interfering in your state of affairs before, I'm afraid that's whittled its way down to absolutely none. It seems my responsibilities have changed since we last met, and I have no power to undo what's been done."

Edgar picked up a thin, shiny object from the desk—a letter opener, by the shape—and shook it at Hamelin. "If you had a heart, I'd slice it out and hide it under the floorboards." With that, he threw the opener at him. It whizzed past Hamelin's head and stuck in the wood of the fireplace mantel like a thrown dart.

Hamelin pulled out the quivering metal—intricately fashioned into a miniature sabre with curled enameled guard and leather grip—bent the point back on itself, and tossed it on the braided rug. He was impervious to physical assault, but no need to leave Edgar thinking he could try again. He approached Edgar slowly to avoid any suggestion that he meant to retaliate.

"I see you're still writing," he said as he tried to read but not hover. "How did the story turn out? You promised I could read it when you finished."

Edgar gave him a dark stare, no doubt inventorying any other office items he had that might be used as weapons.

"Edgar?"

With a blink and a grunt, Edgar snapped out of his murderous mindset, pulled a thick three-ring binder from a desk drawer, and tossed it across the desk. "Here," he said, and then produced three more just like it. He pointed to the fireplace. "Knock yourself out. You've got until the premise tumbles into the deep."

Hamelin glanced out the window. *Overlooking* the water was an understatement, he thought as he watched the silky water roll up to within a few feet of the house and break into sprays of white foam that splashed against the foundation. Occasionally, it wet the window glass. And this on a clear day? "When's the last time you had a good storm, Edgar?"

Edgar continued slamming notebooks of various sizes, shapes, and colors onto the center of the desk—a growing pile that, much like the house, was threatening to slide. "And that's another thing. It's *Edgar McKeithan Parsons*, also known as Herbert Kinney, and Nathaniel Christopher. No past, no future. No nothing. It's all your fault, and I suspect there isn't a scintilla of a chance I can atone for all these extra years you've dumped on me. Take it back, I say." He flounced into the fireside chair and put his head in his hands. The mound of notebooks slid to the floor with a *whump*.

Hamelin cocked an eyebrow. This was new. A human who had been given a second chance at life—received the rare honor of being made a mulligan—asking for *death*? Hamelin would be the first to acknowledge that he didn't track with the minds of mortals anymore, but even to an immortal it didn't make sense. Edgar Allan Poe—in Hamelin's mind one of the greatest American writers, pulled from the clutches of death and given another life so that he could finish the crowning achievement of his literary career—courting death? It was crazy absurdism.

He knelt down next to Edgar, put a hand on his arm, and said, "Ed—"

Edgar moaned and jerked his arm away. "You just don't want to."

No, that wasn't it. Since he had been stripped of his soul-runner role and remanded to earth, Hamelin was incapable of escorting Edgar's soul into the afterlife. And even if he did possess the gift, he would still have to think long and hard on it. At the point of Poe's death, Hamelin had allowed the writer's soul to shuffle into the body of a dying bookkeeper, killed in a buggy accident on Maryland's Eastern Shore. And absent a little paperwork for superiors and after some creative bookkeeping, Poe was free to live a second life. A mulligan as it were. Why? Hamelin's reasoning was simple. Poe was on the verge of finishing the pièce de résistance of a spectacular writing career. Why rob him of that?

"I'm sorry, Edgar. But look at all this you've produced since we last met. You're just having an off day. What do you say we take lunch out at one of the local establishments? My treat. A soft-shell crab sandwich and a bowl of crab soup will do wonders."

"Don't ever mention the word 'crab' again. I'm crustaceaned out. At least free me from this sinking backwater."

Hamelin looked around the room. Edgar had accumulated precious few things since October 7, 1849, when Hamelin had delayed his death, allowed his soul to migrate into the recently deceased Edgar Parsons, and made him a mulligan. The decor was nautical—a large brass bell; a small, scale replica of a skipjack, with fine sails, ropes, and detailing; and several hand-carved duck decoys. The furniture looked to be of the mid-1800s.

Edgar wouldn't be too hard to move out. In fact, they could leave everything except a few mementos and the manuscripts.

"You really want that?" Hamelin asked.

"Do fish stink?" Edgar found a loose thread on the chair arm and began pulling out the stitching on the upholstery.

Hamelin looked at the spray hitting the window glass again, and at Edgar's long face. Did it really matter where Edgar wrote? Perhaps Hamelin did owe him a better landing than this. "All right," he said. "We can do that. Do you have a suitcase? Box? Container of some sort that we can pack your things in?"

Edgar picked up the fireplace poker and began rearranging logs, sending a flurry of sparks up the chimney. "Steal my things? I think not." He swung around and thrust the metal rod into Hamelin's midsection. It went through him as if he were mist. As Edgar went for a second swing, Hamelin parried and then jerked it out of his hand. He bent the poker double and tossed it in the fireplace.

"That was a most unfortunate decision," Hamelin said, backing Edgar up into a corner of the room with the force of his will.

Edgar shielded his eyes with the back of his hand. "Mercy. I'm sorry," he said, beginning to blubber. "I don't know what came over me."

Hamelin stood glaring at him for a moment. Just when Edgar looked as if he were going to plead for his life, Hamelin relaxed. "That settles it. If you're going to bite the hand that feeds you, you can't stay here anymore. Besides, your house is sliding into the bay."

Edgar dropped his hand. There was a gleam in his eye. "So you're telling me there's a chance I may drown? Excellent!"

"Oh, Edgar. At least think of all your manuscripts. All your life's work ruined."

Edgar shrugged. "If readers have managed to survive the past hundred seventy years without them, I think they'll make do just fine for another hundred and seventy. No one will care."

"I'll care."

"If you cared, you'd release me from this prison and let me take my knocks. Just sending me somewhere else solves nothing."

"Well, stabbing me, your only current source of salvation, doesn't solve much, either, does it?"

Edgar stood a moment, apparently weighing options. Finally, he hung his head and said, "The suitcases are upstairs."

That was an understatement. *Everything* was upstairs. The door of the bedroom to the right was closed. With great effort, Hamelin managed to muscle it open. The room was stuffed window to doorsill, tin ceiling to wide plank floor, with old furniture, boxes of clothes, and stuffed animals—mostly black birds—as well as stacks and stacks of newspapers. Hamelin saw no luggage. "Oh, dear." He closed the door.

The door to the left was open. This room was somewhat less cluttered, meaning that it had a narrow pathway through the piles and stacks. Somewhere in the past two centuries, Edgar had become a hoarder.

Hamelin sighed wearily. "Suitcases, Edgar?"

Edgar pushed past him and located an old leather-trimmed steamer trunk hidden under a pile of quilts and clothing. "This will do. The bay can have everything else."

It was nonsense, of course. Just Edgar's writing notebooks and manuscripts would fill the trunk twice over. Hamelin poked through the mess until he found a few boxes filled with worthless odds and ends, dumped the contents, and repurposed the boxes. The sun was melting into the Western Shore by the time they finished collecting and stowing

Edgar's good stuff into his golf cart. Hamelin didn't relish keeping an eye on the author in the failing light, but the sooner he whisked the old crank away from this place, the happier and more settled they both would be.

"Key?" Hamelin asked, hand on the front doorknob.

"Now? Without supper?" Edgar looked to the west with a wide-eyed stare. "I should say not. I'm going to stay here tonight, with a hearty meal and a firm bed. Tomorrow is soon enough." With that, he whisked past Hamelin and returned inside.

"Hold on! I thought you wanted to be done with this." Hamelin didn't get the hesitation. Of course, eating was not a necessity for immortals, so he could bend a little on the eating part. "I'll find you something to eat once we're on the road. Popeyes Chicken? Big Mac with supersized fries? Anything that suits your fancy."

"This suits my fancy right here," Edgar said, talking to the inside of the refrigerator. He pulled out cheese, a strange-looking soup with potatoes floating around in it, and a hard stick of what looked like pepperoni or salami.

Hamelin politely abstained. Instead, he summoned patience and watched Edgar eat enough for both of them as Hamelin bemoaned his own inability to control this little slip of a man. He would let Edgar have his way tonight. Tomorrow morning was another story. It would be an early rise.

After supper, Edgar insisted on finishing up what he had been writing. Hamelin supposed it would be a quiet evening with lots of thoughtful staring out the window and copious amounts of bourbon, so he settled in a comfortable chair, closed his eyes, and found a peaceful place within himself. A soft blue glow soon shimmered around him.

As he should have expected, the evening proved to be anything but tranquil. It started with the shuffling of feet, and Edgar's constant rearranging of his chair as if he had a burr in his britches, and it ended with snorts and hawks that shattered Hamelin's aura into thousands of sparkling shards that flashed once and disappeared.

Hamelin cracked an eye open and found Edgar staring at him with a sly grin. Furious writing quickly replaced that, followed by more staring and a cackle. Memories of "The Cask of Amontillado" and "The Tell-Tale Heart" swept through Hamelin. "I'll be outside," he said, and slouched in the golf cart. Poe couldn't physically hurt him, but he needed an emotional break.

When Edgar retired for the night—nodding off to sleep in the middle of his scribbling, a pen still clutched in his hand—Hamelin searched through his collection of writings. With a little effort, he found what he had been hoping for: the manuscript Poe had been working on when Hamelin first came to escort him to heaven, and the very reason Hamelin had given him more time on earth. When Hamelin read its opening paragraphs that night so long ago, he recognized its brilliance and its potential as one of the greatest horror stories of the nineteenth century. And now he had it here before him again. Hamelin stoked the fire and, leafing carefully through the fragile, foxed pages, began to devour the words. The beginning pages were just as he had remembered: dark, foreboding, and riveting.

# Chapter Three

# Abandoning Ship

Hamelin stood at the bedroom window, watching the eastern horizon color up pink and orange beneath the lifting fog that still blanketed the little island world. The local watermen were no doubt awake, but Edgar remained a creature of late nights and even later risings. He shifted his head on the desk several times in search of a more comfortable position, and there might have been a growl or two, but clearly, he wasn't about to seize the day.

"Edgar," Hamelin said. He reached down and nudged his shoulder. "Time to rise."

Edgar's head popped up, and he blinked several times as if orienting himself. He seemed calmer after a good night's sleep. "Is it time?" He got right up, almost eager to start the next phase of his life.

"I read your story last night," Hamelin said, "or at least the first part of it. Where's the rest? If I'm not mistaken, it's no further along than when last we spoke."

"Yes, yes, exactly," Poe said, putting away his pen and closing the journal he had been writing in. "I've been busy with other things."

Hamelin cocked an eyebrow. "One hundred and seventy years is a long time to be sidetracked. Our deal was that you'd get a reprieve to finish the story and then you'd be on your merry way into the afterlife.

One could almost get the feeling you've been milking the system."

As Edgar rooted around in the chifforobe and began changing clothes, Hamelin took up a position just inside the door.

"Don't be ridiculous, Hamelin. I've asked for only one thing since you've been here. Take it back." Edgar tussled with a sleeve button. "Milking the system indeed," he muttered. The button came loose in his hand, and he flung it across the room. He slipped on a dark suit jacket, primped in the mirror, and then presented himself to Hamelin. "I would think this is presentable. Shall we do it inside, or would you prefer to walk out onto the veranda?"

Hamelin raised an eyebrow. *"Do it?"*

"Maybe at the desk, then, eh? That would be fitting." Edgar took a seat, picked up his pen, and flashed a smile, the first spark of humanity Hamelin had witnessed since his arrival.

Hamelin raised both brows. The man looked as if he was ready for Hamelin to take his picture. Physically he looked okay, but mentally? Perhaps Edgar's short-term memory was on the fritz.

"Well?" Edgar said through gleaming pearly-whites and locked jaw.

"Look, Edgar, it's as I explained it last night. I am in no position to take the gift back." What an understatement. To be honest, Hamelin wasn't sure how any of his life was supposed to work now. He had felt so lucky about being booted back to earth and not being thrown into the eternal burning abyss that he hadn't wanted to tempt fate by asking too many questions of his Weigh Station supervisors. Then there was the quick settlement in an ideal location, and a Bill Gates-size bank account. Now he had even more invested in not rocking anyone's boat. If he kept his nose clean, he didn't have to test his limits. "I'm, uh, no longer in that line of employment, and I can't do anything for you."

"You got thrown out of heaven." Edgar's eyes narrowed, followed shortly thereafter by a soft *hmm.*

"What?"

"So this is what angel looks like." Edgar uncapped his fountain pen and began scribbling furiously.

Hamelin ground his teeth together. Accustomed to absolute authority over the souls he transported, he wasn't used to putting up with such nonsense. He shook his head. "No. I'm not an ang— Oh, forget it." The poor fellow was all over the place. "So you thought if you never finished the manuscript, you could live forever? Well, Edgar, you gamed the system and lost. It seems you've outsmarted yourself, my friend."

The happy expression slid off Edgar's face. He looked as if someone had sucked the air out of him, deflating him into a small, floppy sack of person sitting in a heap at the desk. "But, but, but … I can't take this anymore." He looked wildly around the room. "Then I shall do it myself," he said. In an instant, he was at the window, tugging up the sash.

Hamelin was a split second behind him. "Now, we'll have none of that," he said as he peeled Edgar away from the window and secured the lock. "Taking your own life is frowned upon. First, we change your scenery; then we discuss your options. Okay?" He guided the distraught writer to the chair by the fireplace. "Can I rely on you to stay put a moment and we talk?"

Edgar nodded.

Hamelin studied the little man before him—all five feet of him, with a full head of sandy hair and penetrating gray eyes. When motivated and riled, he was a force of nature. Hamelin had to harness that into something beneficial. He had never had a suicidal mulligan before. All the others relished the extra time he gave them. What would he do with the man, and how would he motivate him to write? Who would transport the soul? Not Hamelin. He'd been stripped of those abilities. Worse yet, how would he explain to the Weigh Station what he had done to Poe after he had just gotten done swearing that he didn't have any more mulligans hanging out there? And then it hit him like a cooling breeze on a sticky-hot day: a job at the Phoenix, Ryan James Thomas's bar in Nevis. Edgar was the perfect employee: quiet, smart, and dedicated. Hamelin would hide him there until he figured out the rest. Ryan would be thrilled.

"Do you swim, Edgar?" Hamelin asked, the workings of a plan beginning to coalesce.

Edgar shook his head.

"Excellent. If you stay here, the house is soon going into the bay and you'll drown. There may be a way I can assist you, but we must be quick about it because if I'm found out, there'll be trouble for the both of us. Gather up what you were working on last night and let's go."

He didn't have to say it twice. Edgar swept up the additional belongings and was halfway out the door before he paused in mid step.

"If I'm going to be around a while, I'll need more clothes."

"I will buy you new ones," Hamelin said.

He pivoted Edgar around and propelled him out of the room. But just when he thought they would break free of the house, Edgar slipped his shoulder out from under Hamelin's gently guiding hand and took an abrupt right.

"Raven! Raven!" he called, heading toward the dining room.

"Come on, Edgar! All your writings are in a box in the cart."

"Confound it!" Edgar said, exiting that room and heading for the sitting room on the other side of the entry hall. "I'm looking for the cat."

"That one?" Hamelin pointed at the yellow tabby watching them from the porch banister.

Edgar studied him a moment as if trying to determine whether a yellow tabby cat sitting on *his* own porch, staring into *his* house, might belong to someone else. "Humph," he said at last. "That'd be him. There's a carrier on the side porch. Bring him and come on."

Hamelin stowed the feline and took a last look at the dwelling. If he was not mistaken—an exceedingly rare occurrence—the house had tilted another inch since he arrived. "Anything else you might be wanting out of here before I lock her up? She might not be here long. Ship's bell? Captain's desk? Human heart stashed under a floorboard in the bedroom?"

"Of course," Edgar grumbled. "Go get those while I get my wooden box. But make it snappy. I'm expecting some rather unwelcome visitors today."

Hamelin's patience snapped like a dry twig. No worldly pain-in-the-ass eccentric was going to give him orders. He marched back into the residence, ripped the bell from its mooring on the wall, scooped the lap desk up, and tossed both into the back of the golf cart.

And Edgar? Still inside and ripping up floorboards, by the sound of the squeaking. Hamelin stayed put outside. If he had to go get the man, he might kill him in righteous indignation—which, when he stopped to consider, might actually be Edgar's plan for ending his dilemma. He sat down on a bumper and waited. And when Edgar eventually left his domicile carrying a small wooden box tucked protectively under his arm, Hamelin didn't inquire further. He seriously doubted it was Pandora's box.

When Ryan Thomas converted an old produce market into a pub named the Phoenix, he had envisioned it becoming the community heart of Nevis. And except for a few bumps and missteps, he had largely succeeded. Bright natural light streaming in the two large front windows gave it a family-friendly neighborhood vibe, while the dark wood decor had the feel of an English pub, wooing patrons to linger for a while and have a few with one's mates. Local businesspeople conducted serious negotiations over a top-notch Colombian Supremo coffee, or a scotch neat if one preferred. There were fiftieth wedding anniversary celebrations, courtships, and four o'clock happy hours that brought in residents seeking an escape from a fast-paced world. The head bartender, Bennie, was beloved by all, the crab soup was to die for, and patrons gravitated toward Phoenix like iron filings to a magnet. And then there were the liquor shelves behind the main bar top, which boasted enough local and micro brews to entice even the hippest of hipsters to put the place at the top of their "favorite hangouts" list. All these attributes were good, but for Hamelin, the appeal was much more personal. Ryan Thomas, Bennie Bertollini, and the rest of the crew were the closest thing he had to family, and their open-mike nights helped satisfy his ever-restless muse.

This morning, while Edgar and his cat slept their lives away at Ms. Wanda's B and B on Third and Apple Streets, Hamelin found the Phoenix less than inviting. Ryan Thomas had no time for him. Sure, Hamelin was violating the thirty-day moratorium that Thomas had instituted against fraternization, but technically speaking, that concerned friendship. This face-to-face was about business.

Hamelin decided to let Ryan work a little frustration off before he started a second round of badgering about hiring Edgar. As the pub's owner moved a stack of boxes from their temporary place by the kitchen door, Hamelin ran a plump tiger-striped cat around in circles chasing the green light from a laser pointer he had found on the prep table.

"Stop it," Ryan said, pulling the laser out of his hand. "You're going to give him a heart attack. He hasn't moved that fast in years."

"Nonsense," Hamelin said, laughing. "He's fit as a fiddle, the terror of the mouse crowd."

Ryan put the laser in a drawer. "Well, then, it's me that's going to flatline. Don't you have something to do? Help me unpack boxes? Take a hike along the beach? I hate for you to be bored. In fact," he said, putting a forefinger along his chin, "didn't we have an agreement?"

Hamelin walked over to a stack of boxes and flipped the top one open. "I don't do manual labor, but I can inventory if you like. By the time we're done, I'll know everything that makes a Thomas Investigative Agency tick." He pulled a notebook out of the box.

Ryan pulled it away and dropped it back in the box. "Your idea of inventorying is my idea of snooping. You know how your celestial manual was for your eyes only? Well, same here. This is confidential material—it's a violation of my PI license to let other people eyeball it."

"So, what do you say?"

"The same thing I told you five minutes ago. No!" Ryan punctuated the word by dropping the crate he was carrying onto the tiled floor with a loud *thump*. "I don't have a job for your friend, and I don't run a charity house. I also don't want to be involved in any of your inevitable escapades."

"Oh, nonsense. Don't be so shortsighted," Hamelin said, dogging the bar owner's every move. "Just look at the potential, my friend."

"If you were a friend of mine, I would tell you that I don't mix business and friendship. What skills could this Edgar possibly have that I might use?"

Anyone else would have been stung by the remark. Not Hamelin.

The two men had a history together, of mulligans, sweet love stories, and unearthly redemption.

"He's a writer," Hamelin said. "He can keep your books. No tax audits, no embezzling, and with his astute eye for economy, a future ripe with a rather large nest egg. And best of all, he can do this on in a very short time frame. He's not settling down permanently in Nevis. It's a sort of pass-through before he's on to greater things. He'll do an outstanding job so long as you don't let him bend his elbow."

"Nest egg, goose eggs—I don't need him. If he's so into books, why don't you take *your* little golden *parachute* and buy him the bookstore across the way. For-sale sign went up this morning. Silas Hutchens passed away late last week, and the property is going to be up for grabs. Wouldn't be surprised if someone razed it and tried to put in condos. You know how much people like a water view."

"Bookstore?" Hamelin peered out the large pub windows at Barnacle Bertie's, the independent bookseller across the street. Not much of a reader himself, he'd never noticed it before. Like Edgar, the place was showing its age. It probably held a few first editions tucked away in the stacks, gathering dust and value, but it also projected a brooding air that threatened to suck the life out of anyone who crossed the threshold. Hamelin liked the big, curve-topped front door, which reminded him of Bilbo Baggins's hobbit hole at Bag End. Tolkien's Middle Earth epic was one of the few longer works he had made time to wade through. Something about those elves ...

"Why, that's perfect!" he said to Ryan's obvious surprise. Noting the RE/MAX sign in the window, he set off for the office on the corner of Seventh and Chestnut Street.

# Chapter Four
## Striking a Deal

The real-estate office was one of three enterprises on the corner that had converted old houses into commercial businesses. Sadly, Hamelin thought, the rest of the rather nice houses on the street would probably follow suit one day.

The stately foyer radiated a feeling of warmth and assurance that the RE/MAX family could make a first-time homebuyer's dream come true. He took an immediate left into a large room where two agents sat. One, an older woman with big gold hoop earrings and bleached-blond hair pulled back into a sophisticated ponytail, sat nearest the window, quietly engaged with a young woman in a tailored navy suit. The other, a young hipster with a red-checked sport shirt and a coordinating flashy tie, greeted him as he entered.

"I'll be with you in a moment," the man said.

"That's fine," Hamelin said, homing in on a dish of party mints next to a stack of open house flyers. "I'm here to buy one of your commercial properties."

A smile spread across the agent's face, and he put down his pen. He offered a handshake and some coffee, both of which Hamelin politely declined, and then settled Hamelin at his desk near the door.

"How may I be of assistance today, Mr. ..."

"Russell," Hamelin said, noting the name *Tom Morgan* on the agent's brass nameplate on his desk. "Barnacle Bertie's, the bookstore? I'd like to buy it."

"Oh, Bertie's, nice listing. Great location. Extremely motivated seller." Morgan selected a file folder from a rack on his desk and began perusing it. "All the inventory conveys, but you could do most anything with that property. And it's a steal—"

"Money isn't a problem. How fast can you draw up the papers?"

"I, uh, well …"

"All cash. Is that a problem?"

The agent shook his head, started to speak, and then shifted his attention to the other agent. Frowns as well as the shaking of heads were exchanged.

"Problem, Mr. Morgan?" Hamelin asked again.

The agent turned back to him. "No, sir. It's just, uh … it seems we have competing offers for the same property."

Hamelin cocked his head toward the young woman in the navy suit, and Morgan nodded. Hamelin had no interest in a bidding war. He considered her for a moment, then leaned in the woman's direction and said in a loud voice, "Are you interested in Barnacle Bertie's?"

She seemed rattled, but she engaged long enough to nod and point at what was on the table and then resumed watching the blonde shuffle her paperwork.

"That really isn't necessary," Hamelin continued. "We have it covered over here."

The woman kept her attention on the desk papers.

Morgan cleared his throat and shoved a form across the desk. "Competing offers are not unusual, Mr. Russell. No need to engage. The buyer will see everything. Just give it your best shot. If you'll just provide me with some inform—"

Hamelin beckoned him close with a crook of an index finger. "Twice whatever she offers," he hissed.

Morgan shot a pleading look at his coworker. She kept her head down and continued pushing through her pile of papers. "Well," he said. "It wouldn't be ethical to violate the confidentiality of her offer, sir. Just give me a number you're comfortable with, and we'll present it to the seller."

Hamelin grabbed the pen out of Morgan's hand, pulled a copy of the listing across the desk, and scrawled a number. After underlining it twice, he tossed the pen on the desk.

"Th-th-three times the . . .?" Morgan side-eyed the other desk and began furiously filling out paperwork. After several minutes of "do you understand?'s" and "sign here's", he picked up the phone and called the seller, cautioning Hamelin with an index finger pressed against his lips.

That was okay with Hamelin. Hard currency would do the talking. Besides, he was much more intrigued by the reaction of the other buyer—scowling—and her agent, who was muttering and slapping paperwork around.

"Done," the agent said, hanging up. "Your signature and a good faith deposit by the end of the day, and the owner would be more than happy to accept your offer."

The woman agent slapped her palm down on the desk like a gavel and rose faster than Paul Hollywood's hot cross buns. "*We* are not finished yet," she said to Mr. Morgan. And then to her client, "You have every right to bid on the property until the seller accepts in writing. How high would you like to go, Ms. Hutchins?" She picked her pen back up.

She got nothing from Morgan. He offered to shake Hamelin's hand, realized his faux pas when Hamelin put his hands behind his back, and gave him a thumbs-up instead. "When should I expect a check from you, Mr. Russell?"

"I'll be back shortly," Hamelin said. He rose and gave Ms. Hutchins—who was staring at him with her mouth open—a pleasant smile. "Sorry if I've ruined your day, ma'am. There was no malintent on my part. This was just one of those very special circumstances. I'm sure you will find something else that tickles your fancy." As he walked away, he could almost feel the heat of her indignation burning his scalp.

When he reached the end of the street, he stopped on the pretense of checking his wristwatch, but what he really wanted was a glance back at the real-estate office. Ms. Hutchins was standing in the doorway at RE/MAX, getting a hard-sell routine from the female agent, but Hamelin doubted she heard a word the agent said, because her eyes were glued to Hamelin. Their gazes met briefly, and then she huffed off toward the silver Volvo parked at the curb. He had encountered her type before: entitled and fiercely competitive. It might take her a while, but she'd get over it, maybe even learn a lesson in civility. If not, the afterlife would be a rude shock.

His trip to First National was much more pleasant. They couldn't do enough for him. By the time he headed back to RE/MAX with a certified check, he was toting a calendar advertising historic sites of Maryland, a miniature foam easy chair to cradle his cell phone, and a certificate for a free Oster toaster. He left everything on Morgan's desk except the chair and soon left the RE/MAX office, a very satisfied man, giddy in the knowledge that Edgar would be pleased.

Apparently, it was his day for meeting attractive professional women. No sooner had he reached the end of the block than he was politely accosted by a serious brunette scurrying after him in high heels.

"Sir, sir," she called. "If I may have a minute?"

He waited, wondering why she needed him and where he had caught her eye.

"No, we haven't met," she said, as if reading his thoughts. "I'm Edelin Jacoby. I co-owned Barnacle Bertie's with my late father, Silas Jacoby. I want to thank you for the quick sale and the more-than-fair price."

Hamelin nodded. "No problem. You look too young to retire. Relocating?"

She laughed, but it was mirthless and uneasy. "Thanks for that, but looks can be deceiving. Yes, I'm leaving town, and I won't be back. If I may, I'd like to leave you with a piece of advice before I do." She hesitated, threw a quick look over her shoulder, and then continued in a hushed, confidential tone. "Whatever you do, read the fine print. *All* of it." Her eyes searched his face as if making sure he understood.

He didn't. "The paperwork's all done and ready for you to sign," he said, frowning. "Am I missing something?"

"No, no," she said, nervously wetting her lips. "We're all done, but when he ..." Again she stopped herself. "Just be careful. And I'm sorry."

With that, she crossed the street and started back the way she had come.

"Wait! What? Where can I contact you?"

"Don't," she called over her shoulder. Despite the stilettos, she bumped it up to a full sprint.

Hamelin looked up to make sure there was still only one sun shining in the sky and that little green men weren't beaming down from spaceships overhead. He had little patience for most people as it was. This morning's overload of crazies warranted some nice poolside alone time and meditation, which would commence directly after he made Edgar's day.

If Hamelin had thought that presenting Edgar with his very own bookstore would perk him up, the author quickly disabused him of that notion.

"Two keys," Hamelin said, handing Edgar two split rings with a single key on each. "The smaller one locks the front door; the other gets the back." He led him behind the front counter and cash register to a room scarcely bigger than a cupboard and pointed to a set of narrow wooden stairs—four steps up, and a tight turn to the right as it wound up to the second floor. The treads looked as if they were sagging, but on closer inspection, they were just worn down in the middle from decades of use. This place was one of the oldest in town, and the realtor included with the settlement papers a photocopy of the original 1795 deed to the property. Hamelin couldn't have cared less, but he thought Edgar might appreciate it. "There are living quarters up there: adequate sleeping accommodations and room for a smallish writing table. You can see both the town and the bay from the window. Shall we go up?"

Edgar grunted his consent, but his demeanor remained unchanged throughout the tour. After a casual snoop in all the corners, a sit on the bed, and a long, silent look out at the water, they returned to the main floor without his uttering a word.

"How long?" Edgar asked, turning weary eyes on Hamelin.

"How about just saying thank you?"

"No, really, how long will it be before you release me from this miserable life? Haven't you plenty of other things I've written? I embrace death. Kill me, please!"

Over the centuries, Hamelin had heard the plea many times from the pained and suffering, and yet he hadn't become inured to it. It never failed to tug at his emotions. "Don't even think it, Edgar. What a terrible waste of talent." One look at the stoic expression on Edgar's face told Hamelin everything he had done so far was for naught. The man was depressed. "Tell you what. Let's give it a month. If you haven't gotten your mojo back by then and finished your manuscript, we'll talk about it again. Sound reasonable?"

He looked in Edgar's eyes and saw there an intensity and pain that Hamelin swore he would remember until he received his own life's judgment. "There is nothing reasonable about keeping someone alive for one hundred and seventy years beyond their death. You are one of the cruelest and most thoughtless men I have ever had the displeasure to meet."

And with that, he turned and marched himself back upstairs. "My things, Russell," he said before rounding the bend in the stair. "The sooner I commence, the sooner I can leave this godforsaken establishment."

# Chapter Five

# The Collector

Daimon Bertland went to bed Thursday night secure in his position as acquisitor and protector of dark muses. He woke up Friday morning less certain. Was his vivid dream a premonition, or just fear that things could not remain perfect?

He got out of bed, dressed, then padded down from his bedroom on the second floor to his closed bookshop below. Who would sell one of his shops without permission? The dream showed no face and provided no name, and the horror of not knowing which shop was sold clung to him like a dank mist. He lit the kindling in the stone fireplace and coaxed the little crackling flame into a hungry, licking roar. Then he retired to his leather easy chair and tried to sort out his nightmare. *Who?* he asked. Who would dare? The insult was almost worse than the chaos that would ensue should it prove true."

And thus, Bertland found himself on a Friday morning, in a year of no particular significance, sitting in the middle of his bookstore, Pickled Peppers, on the Isle of Man, surrounded by first editions, ancient texts, and dozens of his favorite books. Their bouquet of vanilla and a faint hint of grass hung in the air like a comforting friend. He raised his eyes from the fire and looked around. He owned so many stores, controlled them with an iron fist. Or so he thought. He would torch this one before he let it fall into the wrong hands. He chuckled in spite of the alarming turn of events. What an intriguing thought. The locals who didn't already think him strange would be wagging tongues over that. But would it really solve his problem? No. Transfer ownership to a relative? None he trusted. A friend? None to speak of.

He got up and walked down the rows of bookshelves, fingering a particularly lovely leather volume here, a favorite story there. The original owner had chosen well, and Bertland prided himself on his subsequent additions. Recent foot traffic and sales were bleak. Pickled Peppers wasn't needed anymore in a fast world of shiny new Kindles and free downloads. Fortunately, *bookseller* wasn't the only profession he had a hat for.

He was actually more of a collector than a seller—the grandson of Pandora, mother of all the world's evils. She had been badly cast, unaware of what was in the jar that she opened. Regardless, she was expected to make recompense, and now it was up to her and her descendants to collect the unleashed corruption and remove it from the world. As grandchild number six, Bertland was tasked with removing the darkness of the written word, and for eons untold, he had worked tirelessly at it.

Did he feel like a gladiator? A stalwart defender of humanity? Hardly. In fact, he loathed the responsibility. Stories in all their forms should be nurtured and cherished. He despised himself even more than the job thrust upon him by virtue of his birth. He hated looking into the eyes of a dying man or woman, knowing that he was about to rob them of their creative gift. Had they really known what he was about? Had they hated him, too?

Bertland walked to the end of his Renaissance/Middle Ages collection, took several volumes off the shelf, and placed them gently on the floor. Then he rooted around behind the others on the shelf until his hand found the small wooden box he had hidden there. He turned it over in his hands as if looking for the latch to open it. There was none. It opened and closed when he willed it, but he would never open it again. His books might be of great value, but this was the prize without price: the dark muse of Costache Ardelean, a great writer of the macabre and a close confidant of Vlad the Impaler. Bertland took Ardelean's dark muse and imprisoned it here so that his vile, twisted creativity could never again cast its shadow over the earth. All his bookstores warehoused boxes such as this, and one couldn't simply sell the shop and expect things to proceed again in normal fashion. New owners would poke, they would pry, and, gods forbid, they might even dispose of something they didn't fully comprehend.

Bertland shuddered at the thought. Although no box was marked, he connected personally to them all and could associate a name and a face to each. Of all the dark muses he had taken over the eons, one haunted him the most: Edgar Allan Poe's. On the night of acquisition, he had willed it with a heavy heart. What a gifted man. Even the three roses and cognac Bertland left each year at Poe's grave could not mitigate the regret he felt.

On the day of acquisition, Poe had fallen into the hands of rascals conducting voter fraud in Baltimore, Maryland, in the United States. Plied with liquor and drugs, the writer had been forced off the street between the docks and the place he was staying, bundled off to a neighboring voting precinct, and forced to vote numerous times within the city. When Bertland found him, Poe lay incoherent and dying on a city street outside a place called Gunner's Hall. Bertland procured Poe's dark muse through his normal procedures, but as he recalled, a gathering crowd of gawkers prevented him from seeing the man off to his life's final reward. So he had taken a room at a local hotel and remained there until he received word that the gifted writer had passed away in the hospital. Then it was on to the next box. There was always another box.

The job never changed, and with the single exception of Poe, he never looked back. As he held the little black box, more details from his troubling dream came tumbling back to him: skipjacks, a sinking island, and a *For Sale* sign hanging by a chain on the door of a small bookstore. Above the door, a porcelain sign squeaked quietly back and forth on its hanger, and just inside the door lay the physical remains of the late Silas Hutchens. Old Silas was of little consequence, but the door sign made Bertland fume and swear oaths he would later ask forgiveness for. It was one of his oldest stores, in a two-drachma town with little going for it—which meant great privacy and security. "How dare she!" he said loudly enough to send the resident mouse scurrying behind the wall in Children's Fiction. *How dare she!* A written agreement was a sacred trust, and no one had ever broken a commitment to him to protect his boxes. In the old days, he would have retaliated by making an example of her—say, chain her to a rock and let the vultures peck out her eyes. These days required a softer, subtler touch, however. He would know what measures to take once he caught up with her.

He returned the box to where he had found it, and walked back to the fireplace. The fire needed stoking. He ignored it. Instead, he picked up the wrought-iron poker and wedged its tip between the bottom of the brick hearth and the wood floorboard it abutted. With minimal force and the correct angle of leverage, he popped loose the bottom brick and the two above it. Then he knelt and felt about for the box of polished red cedar in the cavity he had exposed. It was twice the size of

Ardlean's, much heavier, and within its chamber rested his most recent acquisitions on his grandmother's behalf.

He pulled it out and set it on the counter, next to the cash register. Standing there, he put pen to paper and wrote a short note in careful, flowing cursive. He reread it twice. Satisfied, he signed his name at the bottom.

From three fish-shaped coat hooks tacked to the wall near the cash register, he selected his favorite oilskin coat and put it on. He slipped the cedar box into the deepest pocket. When he had a moment, he would send it off to someone else for final disposition. He picked a favorite walking stick—oak, ornately carved by Druids he had once bartered with—from the stand by the door and walked out into the evening's drizzle. He locked the door, taped his note to the oval glass, and slipped the key through the mail slot. Then he set off on foot for his boat moored in the small marina at the town dock—never once turning to see the soft glow of the lights spilling out the storefront windows, or his message fluttering off the door and tumbling into the gutter. He looked up at the dark, starless sky. He'd have to wing the journey. With thousands of years of experience, it wouldn't be difficult. He stowed his gear and set off, wondering whether tonight's sleep would bring any new insights into the completely unacceptable—and quite correctable—sale of Barnacle Bertie's.

# Chapter Six

# The Boxes

Edgar ran his dusting cloth along the edge of the shelf marked *A through Cr*. He paused a moment to assess his effort and gauge how long it would take to polish up all the other shelves. He guessed a few hours, and that was perfect. He had already spent too many hours upstairs hunched over his writing desk and, as he might have predicted, hadn't produced anything of substance. The thought of spending additional time there made him feel nauseated. It seemed the only two people who could put an end to his earthly sojourn were he himself and Hamelin Russell. Truthfully, Edgar was incapable, and the soul runner reluctant. And so he cleaned, rearranged, and planned how to waste time that seemed endless in supply.

He studied the other shelves, searching for the letter *P* or, more correctly, the *Po*'s, and, even more precisely, the *Poe*'s. It was the first place he wanted to rush to when Hamelin left him on his own, but he fought the vanity of it. Even a reconnaissance trip past the *P*'s to the *Q*'s seemed blatantly transparent. He guessed his own literary works to be in the back right corner—half a dozen shelves from where he now stood.

Edgar pulled his timepiece from his trousers pocket—a concession to Hamelin, who insisted that wearing it on a fob and chain would make him appear too eccentric. The time was four o'clock on his second day at Bertie's. Surely, sufficient time had passed that vanity could now be considered mere curiosity. Edgar turned the shop sign around to read *Closed*, locked the front door, pulled the blinds down, and headed for the far back corner. Only Hamelin would mind the momentary closing, and what he didn't know wouldn't upset him. As Edgar approached the *P*'s, his heartbeat quickened at the sight of his favorite works: "The Raven," "The Black Cat," "The Fall of the House of Usher," and *The Narrative of Arthur Gordon Pym of Nantucket.*

He pulled out "The Black Cat." It smelled of must, vanilla, and grass—a first edition, he noted with satisfaction. He was about to slide it back into its slot when he saw something sitting on the shelf behind it. What, pray tell, was this? He removed several volumes of his works and reached in and pulled out a small dark lacquered box the size of his fist. It had no markings and no visible seams or hinges. He shook it, but nothing rattled inside. Pushing, prying, and squeezing produced the same result.

He looked down the row. Were there more? He pulled, slid, and replaced books until he had searched the length of the shelf. He found another small wooden box at the end of the row, and, when he tackled the rest of the shelves, six more. When he had satisfied himself that he had them all, he took the armload of little wooden boxes up to the checkout counter and dumped them beside the cash register. They were similar but not indistinguishable. No matter which way he arranged them, he immediately knew—though he couldn't say how—which was the box he had found behind his own books. He might indeed be crazy, as his detractors had long said, but that box seemed to warm at his touch. He lined them all up end to end by the cash register and sat down to wait. Hamelin would know what they were. Hamelin knew everything.

"Nope, Edgar sorry. Not a clue," Hamelin said rotating one of the boxes around in his hands once and then putting it back down with the rest. "Contrary to what some people think, runners know only what they need to know. I thought we had an agreement that you would be *writing*. Where did you buy these?"

"I am, I am," Edgar said, his hand hovering over the row of boxes before picking one up from the middle. "But everyone needs a break sometime, and no, I haven't been shopping. I found them right here at Bertie's. I was cleaning up a bit, taking an informal inventory of what was shelved, and I found them behind some books. They're not heavy enough to be bookends. My guess is, they might open, but I don't see a clasp or hinge. Given, ahem, your *special* gifts, maybe you can open them. This one first," he said, and gave Hamelin the box he was holding.

It was decidedly heavier than the first one Hamelin picked up, and it seemed to grow and warm up in his hand. It felt almost supernatural. Animate. Hamelin quickly set it down. "It doesn't open. Hand me one of the plastic bags over there and I'll dispose of these."

Edgar started to protest, then said, "I used the last bag, but I can dispense with them as soon as I can figure out where they kept the supplies."

For a moment, Hamelin's gaze bounced back and forth between Edgar and the blocks of wood. Edgar was as transparent as a windowpane—he had no intention of getting rid of them. "I'm glad to see you getting into the swing of things," Hamelin said, "but you should be writing. I'll handle it."

Edgar gave him an odd look and went back upstairs.

Hamelin scooped up the blocks, but before he could walk away with them, the bell on the front door jingled and a short, well-dressed man with fiery red hair, and a sun-kissed complexion entered. He didn't stop to browse, but waltzed in as if he owned the place, fixing a steely gaze on Hamelin that stayed there until he reached the sales counter. Hamelin had never seen eyes so deep blue.

"Is the new owner about?" the man asked.

"Who's asking? Hamelin replied.

"Bertland. Daimon Bertland."

"That would be me, Mr. Bertland," Hamelin said, taking an immediate dislike to the stranger for his directness and failure to exchange even the most basic pleasantries.

The stranger's gaze shifted to the wooden boxes. "It seems there has been an unfortunate mistake," Bertland said. "I've come to invalidate the sale of Bertie's. You see, I had an oral arrangement with Silas Hutchins and his daughter Edelin. It was …" He dismissed the rest of the thought with a wave of his hand. "The particulars aren't important. We just need to void the sale, and all will be well."

"An oral agreement, you say?" Hamelin shook his head. "No, the specifics aren't important at all. Oral agreements regarding real property are not enforceable. The sale was legally binding, and there won't be any voiding of anything." Hamelin smiled broadly, wondering where the man got off feeling so entitled. "Now, if you would like a book, we can help you. Otherwise, I must bid good day to you, sir. I'm afraid we have a lot to do at the moment."

Bertland's eyebrows arched. "I will give you twice what you paid for the place. Considering how much you shelled out to buy it, that's a rather handsome profit. You can buy several stores. I believe we can come up with some arrangement. No need for lawyers. Just a simple agreement without any bothersome fine print."

The words of Edelin Jacoby slammed into Hamelin like a breaking wave he had turned his back on: *Whatever you do, read the fine print. All of it.* He tumbled about in the surf for a moment while trying to figure out what he had fallen into.

"I don't know," Hamelin said, leading Bertland toward the door. "This is all a whirlwind. Do you have a card? I can call you back after I've had a chance to think about it." He ushered his strange guest to the door.

Halfway back to the sales counter, Hamelin turned around to find that Bertland was following him back to the cash register.

"Well, of course, you should think about it," Bertland said, "but I can't believe anyone would turn down such a lucrative offer. What can I do here to assuage some of your concerns?"

"Oh, rest assured, it's nothing you have said or failed to say," Hamelin said. "I'm somewhat anal, and I never act on impulse. If you don't have a card, I'll just jot down your information and you can get on with your day."

Bertland raised his palm. "No, I have one here," he said, producing a card from an inside jacket pocket. "The offer is good for twenty-four hours. If I don't hear back from you tomorrow, I'll have to make other decisions." He gave a half salute and left.

If failing to call Bertland was all Hamelin had to do to get rid of the man, why bother to call at all? Hamelin knew trouble when he saw it. He shoved the card under the edge of the cash register and vowed not to pull it out again.

# Chapter Seven

# The Keeper

After Edelin Jacoby's pronouncement that she was leaving town, and her brusque departure on the street, Hamelin was surprised when he ran into her at happy hour. Her face was long, and her liquor glass nearly empty.

Hamelin had seen many oddities over his long soul-running tenure, and he found the Jacoby woman decidedly strange. He acknowledged her with a nod and took his customary seat at the end of bar, where Bennie promptly served him his usual: water—no ice, no lemon. When their eyes met, her expression brightened considerably, and she immediately left her window table and joined him at the bar. She reeked of booze.

"I thought you were skipping town," he said, trying to be polite. It was not his forte, and he regretted not making her work for a conversation starter. Maybe she would flit away just as quickly as the first time they met.

"What are we doing, Hamelin?"

He searched her face for some sort of context, but her stoic expression was of little help. "Concerning what?" he asked as he considered changing his water order to takeout.

"Don't you feel that you were meant for bigger things than a small town that is holding on by its fingernails to keep from sliding into the bay?"

"A little harsh, don't you think?" he waffled, still unsure of the conversation. "Owning a small business is noble work."

"Help me be happy," she said, looking at him with eyes that brimmed with sudden pain. Her hand shook as she sipped her drink.

Ah, now he understood. He resembled her shrink, who was momentarily inaccessible. He pushed his glass away and stood up. "Look, I'd love to help you, but I've got to run."

"I've made a mistake," she continued, oblivious of his impending departure. "I need the shop back. We can do it any way you want. Canceling the sale would be the easiest, but if you'd rather I bought it back outright, I'm good with that, too. Of course, I'll cover all expenses related to the sale."

She mumbled something else that Hamelin didn't catch, but he didn't want clarification. "Sorry. Other parties are involved, and they would never sign off on that." He flipped two bucks on the counter for Bennie and turned to go.

"Wait!" she said, catching his sleeve. "There is another way. Not the best, but I'll wing the rest of it."

He yanked his arm free. How dare she! He had killed people for as much—the mere touch of a soul runner was instant death and transport to the afterlife. "Don't. Touch. Me," he said, glaring at her.

She pulled back, lower lip trembling.

"I paid you far more for that property than it was worth. Go buy another one. It's that simple."

Her eyes welled up, and she looked away. "No, it isn't."

He should have walked away, but he felt a strange pull, an inexplicable need to offer some sort of assistance. He sat again, not comfortably but on the edge of the stool, as if on the verge of bolting. "Well, then, let me hear this other way. But I'm not promising anything, and you're making me late for an appointment," he lied. "And if you so much as extend a hand in my direction …"

"I'm going to be totally honest—"

"Well, I would expect so considering you've asked a very big favor from a complete stranger."

Her head bobbled a moment as she glanced over at him. Then she concentrated on jiggling the ice in her drink. "It's not so much the building I want as something inside."

"Oh, why didn't you say so? Just drop by later, and Edgar will be happy to find it for you."

She shook her head. "You need to get it for me."

Okay, he got it—something to do with personal information. "So what—bank statements? Diaries? What are we talking about here, Ms. Jacoby?"

"*Edelin.* Have you ever noticed the small wooden boxes scattered amongst the shelved books?"

Hamelin pictured the polished wooden blocks. Oh. Funerary urns? Rare oriental art? What was the use of having art if you were going to hide it? And why was it only now occurring to her to collect them? He couldn't see the attraction of having the cremated remains of a loved one hanging around anywhere, let alone serving as a bookend. Edelin Jacoby was one twisted person. "Yeah, I've seen them. They're all yours. You bring the cardboard box."

"Oh, no, that won't be necessary. I only want one of them."

Hamelin cocked an eyebrow. She was playing favorites? "Which one?"

"I'd rather not say, but I can direct you to the right one, you can give it to me, and then I won't bother you anymore."

"How about you come back with me and take all of them?"

"Oh, no. That wouldn't be proper. And I really just need the one. You're the keeper now. You have to give it to me."

"*Keeper?* And how do you suggest I dispose of the rest?"

"You don't."

Hamelin was appalled by her lack of respect for the dead. "Hey, I bought a bookstore, not a mausoleum. It's all or nothing, *Edelin*."

Edelin's smile sagged into something ugly and forlorn. Tears burst forth, and she sobbed, "I supposed you've never made any mistakes, Mr. *Perfect*. If the owner of the one box finds out I've sold the store …" There followed several hiccups, a whimper, and a sigh to fill the Grand Canyon.

"Somebody's going to kill you over a bunch of *ashes?* You're right, Edelin, it does sound complicated. So stop, take one more deep breath, and bring it back to simple. Come get all the urns, and everybody— you, me, and the person leaning on you—will be jubilant."

The look in her eyes said no.

"It's either that or I dump it in the lap of the local constabulary. Dead people aren't my job anymore." He fully expected the next thing out of her mouth to be a question. It wasn't.

"They aren't ashes," she whispered.

"They're …?" he offered, rotating his hands around in small circles as he tried to goose the conversation along. When that failed, he said, "Maybe I should just give them to Mr. Bertland. You can negotiate with him."

"Bertland's in town?" Edelin closed her eyes, and a shudder ran through her. "I've got to go," she said. And scooping up her purse, she fled.

"Your loss," Hamelin mumbled. He signaled Bennie to top off his drink. He had a better solution than trying to strike a deal with an unstable woman: curbside service where the garbage man could collect the boxes in the morning. Boxes gone. Edelin gone. Problem solved.

If Hamelin thought he had seen the last of Edelin Jacoby, maybe he wasn't Mr. Perfect, after all. Early the next morning, before he could put the trash out or Edgar could flip over the closed sign on the door, the woman knocked on Bertie's door, imploring Hamelin to speak with her again.

Hamelin never expected her to be such a hard case. Evidently, she had bad-mouthed him at the bank, and the same helpful source told him she had been scouring property and other official records all week, trying to reverse the sale on a technicality of one sort or another. The former was petty, and the latter, seeing that whatever dirt she dug up would also apply to her and any other subsequent owners, was just plain stupid.

Hamelin instructed Edgar to pull the door and window shades down and left her outside to amuse herself. After an hour or so, she stopped talking and pounding. Hamelin conducted a brief reconnaissance mission around the block and didn't see her. Bertie's was back in business again.

Hamelin put his pen behind his ear. Calculating sums was not his thing. After centuries of existence without money, his skills were creaky, although, if he were honest, mathematics had never been a strength. His father had boxed his ears more than once when he charged incorrect amounts for his father's leather goods. Eventually, his father had lost all patience and apprenticed him to the town baker. After several months of similar treatment there, Hamelin had run away to Tuscany and, in exchange for a bed and two meager meals a day, apprenticed himself to Berlinghiero of Lucca. There he swept, he cleaned, he learned to paint, and he flourished. The first painting he had ever been allowed to start—

He jolted out of his daydream to the clearing of a throat, and a woman's voice. "I suppose you've included credits and returns?" It was Edelin Jacoby, with a haughty air about her.

"That could be it," he said, realizing there was no column for such information. "You're becoming quite tiresome, Ms. Jacoby," he said, glaring at her. "And I can become quite vindictive when annoyed. I'll give you one final chance to make your case, and then my advice is to beat it."

"I'd like to buy—"

"No!"

"... a copy of 'The Purloined Letter,' by Edgar Allan Poe," she said, eyes roving the area behind him.

He closed the ledger and put it on the counter behind him, taking the opportunity to look around for Edgar. Hamelin didn't see him, which suggested he was upstairs—writing, hopefully. He jerked the curtain shut behind him and blocked her view of the rear room and staircase. She was out of luck if that was who she sought. "It's on back order," he said. "If you like, I can give you a call when it comes in."

She shook her head and pressed her lips together. The perky cupid's bow on her upper lip disappeared. "Actually, it doesn't have to be that one. If you'll just point me toward the *P*'s, I'm sure I can find something else."

"I'm afraid everything from that catalogue is on back order. Give me your phone number and I'll contact you the moment they arrive. Next week, no doubt."

"James Patterson, then?"

"Out."

"Jodi Picoult, Terry Pratchett, Sylvia Plath?"

Hamelin shook his head at each mention. "Actually," he said, crooking his finger to draw her closer, "it's somewhat more complicated than that. We're dealing with a mold issue in that section. The proximity to the bay, bad flooring, bad ventilation," he said, gesturing in several directions. "We'll have to replace all the stock." He was rather proud of his lie, but her narrowed eyes told him she wasn't buying any of it.

"Sounds expensive. Take it all off your hands—"

"Get out!" Hamelin said, and he picked up his pencil and pulled his accounts book back in front of him.

"You don't understand," she said.

"A sale is a sale. And if you don't leave immediately, I'll be forced to do something you will wish never happened."

"It's not you I fear," she said, side eyeing the door. "I've come on behalf of someone else. If I don't bring him the box, he's going to hurt me far worse than anything you could do to me. Please let me have it. *Please.*"

Mortals. Everything was a matter of life and death. Hamelin tilted his head and beckoned her to follow him to the window. "See the dark-red building down there next to the green striped awning?" he said, pointing. "J. Bean and Associates. They should be able to help you with a protective order and any court proceedings you may need to navigate through. Now, leave us alone." With that, he opened the door, ushered her out, and latched the dead bolt behind her.

"You'll be sorry," she said, pointing a finger at him.

Hamelin returned to his arithmetic. He was already sorry.

## Chapter Eight
# When Immortals Dance

Hamelin remained vigilant and kept Bertie's door locked, letting customers in only when they knocked. But Edelin never returned, and he began to feel that he had driven his point home. Apparently, Mr. Bertland had also gotten the message, because he hadn't shown his face again, either.

Hamelin's peace was short-lived. At close of business, he again heard three familiar raps on the door. He wondered if it was some sort of secret code among mortals, which he had somehow missed along the way. The register was counted out, and he was tempted to remain hidden in the stacks until the caller left. Still, he couldn't be positive it was Edelin, and if he was going to assume the role of businessman, good business meant, among other things, good customer access. Bernie Bertollini had told him the customer was *always* right. Hamelin doubted that, but he kept reminding himself that it would be a lesson in humility and, when practiced with great feeling, a stepping-stone toward restoring his place in the afterlife. He opened the door to Bertland.

"I'd like a word with Edelin Jacoby," Bertland said, heading for the customer counter.

"I'm afraid she's moved on," Hamelin said, wondering how on earth he would get rid of these crazy people who wouldn't take no for an answer.

"And the shop?" Bertland asked in a rush.

"Still sold to me."

"Oh." Bertland rapped his knuckles on the counter, leaned back, and sighted down the nearest row of shelves. "I left some things in her keeping that she stored here. I need to retrieve them. The small polished boxes she decorated the shelves with. I need those."

*Them again.* Hamelin looked the man up and down: Calm blue eyes and an ageless face without deep creases or age spots. He didn't look like the type to snuff an attractive woman over a box of ashes. "So you and Edelin are working together, or what?"

"I've come myself. If I may borrow that," he said, pointing to an empty cardboard box sitting on the floor near the register. "Five minutes from now, you won't even remember I was here."

To anyone else's ears, Bertland's statement might have sounded polite and considerate. To Hamelin's finely tuned sensibilities? Suspicious as hell.

Hamelin shook his head. "I doubt that." He took a moment and studied the man's aura. It was wispy, colorless, and constantly in motion, but not because it was in tune with any particular mood or quality in the man. Quite the opposite, it bopped and weaved like a boxer—an evasive tactic to keep prying discernment out. Hamelin disengaged as he realized that Bertland was giving him the same sort of once-over.

"Mr. Bertland. "Let's stop the merry dance, okay? The most obvious: you're not mortal."

For an instant, Bertie's eyes brightened. But he quickly mastered himself, and his eyes hooded as he lined up the edges of the books stacked on the counter before him. "Nor you."

Hamelin said nothing and waited.

Bertland shrugged. "Call it a legacy, call it a curse. It is what it is."

"I take it the boxes aren't filled with ashes. What do you really want? As Ms. Jacoby was specifically asking about Mr. Poe, what do you want with Edgar?"

"Nothing."

Hamelin sighed. It was going to be a game of twenty questions, was it? "How are you and Edgar connected?"

"I believe it's called *mojo*."

Hamelin didn't hear any movement upstairs—no creaking of floorboards, or frustrated slamming of cabinets and doors. Hopefully, Edgar would stay quietly in his room for a while. Hamelin arched an eyebrow at Bertland and waited.

"I don't make a point of discussing business, but you, Mr. Russell, intrigue me. What does an immortal want with a run-down bookshop in a got-nothing-going-for-it town in the boring state of Maryland?"

Bertie had a smug look, so Hamelin took it as a rhetorical question and just smiled.

Bertland pushed on. "With remarkable talents: Renaissance art, Mississippi Delta blues guitar, just to name two. The first was righteous and good, but the latter talent ... I do believe we might deal on that one."

"Deal?"

"You stay out of my way, and I won't delve into the blackness by which you learned your musical craft from Robert Johnson."

Hamelin's stomach lurched. *Robert Johnson?* Back in his soul-running days, Hamelin had struck a deal of his own with the great bluesman. In exchange for a few more hours of life, the bluesman had imparted the finer skills of bottleneck slide guitar. It violated every guideline in Hamelin's celestial rule book, but he'd gotten away with it at the time, acquiring a virtuosity that made his playing almost indistinguishable from the man known as the Father of the Blues.

He fixed his presumptuous visitor with a cold stare. "Who *are* you?"

Bertland sat down at one of the reading tables and took a moment to make himself comfortable. "My business is tit for tat, Mr. Russell. Fair exchange of goods and information for services rendered. I give you something and you, in turn, give me something I want."

"Not interested. That's your business, not mine."

Bertland seemed amused. "Oh, you will be interested. You will." He extended a hand, which Hamelin ignored. Bertland chortled, his head bouncing strangely up and down like a bobblehead. "You don't seal deals with a handshake? It won't take me long to have you sorted out. It's what I do. What *you* do."

Hamelin circled around until he stood between Bertland and the stairs to the upper floor, where Edgar was writing. "I resent all your assumptions. I do nothing of the sort." Which was mostly true. As a soul runner, Hamelin never had the power to determine who died—he might delay a while, perhaps, but he would never change the date when someone's life was supposed to end, or the destination of the deceased. He merely followed orders. "Don't waste your time sorting. The only way I'll discuss the boxes is if I know who I'm really dealing with. Obviously, you need permission to take them. Otherwise, you would have taken them already and booked out of here. No pun intended. So, if you want to do business, tell me what you're about. For the last time, who are you?"

"Commodore Daimon '*Barnacle*' Bertland."

"*Barnacle Bertie?* This store is over a hundred years old. You're named after it?"

"Has it really been that long?" Bertland said with a chuckle. "No, I built it." He stopped a moment as if struggling to put his thought into words. "Let's just say building bookstores—and I have a few—fit well with important pursuits in my life, and leave it at that. I've never been a merchant per se, just a *procurer* of sorts."

"Procuring what?"

"Evil," Bertland said, his eyes flashing with a fire that suited the blazing red of his hair. "Evil as it relates to the written word."

"And who sends you? Surely it's not a godly mission."

"We all have our gods. I have given you an English translation of my name. I won't bore you with the longer version in my native tongue. I am a grandson of Pandora and, like all her descendants, doomed to roam the ends of the earth trying to put all the ills of the world back into her little dark jar. It is our fate until the earth passes away or a new world order is established."

"Amazing." Hamelin dropped into a nearby chair. "Pandora's box? And the little boxes here—they're parts of a bigger whole."

Bertland nodded. "*Jar, box*—as you wish."

The air around Hamelin began shimmering a soft blue. Before him sat … who? A Greek god in the flesh? He quickly ran through his understanding of the Pandora myth, trying to position her in the pantheon of the Greek gods. Pandora had been created as the world's first woman and not a god at all. Endowed by all the gods with special gifts, she had unleashed misery and torment upon man when she ignored Zeus's prohibition and opened the jar given to her.

"So that would make you the son of Pyrrha and your father …?"

"Deucalion."

"Fascinating!" Hamelin's aura went from shimmering to throbbing.

"Yes, you've made that clear," Bertland said. "Now you know my mission and should understand that I will never give up and go elsewhere. These boxes are part of who I am. Give them back to me and I'll leave you alone."

"So why can't you just take them and be gone?"

"Would that I could, but they're entrusted to the shop, and I just can't *take* them. I cut a deal with Edelin and her father a while ago. So long as they were caretakers, I agreed not to add either of them to a box. She violated our agreement by selling this place. When this brouhaha gets straightened out, I'll discuss her recompense."

Based on Edelin's Herculean efforts to retrieve the boxes, Hamelin was certain she already had a good idea what that would be. "Edelin Jacoby seemed a lovely woman. She has a dark side?"

"Everybody has a dark side. Even you, Mr. Russell. If they didn't, we wouldn't even be having this conversation."

"Be careful with that," Hamelin said, poking a finger at him. "There's dark and then there's *dark*."

Bertland smiled affably. "It may be hard to believe, but it all comes from the same place. That little religious from Calcutta? Fought darkness all the time. The difference was, she won even the most difficult battle."

Hamelin offered him a cool smile. "I'm glad you appreciate a good fight, but there is a simpler solution to all this. Release *hope*. Then there's no need to cart around and store all these boxes."

"A scholar, I see," Bertland said, smiling broadly. "See, here's the thing. I don't have authority to open the jar again. Whatever's still inside, good or bad, will remain so. I don't—"

The sound of someone descending the staircase brought both their heads around. The curtain to the back room parted, and Edgar appeared.

"Don't give him anything, Hamelin," Edgar growled. "For the last hundred and seventy years, as I have knelt each evening at the foot of my bed before my God, there has been but one prayer on my lips: that I should see you, Daimon Bertland, one more time and curse you to the ends of the earth."

Hamelin felt his own aura still and vanish. "You know him?" he asked, rising from his chair.

"Unfortunately, yes. He's a con man," Edgar said. "As I lay dying in the street, I thought he was going to help me, but he's a scoundrel. His contracts are full of fine print that benefits him alone. Instead of saving me, he purloined my creative side." He glared at Bertland. "Don't think I don't know. It's locked in one of the boxes here."

Bertland raised his hands as if fending off the criticism. "I operated in good faith. I knew that your life was short. At least, those were the indications when I first approached you. As I recall, you didn't object to our agreement. And I did get help. It was I who sent kindly Mr. Walker, the printer, to find you. It was because of me that you died with some dignity at Washington College Hospital and not in the gutter outside Gunner's."

"Oh, come on," Hamelin said, butting in before Edgar could reply. "Edgar was drugged out of his mind—a day of cooping gone totally wrong. You really think he was capable of consent?"

"I wasn't privy to that."

Hamelin turned to Edgar. "That's why you didn't finish your last story?"

Edgar nodded. "Couldn't. This trickster sucked my creative juices dry."

Hamelin turned to Bertland. "Ah, now I see you."

"Be fascinated on your own time," Bertland snapped. "Let me have the wooden boxes, and I'll be out of your hair."

Hamelin sat down on the edge of the table. "No, now, wait a second. Tell me if I'm missing something. These boxes don't contain anyone's ashes, but rather the darker muses of writers? If that's the real skinny, I would hate to leave them all in the lurch. How many are still alive?"

"None but Edgar," Bertland said. "That one would be on you, bud. I'm not sure how, but don't you worry, I'll figure it out."

Hamelin shrugged. "If you want to waste time on me, the most pedestrian person on the planet, knock yourself out. But seriously, what if I refuse your request?"

"You can't refuse. As I said, my sole reason for existence is collection and maintenance."

A sly smile crept across Hamelin's face. "If I refuse, do you go *poof* immediately, or is it more of a slow dissolve into a gooey puddle on the floor, à la the Wicked Witch of the West?"

Bertland scrambled to his feet. "You wouldn't! It's a useless game that just postpones the inevitable. Th-th-there would be others seeking them."

Hamelin swung a leg and examined his cuticles. "Edgar and I've got time to spare."

Bertland sputtered a few unintelligible syllables and kicked over his chair. "You're next, by golly. You're next!" he said, stabbing a finger at Hamelin. He made a move toward the pile of packing boxes by the register, but Hamelin slid in front of him, blocking his way.

"Take your best shot," Hamelin said, spreading his arms wide. And then he laughed, sending Bertland into a coughing fit of rage.

Hamelin supposed that Bertland wasn't *evil*, but just a neutral party doing his job. Oh, and couldn't he relate to that! But then there was this other thing. Bertland was a loyal foot soldier, apparently unwilling or unable to question authority, and for that, Hamelin despised him. There was right and there was wrong, there was black and there was white, and sometimes, there was something in the middle that worked out best for the most people. "Take a deep breath, Bertland, and dial it back. Don't feel like I don't want to work with you. Not all is lost. Give Edgar his so-called mojo back so he can finish his writing, and then maybe we can strike a deal. Everybody wins."

Bertland reigned in his emotions with frightening speed. His face became serene and his eyes calm. He studied Hamelin a moment, then shifted his gaze toward Edgar. "Can't be done. If I open one box, they all open."

"And?" Hamelin said. "So what? Where could they possibly go? Those people have moved on. It's not as if they're going to care about any dark thoughts flitting about. Once Edgar's mojo is free, can't you scoop the rest up and put them back in the boxes? Snag 'em with a big butterfly net or something? We might even be able to call in some specialists to help move them along to the final destination of their owners."

"You have no idea what a large, malevolent force like that is capable of," Bertland said.

Hamelin felt Bertland assessing him again, and he used the opportunity to do some snooping of his own. Bertland's aura was a dull gray and smacked of trouble.

Bertland suddenly brightened. "I certainly didn't expect you, Mr. Russell, to come along and change his life's timeline. What are you all about, sir? Why didn't Edgar move along with the rest of them? And who are these *specialists* you speak of? You seem well acquainted."

Bertland's expression was serious. The man was desperate. He would make promises all day long, but every one would have loopholes you could drive a bus through. Hamelin could play that game. "Look, Edgar doesn't want to hang around any longer than necessary," he said. "Give him some space to write his masterpiece, and then we'll sit down and address your concerns. Right, Edgar?"

Edgar started to argue, reconsidered, and then said, "Right. Manuscript first. Then discuss."

Hamelin nodded. "That's our one and only offer, Bertland. Otherwise, toddle off to wherever it is the grandchildren of Greek tragedy fade away to."

Bertland's fingers drummed the side of his pant leg. "As stated previously, there will be others to take the baton from me. Your best bet is to strike something here and now with me."

"Uh-huh," Hamelin said, nodding. "Because you like me."

"Oh, I do, I do," Bertland said, and he slapped Hamelin on the back. Bertland's cordial demeanor changed suddenly into a spirited yelp and a face pinched with pain. He yanked his hand back and shook it fiercely.

A slow, satisfied smile spread across Hamelin's face, and his eyes flashed with menace. "Now, don't you feel a little foolish for putting on pretenses? If you knew me as well as you have intimated, you would have known not to do that."

"I assure you, it won't happen again," Bertland said. "You stick to your guns, and I like that. So much, in fact, that I'm going to offer you a once-in-a-lifetime opportunity. I will open Edgar's box and give him temporary use of his talent, and five days—"

"A week," Hamelin interjected.

"*Five* days to complete his writing. At the end of that period, all the boxes revert to me."

"I thought you said you couldn't open just one box."

Bertland shrugged. "Sometimes I lie."

"A good reason for me not to strike any deal with you. How do I know you'll be acting in good faith?"

"We'll shake on it. Isn't that the way *you* do business, Mr. Russell?"

A flash of alarm coursed like hot lead through Hamelin's veins. For he *had* clasped many a hand over the centuries, ensuring the newly deceased rapid egress from earth to the heavenly gates or one of the seven fiery rings. But those professional duties were done in anonymity. How had Bertland discerned so much?

"All right," Hamelin said, nodding. "But if I catch you in a falsehood, you'll wish you'd never met me."

"Oh, no, my word is my bond," Bertland said, and thrust out his right hand. Hamelin ignored it and raised his right hand. Bertland did the same.

In that instant, Hamelin read Bertland's soul from inside to out, taking the measure of every honorable act and every infraction. He found no deceit in Bertland's current promise, although there seemed to be an awareness that if he could change circumstances and push the odds more in his favor, he would. Hamelin would have to keep this in mind.

He felt Bertland sizing him up, too. Hamelin had no fear of him. Bertland specialized in writers, and Hamelin wasn't given to writing anything down. If there was any dark talent in him that needed to go back into Pandora's box, someone else must reap it, and most assuredly, the Weigh Station had called dibs on it long ago.

Bertland lowered his hand first. "Excellent," he said, and looked at Edgar. "Go get the boxes.

Hamelin retrieved the boxes from a basket stored below the front counter. "Which one?"

Without hesitation, Edgar pulled one out and handed it to Bertland. Edgar beamed with a wide-eyed delight and eagerness that Hamelin had never seen in him. Any misgivings he had about dealing with Bertland dissipated—the biggest, loudest-screaming ones, at any rate.

Bertland took the innocuous-looking little dark box and walked over to the counter with it. Hamelin and Edgar gathered around him.

"How does it work?" Edgar whispered.

Bertland cleared his throat, took Edgar by the shoulders, and walked him back several paces. "Never you mind. Just know you don't have to hang all over it to make things work." He held the dark, gleaming wood in the open palm of his hand as if it were a prop in a magic show. And then he placed the index fingertip of his other hand on the center of the box top. "Unlock," he whispered, and gently blew on it. There was an almost inaudible click.

Hamelin drew back, frowning. He had always felt that mortals needed a bit of flash and spectacle to fully appreciate things beyond their ken. If the razzmatazz wasn't naturally there, one sometimes had to improvise and embellish. "That's *it*?"

Bertland raised a finger. "No. I've merely unlocked it. Wisdom lies in the use. I'm going to open this for the briefest moment—just long enough for Edgar to get a smidgeon of his mojo back, but not long enough to empty the box completely. That wouldn't be necessary for what we're trying to accomplish. Understand what's in here: a concentration of darkness and malevolence that has been planning and plotting for almost two centuries. To loose it all back into the world at once would be too powerful a surge. It would unleash havoc all around us. No, we go small." He looked at Edgar. "Ready?"

Edgar nodded, his eyes never leaving the box.

"Openclose." Bertland said it fast.

The box remained a solid block of wood without lid or opening.

Edgar's eyes narrowed. He gave Bertland the stink-eye. "What are you trying to pull?" And then he turned to Hamelin. "He's no better than a carnival sideshow. Can't you do something with this charlatan?"

"Relax," Bertland said. "No need to be flashy. It's done." He gave Hamelin a quick look and began to pocket the box.

"No, sir!" Hamelin said, thrusting a finger an inch from Bertland's face but not touching him. "The box stays here until he finishes his writing."

"That would be most unwise," Bertland said, taking a step back. "The box shouldn't be tampered with again until all is done. It is safest with me."

"It's not our agreement. Give me the box. *Now.*"

"No good will come of this," Bertland said holding the box aloft, just out of Hamelin's grasp.

Hamelin's hand shot out and snatched the box. "I didn't think you were trustworthy."

Bertland shrugged and put his hands in his pocket. "No, we're good. The agreement is binding on all parties. I'll be back in five days with Edelin to collect all the boxes. Best get cracking, Edgar."

He turned to leave, then stopped at the front door. "One final admonishment, and if you are wise, you'll abide by what I have to say. Edgar has enough of his muse back. If she decides to give wings to his pen, he'll pour his heart out on the page. If she doesn't, however, you are out of luck. But whatever you do, don't open the box again. Ever. More isn't better. Oh, no, it's infinitely worse." And with that, he was gone.

"Let me have the box, Hamelin," Edgar said, coming closer, hand outstretched.

Hamelin shook his head. "There is no agreement between you and me, Edgar, and quite frankly, I trust you even less than I do that man. It stays with me."

Edgar dropped his hand, and his expression dimmed somewhat. "Yes, it doesn't really matter, does it? Now, if you'll excuse me, I'm heading upstairs to write. The sooner I get it done, the sooner I can move on from this place."

He headed up the stairs, and when Hamelin heard the click of the door, he was satisfied that his deal was a good one. Five days hence, the world would have a new wonder from the great Edgar Allan Poe, the author would take his designated place in the afterlife, and Bertland would be dispatched to ply his macabre trade elsewhere.

Edgar sat down at his desk and set pen to paper. For the next hour, he tapped that pen, drew squiggles on the page margins, and chided himself for having absolutely nothing of worth to say. Obviously, Bertland had closed the box too quickly.

When at last he could tolerate no more, he eased his door open and sneaked down the staircase, hugging the wall and moving stealthily to keep the old treads from creaking. When he reached the bottom, he peered out just far enough to see Hamelin sitting at the table, holding one of the boxes. *Waddlespot.* Would he have to wait all night to get his hands on his own muse? Edgar crept halfway back up the stairs and sat. As long as he might possibly reacquire the rest of his mojo from that box, he could wait. Whether Edgar entered the promised land or the fiery pits of hell, he wanted all his faculties intact. In the end, Hamelin would have his back. Hamelin might be a controlling son of a gun, but he would never leave Edgar at the mercy of such a man as Daimon Bertland.

# Chapter Nine
# Sunny with a Chance of Trouble

Ryan leaned across the bar top and tipped his head toward Bertland in the far corner booth. "You want I should run him out?" he whispered to Hamelin in his best imitation of Bennie the bartender. "Most people don't enjoy being stared at."

Bennie stopped serving mojitos at the other end of the bar and looked their way. "I heard that."

Ryan chuckled, but Hamelin gave Ryan a cool look and resumed his staring. "If you must know, I was *thinking*."

"About what to do with Mr. Bertland? He's not another of your wayward mulli—"

"Shush! That's an antiquated term. You know those days are over."

"Really? To quote ancient wisdom, 'A hog in a silk waistcoat is still a hog.' I coulda' sworn—despite the modern-day suit—that whoever you have over there in your little book emporium is also a bit antiquated. The speech is off, and he's a little too stiff collared. Should I make you more uncomfortable by throwing lots of guesses at you, or can you just tell me when he was born and who he really is?"

Despite having ordered only water, Hamelin smacked five dollars down and stood up. Then he picked up his glass and headed for Bertland's table. "May I join you?" he asked when he got there.

Bertland shoved a chair at him with his foot. "Beats staring at me from over there. Is there an actual problem, or just general mistrust?"

"Oh, none," Hamelin said. "Just wondering at your need to hover so closely during the agreed-upon time period. Don't you have other pressing issues to attend to?"

"Light schedule. Just like yours. Where's the box?"

"Hidden away for safe keeping."

"You do realize he's struggling and wants to open it again."

"Of course." Actually, Hamelin didn't have an inkling of Edgar's current thought processes, but from daybreak to dark he was where he should be, doing what they all expected of him: scribbling away upstairs at his bun-footed davenport desk. Bertland's in-the-know self-assurance made him feel inadequate. "You doubt he can do this?"

Bertland's eyes shifted from Hamelin to the bookstore across the street. "You don't feel it, do you? The vibe. It's all wrong. The forces swirling about the place," he said, making a whirly motion with his index finger, "should be dark and menacing. Instead, I see sunshine, sparkling water, and sailboats. There is a troubling equilibrium about the place, and I can assure you that there's nothing Poe-esque flowing from his pen. He's creating nothing dark and new. We should save ourselves the downtime and let me take the box, because the dark lyricism of Edgar Allan Poe is dead."

Truth be told, Hamelin hadn't studied Edgar's aura of late, and he didn't use the weather forecast to judge how things in the world were going. He shrugged. "Perhaps you could give the old 'openclose' another go. Maybe you didn't give him back enough creative juice. He really shouldn't have to beg for it at all, you know. The muse is his own God-given talent. It doesn't take anything from anybody. To the contrary, it's given millions of readers untold enjoyment through

Edgar's works. You should be ashamed of yourself. If I had the power, I would put you in the deepest, darkest hole I could find, and fill it in with dirt."

Bertland laughed. "Do you really want to have a discussion of what you're capable of?" When Hamelin didn't respond, Bertland waved him off and said, "I gave him more than enough to finish. For his and all our sakes, keep the box away from him."

Hamelin leaned far enough across the table to make Bertland sit back in his chair. "Look, other than a few short walks to clear his head, he hasn't moved away from his desk. Everything is fine. Now, how about you shove off for other destinations? You're like a vulture sitting on a rooftop, waiting for roadkill."

Bertland signaled for his tab. "Can't. I'm meeting Ms. Jacoby later. We're having a heart-to-heart."

"Maybe you should just leave her alone. What's done is done. She made a mistake and tried hard to correct it."

Bertland stacked several bills on top of his check and slid it to the table's edge. "There are some things that can't be fixed. In my business, a contract is a contract. You, of all people, should understand that."

In the vernacular of the street, Bertland was a grade A, thoroughgoing asshole. In Hamelin's soul-running days, he had encountered his share of individuals—the black-hearted Ryan Llewellyn Thomas came to mind—who thought themselves clever enough to outwit even death and the tax man. Hamelin cut them no slack. And if he still had his runner faculties, Bertland would be ruing the day he ever thought he could outwit a soul runner. Still, if it was the last thing he did, Hamelin would see that Bertland personally reaped all the discord and unhappiness he had sown in Edgar's and countless other people's lives.

"Why don't you take it up with Edelin at the end of our agreement? By then, it should be no harm, no foul."

Bertland stood up. "Now, what idea would that give all the other custodians along my supply chain? I would be foolish to get myself booted out of a comfortable life because I didn't take things seriously. Know what I mean? Take care, Mr. Russell."

*Booted?* There it was. Again and again, Bertland seemed to know more about Hamelin's personal business than necessary or prudent. How did he do that? With his unworldly intuition—or maybe insider's knowledge— why was he allowed to roam freely on the earth, interfering with mortals and immortals? Just maybe, Hamelin thought, he wasn't all he claimed to be. Just maybe, Bertland had a little mind-reading talent, a lot of chutzpah, and the ability to run an excellent game of three-card monte.

At any rate, nothing good would come if Hamelin could not live unnoticed in the mortal world. For an instant, he wondered whether he should contact the Weigh Station and see if someone of higher authority might assess Bertland as a threat and move him along if necessary. Then he promptly decided against it. Bertland couldn't possibly be operating under the radar of the afterlife. Maybe this was one more trial being thrown at Hamelin on his path to redemption. He would deal with the trickster alone. Seen or unseen, there were many dangers in the world—even for an immortal.

Hamelin watched Pandora's grandson-cum-shyster turn right as he exited from the Phoenix and head toward the town green. He needed that fellow gone.

Edgar pulled the cardboard box down from the top of his closet and dumped the contents on his bed: a flashlight and two small surveillance cameras capable of recording in real time, which he had bought for four hundred dollars from Bob's Electronics around the corner. For an additional eight hundred dollars, Bob's had installed four more cameras in the stacks and given him a quick lesson in how to use them. Edgar considered it money well spent. He wasn't much for electronic gadgets, especially cell phones. They might make a lot of tasks easier to accomplish, but they seemed more addictive than opium.

Edgar pushed aside a pile of rumpled clothes on the floor and uncovered the DVR/television combo unit he had also purchased. He turned it on and began watching the playback of footage recorded earlier in the night. The picture clarity was excellent, with not a blur in any of Hamelin's movements around the store. So far, Edgar's surveillance had produced nothing except Hamelin's back disappearing out of range into the far recesses of the store. But after the addition of several new cameras at various intersections throughout the shelves, he felt he would soon know where Hamelin was hiding the box that Edgar so coveted.

He watched Hamelin go through his now familiar ritual of locking the cash register, drawing the shades, and heading down to the end of one of the darkened stacks. He disappeared around the corner and then quickly reappeared as he fell in frame of the newest camera installed. Edgar chewed his lip as Hamelin walked to the end of that aisle and paused, checking his surroundings. Seemingly satisfied that he was alone, Hamelin pulled a book from a top shelf, slid something behind it, and repositioned the book. Seconds later, he locked the front door and left.

Hamelin wasn't necessarily a punctual person, but Edgar knew he wouldn't be back until morning. Still, he waited, every fiber of his being tingling with excitement as he watched the motion-triggered camera go black. Then he listened attentively for sounds of activity downstairs. He didn't expect Hamelin to break routine, but it seemed too easy, and Hamelin a little too trusting. The immortal was slipping.

When he could stand it no longer, Edgar crept down the steps and bolted for the hiding place: the "T" section behind a red oversize volume of J. R. R. Tolkien's *The Lord of the Rings* in an ornate slipcover. He yanked it out and patted down the space behind it, his heart pounding like a telltale heart as his fingers locked on the cool, polished wood. It began to warm immediately.

He pulled it out and paused. Now that he had it, should he open it here, or sneak it away to his room? There was little chance Hamelin would return soon––Edgar had verified that night after night, hadn't he? He snatched up the Tolkien volume to return it to its place. But in his haste, juggling book and box, he fumbled the box. He watched with horror as it rolled under the shelving.

"No, no, no," he groaned, falling to his knees. He swept the beam of the flashlight right to left but couldn't see the dark box. He ran a hand underneath the shelves on either side and came up with only an ink-pen cap and a hand covered in cobwebs. He fished about on the floor until he had found it, at last, resting against the baseboard a few paces beyond the end of the shelving. Clutching the box to his bosom, he settled back against the opposite shelf to sort himself out.

He would cut his risks. "Openclose," he said, running the words together in imitation of Bertland's voice. No click. He tried again, changing the intonation ever so slightly. Again, nothing. "Open, open, open," he intoned, caressing, shaking and clawing at its edges. It remained as impregnable as when he first found it. Off in the distance, he heard a boom of thunder. This was good. Hamelin would never return in the middle of a storm.

He sat listening to the syncopated beat of his heart. What had he missed? And then it dawned on him that perhaps Bertland couldn't resist the dramatic, that only he could open the box and it had nothing to do with precise touches, voice inflections, or the like. He sat on the hard floor of the shop in the absolute still and darkness and felt all hope drain from him. His crowning achievement would remain unwritten, and he would be forced to roam the earth forever.

Suddenly, inexplicably, he gave the box a sniff—a sniff that was repeated, but not by him. Then he realized it was not a sniff at all, but the sound of gravel underfoot. He bolted to his feet. Someone was milling about outside. Then followed a scratching at the door, and the click of the front door lock. Hamelin?

Edgar slid his prize under his nightshirt and fled upstairs and slipped back in bed. The speed and pounding with which the visitor attacked the stairs told Edgar this couldn't possibly go well. He'd been found out. He freed the box from the covers and whispered *open* half a dozen times while running his fingers around the edges of the box. "For goodness sake," he hissed. "Unlock. Openclose."

As his bedroom door swung open, light burst forth from the box and flashed against the ceiling. It bounced around the room in a kaleidoscope of colors before gathering itself into a tight swirl in one of the corners. It hung there a moment, spinning faster and faster as it seethed and sparkled. Then, with a flash and a roar, it hurtled like a comet at the window, shattering the glass and disappearing into the night.

Hamelin streaked across the room in three long strides, yanked the box from Edgar, and intoned, "Close." There was an audible click. "What have you done!" he asked, locking eyes with Edgar. "What have you done?"

"I—I—I don't know," Edgar said, blinking rapidly as he wiped a speck of blood from his cheek. "But perhaps it was ill-conceived. Do you think we can put it back?"

Hamelin picked his way through shards of broken glass and moved to the window. Nevis was pitch black and deathly quiet. There was no sign of the light show. He walked back over to Edgar. "Sure, we can. I'll hop downstairs and give Bertland a quick call. He'll be glad to come over and end our little experiment."

"Oh," Edgar whispered. "I'm afraid I've screwed up immensely, haven't I?"

Hamelin looked at the shaken little man cowering in his bed. Maybe the call should be to Luke, his soul-running friend in the afterlife. Perhaps, he should let Edgar's literary achievements rest on his published laurels, and bring this mess to a close. It would be as easy as ordering a new Jaguar.

Edgar shifted from contrition to offense. "Actually, this is all your fault. Why on earth did you leave the box here? Surely, you knew I couldn't resist the siren's call!"

Hamelin poked him in the chest with the box. Twice. The second was hard enough to make him wince. "Considering your precarious circumstances, I'd suggest taking ownership rather than trying to place blame elsewhere. And I'd start worrying about Bertland. He's a most unforgiving man, and when he finds out you messed with his box, he's going to demand payment." And then, in answer to the unspoken question in Edgar's wide eyes, he added, "I have no idea when that will be."

Hamelin looked about the small bedroom. It was remarkably tidy for a packrat like Edgar. His gaze fell on the DVRD on the floor. If the troublesome writer just spent as much time pounding out a story as he did hatching plots to end his life ... "How far along is your manuscript?"

"Halfway ... maybe."

Hamelin gazed out the window again. They had about six hours until daybreak. "I don't like people screwing with me, Edgar. I also don't like wasting time, misplacing my trust, or making things any more complicated for myself than need be. So you're going to put pen to paper and sit at that desk over there and finish your story in the next twenty-four hours. I'm going to be right here, glaring at you, for the duration, and I'll fend off Bertland. And at the end of that period? Our association is at an end. I'll have a friend come and escort you into the afterlife. Got it?"

Edgar hung his head. "Yes, sir."

Edgar hauled his manuscript out and began writing—in silence for the most part, except for brief periods of mumbling, which were punctuated by ungodly oaths and scratchings-out so vigorous that they threatened to tear a hole through his writing pad.

Hamelin took up a chair by the door and drifted into an uneasy meditation as he waited for the inevitable arrival of Pandora's grandson. His aura—usually a shimmering, peaceful blue—hung limply about him in an ominous shade of storm cloud gray.

About an hour later, Hamelin stirred in his chair. Edgar sat hunched over his manuscript, still writing. "Are you making headway?" Hamelin asked.

Edgar nodded and kept writing. "Getting there."

A flash of lightning lit the night, and a thunderclap shook the walls of the shop. Both men popped out of their chairs. Hamelin reached the window first. Across town and to the south, a raging inferno illuminated a church bell tower as orange and yellow flames licked their way up the spire, reaching hungrily for the cross at the top. The air was filled with the smell of burning wood. In the distance, the firehouse sirens began to wail, and emergency vehicles soon added their eerie whine. Hamelin looked out across the water. The night sky was dark but clear, its dark canvas sprinkled with hundreds of points of starlight.

*Dear God, Edgar, what have you loosed upon us?*

# Chapter Ten

# Stilling the Raging Darkness

Bertland threw on his street clothes and left his room at the inn. He was in no dream this time. The real world beyond his window was alight with fire. He had been right. He never should have trusted Hamelin Russell.

He made his way down Bayside Avenue as far as the police would let him go. A block farther down, he saw a building fully engulfed in flames. The area looked like a disturbed anthill as firefighters swarmed the scene with their water hoses and working grappling hooks. What a shame. It had been a lovely church. Bertland closed his eyes a moment, willing his body to relax as he sought a centering and subjugation of the chaos swirling inside him. The muse was here; he felt it. His inner eye found it as it hopped from window to rafter, to crumbling belfry, performing a macabre victory dance in the destruction it had just wreaked. Bertland needed to put a name on it, but that would be impossible until the kinetic force remained stationary long enough for him to sense its essence. His actions were a necessary formality. He knew what raged here. Edgar Allan Poe's most terrifying achievement would not be his writing, but the unleashing of his own inner darkness on an unsuspecting world. As long as Bertland was present, the world would be unsuspecting but not defenseless.

As Bertland stood ramrod straight and silent, watching and listening, additional sirens approached, screaming in the night. The shadow suddenly stopped, bounced again, then settled once more, turning its attention to *him*. He felt its defiance and mockery. Bertland locked on the creature, embraced it, absorbed its every scintilla of energy and thought. "Got you, Edgar Poe," he whispered, smiling. With a shrill whistle that sounded like an incoming rocket, the shadow hurtled out into the darkness and vanished. Bertland let it go. The game was on, but once he had a name, flight was useless.

Bertland stepped away from the crowd of gawkers, which was growing by the minute with pajamaed and nightshirted townspeople rolling out of bed to witness the ruckus, and strode off in the direction of Barnacle Bertie's. When the muse calmed down, it would seek out Poe. He needed the body to entice the muse.

He found a light on upstairs—a bedroom, no doubt—and the store itself dark. He tried the door handle and found it locked. "By Zeus," he muttered, shaking the doors hard enough to rattle the glass and bounce the *closed* sign around on its chain. He bowed his head and willed himself away from the place.

A moment later, Bertland entered his grandmother's house, his khakis and polo shirt exchanged for a flowing Ionic chiton in off-white. He padded across the marble floor of the expansive stone hall, under the searing gaze of Pandora, which focused on him like a raven sizing up its next meal. Her demeanor suggested a foul mood and that she already knew much of what he would say. When he reached her, he nodded in deference, and when she returned the greeting, he sat down beside her as she dined at table. "Grandmother, we have a problem."

"I have seen," she said. "Tell me as you see it."

Bertland looked across the table at the man sitting with her. He was a demon, with a countenance as dark as his clothes. He was an eagle to Pandora's raven, a keen hunter but without the nobility of the stately raptor. "Here?"

"He's of no consequence," she said, dismissing the stranger's presence with a wave of her hand.

"Someone has broken faith and sold one of my collection facilities."

"Is an oath no longer sacred?" she asked, turning to address the man. She didn't seem to expect an answer, and turning back to Bertland, she said, "You dealt with them swiftly?"

"Soon," he promised.

"So, you need the assistance of Daemopoulos?"

Could nothing be accomplished without his help? Bertland bit his tongue and shook his head. "Nothing I can't handle. But there is something more troubling. Someone has opened one of my collection boxes."

Her eyes grew beady, and she put down the kylix she had been drinking from. "Just one?"

"As far as I can determine, the darkness of Edgar Allan Poe. It torched a church—"

"*A church?* That invites the worst kind of scrutiny." She fussed for a moment with the folds of her long chiton, the iridescent fabric shimmering and shifting in color. "I'm disappointed in you, Bertland. How is it that you lost control of your charges?"

"Not through lack of vigilance on my part, but through the duplicity of another who was bound by contract and honor to protect them. My storage house in Nevis, Maryland, has been sold and I've lost access to all my boxes there."

"Who sold the bookstore, and who bought it?"

"A woman named Edelin Jacoby sold it to a man by the name of Hamelin Russell."

"You should have known not to trust a woman," Pandora said.

The demon straightened in his chair. "The soul runner? I know this immortal. He is a troublemaker and a threat to everything we represent. First, it's one box; then it's *all* the boxes. It snowballs from there. Let me handle Hamelin Russell for you, Pandora. We have met before, and I know how to handle him."

Pandora walked to an open window that looked out on a garden full of flowers in every hue. She scooped a handful of birdseed from a red-figure ware fish plate sitting on the sill, and cast it outside. "Make sure Edelin Jacoby understands her mistake, Bertland. If you must, bring her here. I'll leave that up to you. The same goes for Russell Hamelin. Make it clear he is to stay out of your way. As for Mr. Poe," she said, turning back around, "Go back to the bookshop. The dark muse will be drawn back there. When it returns, you are not to store it, understand? Bring it here to me. If you can't handle it, Daemopoulis will clean up the mess."

"And you," she said, addressing the demon. "Take care of Mr. Russell for me."

He gave her an obsequious nod. "At your service. My services do come at a price," he said, "but the resulting personal satisfaction for both of us will be well worth it."

"I pay well," she said. And pointing toward the archway leading out of her salon, she added, "Just do it."


Hamelin joined the whispering bystanders gathered at the bottom of Bayside Avenue and studied the smoking rubble that was once the First United Methodist Church. Its stately wooden structure was reduced to burning timbers, smelly ash, and a heap of colonial bricks. She'd been a looker, pride of the town with a stately spire that rose to a breath-catching gold-plated cross at its tip.

Although Hamelin preferred to commune with the omnipotent Creator in the peaceful solitude of nature, he had been inside once and found its simple space of carved oak pews and pulpit to be a delight. He'd read its interesting history on a historic marker placed out front. He assumed that the placard was also now ash.

First Methodist hadn't always stood here. Originally, the structure sat at the water's edge and many parishioners came to services by boat. It survived gales and nor'easters and even the great town fire in the 1850s that wiped out most of Nevis's southern section. What it couldn't withstand was the folly of man: first the ill-advised excavating near the foundation to create a culvert for one of the local creeks, and now the self-centered needs of a 170-year-old curmudgeon who couldn't follow the simplest of directions. The town had averted disaster in the former by putting the structure on rollers and, over a period of months, dragging it uphill to its present location. Heartbreakingly, it was too late to address the latter.

Hamelin looked around him at the odd collection of vintage shops, houses, and buildings of various eras that seemed misplaced on their own but, taken together, told the story of the town more eloquently than any history book. Boom and bust, religious and secular—which would Edgar's folly light up next? And there would be a next. Of that, Hamelin was certain. He shook his head, no longer sure whether Edgar was worth protecting. He had to find the muse.

He flagged down the fire marshal still barking orders despite the obvious total loss of property. "Anyone hurt?" Hamelin asked.

"Just civic identity," the marshal muttered without stopping to chat.

Hamelin followed after. "Arson?"

"Lightning." The marshall halted in mid step and turned around, eyes narrowed. "Nobody's said anything about arson. Didn't get your name." He pushed his helmet back off his forehead for a better look.

"Hamelin Russell, owner of Barnacle Bertie's."

"New to town," the fire marshall said, his eyes flashing interest. He gave Hamelin the head to toe and then turned, seemingly taking stock of the distance between the bookstore and the church. Hamelin must have disappointed his suspicions, though, because the fireman was soon in motion again, yelling out more instructions for his crew. "Get behind the perimeter tape, Mr. Russell. It's dangerous out here."

*If you knew the half of it ...* Hamelin ducked back under the yellow tape, avoiding the stares of the growing crowd of spectators, all yearning for information but too polite to ask.

"Thinking of setting something on fire?" asked a quiet voice behind him.

Hamelin grabbed Ryan Thomas by the elbow and guided him out of the crowd. "Trying to get me arrested?"

Ryan laughed and then, reassessing Hamelin's mood, checked his mirth. "Leave your sense of humor in bed?"

"You know I don't sleep. I might ask why you are downtown at this late hour."

"Replacing the kitchen floor while we're closed. Can't have the downtime in the middle of the day. You're awfully pissy, you know that? One of your friends short out the church electrical system?"

"Shh! The fire marshall already thinks I'm good for it." Hamelin shook his head in answer to the perplexed look on Ryan's face. "I'm afraid I asked questions that were ill-timed—"

Ryan burst into laughter, drawing indignant stares from some along the sidewalk. He leaned in to Hamelin and whispered, "So you *do* have some involvement in this?"

"No."

"Really?"

Hamelin's gaze skimmed the destruction across the street. "No. I mean, I'm not sure." He ended with a mumbled, "Perhaps."

"You are so naive," Ryan said. "One never revisits the scene of one's crime." He tipped his head in the direction of the Phoenix. "My place."

# Chapter Eleven
# Divining the Fibonacci

In the quiet of the closed pub, Ryan poured two fingers of scotch for himself and an iced tea for Hamelin, and they sat down at the bar with a bowl of shelled peanuts.

Hamelin pointed at his drink. "Long Island?"

Ryan shook his head. "No, just plain old sweet tea. How many times do I have to apologize for slipping you some alcohol?"

"Until I trust you again," Hamelin said. He sniffed the drink, then took a few tentative sips.

"So you're in trouble with the fire marshal. I can help. Sean Fisher is a friend of mine. Unless this is some new contest for your old acquaintances in the great beyond, in which case I'm not getting involved. The bar contest was more than enough."

Hamelin rolled his eyes and began arranging peanuts into a pattern on the bar top. Mortals could be entertaining, even endearing, but *helpful?* Absurd. "It has nothing to do with that."

"What, then? Spill the deets because we only have three more churches in town and you're acting guilty as hell. You know something."

Hamelin's head bobbed. "Do you know the story of Pandora's box?"

"From Greek mythology? Sure. When I attended James Ryder Randall Elementary School, I had eternal dibs on D'Aulaire's *Book of Greek Myths.*

The librarian threatened to ban me from the library if I didn't start checking out other books. As I recall, it wasn't a box, though. It was a jar."

"You remember correctly. It was a jar, and now it is a box. Funny how that worked out."

Ryan jiggled the ice cubes in his drink. "I can go either way with it. What's it got to do with the fire? Pandora married *Epi*metheus, not *Pro*metheus."

"I'm not certain yet, but I can assure you it is most assuredly connected in some fashion."

"A little more information, Hamelin."

"Do you know why I made Edgar Allan Poe a mulligan?"

Ryan thumped down his glass. "Oh, dear God, I knew there was something wrong with that guy!"

Hamelin drew back, scowling at him. "There's nothing wrong with *that* guy—at least, nothing more than can be said about *you,* fellow mulligan. As I was saying, I made him a mulligan because when I came for him, he was on the verge of finishing a masterpiece of literature."

"You researched all your transportees that closely?"

Hamelin's head bobbed. "Not research per se. If they were in the arts, I took particular interest in what they accomplished, and usually poked around in the history of their careers. As I shared the review of their life story right before death, I got special insights into what they were all about. Edgar's inventiveness was staggering. To let him slip away from this earthly plane after he had been treated so poorly seemed almost sinful."

Hamelin looked at Ryan's furrowed brow. "For heaven's sake, he's father of the modern-day detective story. Have you never read 'The Murders in the Rue Morgue'?"

"Of course I've read it," Ryan said with a sneer. "Contrary to what you might think, I do have some education under my belt. I'm just wondering what it was like to actually meet him. Was he a depressed man, Hamelin? Because I can't imagine someone writing the dark things that he expressed and not getting dragged down by them."

"No," Hamelin said, reflecting back on the writer's intimate last moments. "I saw a gentle man who lived a good life doing the best he could with those extraordinary gifts he had. He may have entertained a dark muse, but his aura certainly wasn't dark. That's why I can't understand ..." He suddenly checked himself and shook the thought out of his head.

"Understand what, Hamelin?"

"To get back to the tale about Pandora's box. Her grandson, Bertland, walks this earth, forever commissioned to put back in the jar the evils his grandmother released. It's fruitless, but he's determined."

"Wait! Are you saying Pandora's box is more than just a story?"

Hamelin turned wide eyes on him. "You don't think all those fables and myths are based on *something*? One has to start somewhere."

Ryan put his hands over his ears. "Wait, wait, *wait,* Hamelin. Slow down. Are you saying the Greek myths are based in truth? That all those gods are more than a collective cultural fantasy? Because I don't think I can take that."

"That blasphemy would never come out of my mouth. No, what I'm saying is that humans have always made up stories to help deal with things they don't understand. Bertland is presenting himself as part of a polytheistic world. Well, don't you believe it for a second. There is but one God—eternal and loving. But that doesn't preclude the existence of powerful rulers and forces who, for eons, have tried to control the destiny of man."

"Okay, good," Ryan said, putting his hands down. "He's delusional and set the First Methodist church on fire in tribute to Great-Great-Uncle Prometheus, the Titan of fire?"

"Or running some sort of scam," Hamelin said, adding more peanuts to his design, which had grown from a single nut in the center into two swirls moving in opposite directions around it. "While Bertland may not be the son of Pyrrha and Deucalion, that doesn't necessarily mean he's just some crazy mortal. There are many more things at play in this universe than you suspect."

"Crazy *im*mortal, then."

Hamelin shrugged. "Perhaps. Or at worst, a troublesome demon out to make mischief." He arched an eyebrow as Ryan topped off his tea.

Ryan put down the pitcher and snorted. "Go ahead, do your sniff test again. Do you think he knows what you are?"

Hamelin pushed the glass aside. "I don't believe so, although he's certainly tried to suss me out." He chuckled softly. "It's an interesting chess match, I must say."

"Until now. Burning down places of worship goes way past gaming. Imagine what would have happened if there had been people in that church. What does he want, Hamelin?"

"Oh, that wasn't his doing. All those pyrotechnics were Edgar's fault." Hamelin fished a bit of shell out of the bowl of peanuts and put it on the bar top. "In a nutshell, Bertland came here to retrieve Edgar's dark muse, which he claims is, or was, trapped in a little polished cypress box on a shelf at Bertie's. Supposedly, a number of other artists' muses are trapped in boxes at Bertie's, too, although Edgar is the only soul that hasn't been transported."

Ryan started to laugh.

"Why is that so funny?"

Ryan took a moment to compose himself. "You do realize, I may be the only person in the world you could get to believe this cockamamie story?"

Hamelin gave him a death stare and slid off his stool. "I might have known—"

Ryan held up two hands to stay him. "Wait! I'm trying. I'm really trying, Hamelin. Why not just give the muse back?"

"Because while Bertland says he wants Edgar's dark muse back, I'm not entirely certain he's ever had it. Edgar was out of his mind, delirious and dying on a Baltimore street, when he made a deal with Bertland to take his dark muse. Neither party has said what Edgar was to receive in exchange for giving Bertland his muse. I suspect it was a promise that the darkness Edgar brought into the world through his writing wouldn't be used against him in his final judgment. You and I might consider that to be a ludicrous, bogus deal—no one has the authority to influence what the good Lord considers. He sees all, hears all. But what's to say a dying man wouldn't cling to that? I doubt it would have taken much for a powerful entity like Bertland to convince a weakened Edgar that he took his muse when, in fact, he didn't—hypnosis, for example, might take care of it. Then I come along close behind, set Edgar up in a new life, and after several bad days of writing, Edgar really believes Bertland hoodwinked him into giving up his talent. Next thing he knows, Edgar is hopelessly writer-blocked."

Hamelin shook his head and continued. "No, maybe these aren't muses at all, but some sort of demon army Bertland has at the ready. I just don't know."

Ryan tossed the peanut shell into the trash can behind the bar and studied the century-old crabbing photo above the whiskey shelf. "It's a crazy world, but considering some of the other wild things you've told me that turned out to be true, I'll go with it. My question for you is, what if Bertland is lying about what he wants? Maybe he has a different motive for getting all up in your business."

"Oh, he's a liar, all right, and cunning. He freely admitted it, and his aura is tinged with ugly shades of prevarication. Deceit is his nature. But you don't have to worry about me. I'm watching him."

"What does Edgar want? Don't his wishes count?"

"He doesn't know what's good for him."

Ryan side-eyed him. "And you do? Come on, Hamelin. You're trying to play God. I would have thought you'd learned your lesson when they booted you out of heaven. Most guys would have got the message."

"It wasn't heaven, and they didn't give me the boot," Hamelin said, scowling. "They merely redirected my efforts."

Ryan studied him a moment. "I'm going to say this as a friend, so don't go nuclear on me, all right?" He waited until Hamelin nodded. "Release Edgar from this mortal life, and all these problems disappear. No more destruction of property, no potential loss of life or limb, he's content, and no violation of your probation. He's lived, what, two hundred years too long? What kind of life could he possibly live hiding in a bookshop all day? He's a fish out of water. What else is there to consider?"

Hamelin drew his hand back from the bar top and admired his peanut design. Then he looked at Ryan and cocked his head. "One, two, three, five, eight, thirteen ..."

"It's wonderful," Ryan deadpanned. "And it solves *everything*."

"It's the Fibonacci sequence, and yes, it does. Sunflowers? Pinecones? Seashells? The curve on an incoming ocean wave? They all exhibit the Fibonacci spiral. There is a pattern to everything in the universe. You just have to look at it in the right way." He saw confusion in Ryan's face. "If you had an ounce of the artistic in you, you would understand." With his hand, he swept the peanuts into a pile in the center of the bar top. "And if you paid attention. You haven't heard a word I've said since I moved in next door to you. I can't transport him, because I'm not a soul runner anymore. I'm no longer permitted those powers. As I said at the beginning of this conversation, simple solutions won't do. Bertland isn't mortal, and while I have crafted a temporary understanding with him, he can't be trusted over the long haul. We start with one Pandora brat, then there's two, and before you know it, the sequence has taken on a life of its own—three, five, eight ... No need to attract that sort of trouble."

"But why would heaven acknowledge polytheists in the first place?" Ryan said. "Seems to me they'd stamp out Pandora's operation in a St. Peter minute."

"Trust me. They miss very little, but I'm not privy to the inner workings. Whatever is involved is too far above my above my pay grade."

Ryan raised an eyebrow.

"*Was* above my pay grade," Hamelin said, correcting himself. "At any rate, I suspect something has gone off track here, because I can't imagine heaven letting *anyone* delay the delivery of complete souls to their destination. Even though I fear for the likes of Stephen King and Dean Koontz, how do I really know that he is just collecting dark muses of the writing elite? There is darkness in all of us, Ryan James: envy, duplicity, mistrust. Who's to say who Bertland might target next? You? Your mother, Vanessa?"

Hamelin watched Ryan weighing the consequences of letting Pandora's offspring roam free to wreak havoc in his orbit. "Your beloved Marie at Nonnis?" he added, piling on. "You see? I must stop him *now*. It's my duty."

"Enough," Ryan said, putting up his hand. "I got the picture. How do you intend to put an end to his mischief?"

Hamelin drained his glass. "I don't know yet, but I have a little less than five days to find out and then crush him."

Ryan bussed Hamelin's glass and swept the peanuts into a white bar towel. "Even if I wanted to get involved, I'm no match for an immortal, and I'm not willing to antagonize him and put my loved ones or any of my patrons at risk. I might be able to subtly encourage him to move along, or I can let him make this his second home. You tell me what helps you most in rooting him out. But's that's as far as I'm willing to go. Our adventure days together, Hamelin, are done-zo."

"Don't run him off. Haven't you ever heard of holding your enemies close? If he's remaining close by, he's probably content to let our little agreement run its course. A little tally of who he hangs with would be helpful, though, if you think you can handle that."

Ryan cut eyes at him. "Why are you always so condescending?"

"If I had more time, I would list the reasons, but right now my concern is Edelin Jacoby. I need to run her down."

"We're not talking literally, right?"

Hamelin gave him a disgusted look. "What do you think, Einstein? Edelin is the only other working part I know of. She may know how to recapture the muse. What do you know about her?"

"And this Edelin would be …?"

"Former owner of Barnacle Bertie's. You know, the business right across the street from you? Jeesh, are you really that antisocial?"

"Oh, her," Ryan said, not rising to the slight. "Tall, figure out of Victoria's Secret? Never got a name. I can save you some running. She was in here last night."

Hamelin brightened. "With Bertland?"

"Uh-uh. Alone. Lately, she's in here all the time. Now, *there's* your Long Island ice tea drinker. She's the antisocial one—orders the Long Island and keeps 'em coming until she's so hammered, she forgets whatever it is that's bugging her. Bennie did have to cut her off last night. Don't know whether that will change her mind about coming here again. There's always Clancy's down the street, although I suspect they would cut her off, too. I thought you threw big bucks at her for Bertie's. She shouldn't have a care in the world."

"By now, I would have thought she would be soaking up the sun on Capri," Hamelin said, his brow furrowing. "She was in such a hurry to leave town after the sale. Sometimes, a windfall can come with a heavy price. Do you have any idea where she's staying?"

Ryan shook his head. "No, but I can ask around. If I don't get any nibbles, I can always bring in my friend Maggie Sullivan. She's a top-notch researcher I worked with when I was based in New York."

"When you were running with organized crime, you mean?" Hamelin shook his head. "Forget it! I've already got the fire marshal looking askance at me. Adding the scrutiny of the po-po is not a smart move."

"I never *ran* with organized *anything*," Ryan said, giving him a heated look. "Before you mulliganed me, I was a law-abiding college student. Remember? You conjoined my soul with that of the criminally minded sociopath Ryan Llewellyn Thomas. I still can't figure out how he even *had* a soul to transport."

"I fixed that," Hamelin growled. "And thanks to me, here you sit, blessed with a second chance at life." He stopped and pondered the ceiling. "Come to think of it, I don't recall that you ever actually thanked me for that."

"Thank you!" Ryan spat the words out as if they burned his mouth.

"Change the subject before we're not speaking again."

"Yeah, how long did that last?" Hamelin mumbled, giving him an injured look. "Tell me about this Maggie Sullivan."

"She's been working in the investigative agency I've got going on the side. Late last week, she relocated from New York to Nevis. Part of our deal is, she gets out from behind the desk once in a while. With the exception of Vanessa, nobody here knows her. How about we set her up in the Phoenix, have her bump into our friend Edelin and get chummy? She's a charming lady, and if anyone can find out where Edelin fits into this, it's Maggie Sullivan."

"I already know her role in all this. I just need to know where she is."

Ryan shrugged.

"All right," Hamelin said, nodding slowly. "If I haven't found her by the end of the day, I'll take you up on your offer, but I don't want any side issues popping up because of her past associations. Understood? And don't give Ms. Sullivan too many specifics. It's safer that way. I'd hate to have to consider her a loose end when this is over."

"You wouldn't harm her—"

Hamelin rolled his eyes. "You are even more gullible than usual if that's possible."

"Bastard!"

"Yes, actually. But I don't see why you need to bring that into all this."

Ryan put his hand to his forehead. "Sorry, Hamelin. I didn't mean that literally."

"Nothing to be sorry about. It was my stepfather who was the real bastard. Now, about Ms. Sullivan?"

"I can limit Maggie to the basics—nothing in depth and no side issues. If I thought her past associations would ever cause a problem, I would never have promoted a working relationship with her, but she hasn't heard from her crazy-ass ex for ages. As far as we know, he's still living it up in the Caymans on his boatload of ill-gotten dough."

"Just make sure." Hamelin slid off his stool. "I'm not going to solve this by sitting here."

"I wish I could offer more, Hamelin, but like I said, this is kinda out of my sphere of influence. Can't you call *them*?"

Call *them*? Did Hamelin really want to explain that when he left the Weigh Station behind, it was not just a relocation, but a complete cutting of the cord? He was on his own with life, death, a crazy dark muse tearing up Nevis, and a less-than-transparent immortal who stood for everything a good soul runner would despise. Hamelin was an orphan, which was a thousand times worse than being a bastard.

# Chapter Twelve

# Fluctuation

At the Weight Station, the sweet-faced youth stood at his desk, staring at two computer monitors. "Excuse me," he said to his visitor, and turned to call over the cloth partition to the next cubicle. "Claudia."

"What is it now, Mark?" a voice answered back.

"Come look at this?"

Ezekiel listened to the squeak of Claudia's chair and watched as Mark made peevish eye contact with his neighbor.

"There's a problem in sector four-four-z-z." Mark pivoted his monitor so Claudia could see it. "There, in the upper right corner. Fluctuation."

Claudia took Mark's mouse and began clicking computer windows. "When did this happen?" She ran through half a dozen in a matter of seconds and then muttered something indelicate. "Go get Ezekiel. This is going to be chaos."

"I'm Ezekiel," the visitor said, moving closer to get a better look at the screen.

"*You're* him?" Claudia extended a hand. "No offense intended, sir. It's an honor. You're the man."

Ezekiel ignored the flattery and concentrated on the graph showing sector 44zz. "Here?' he asked, indicating a sudden rise on the graph.

"Right. Everything normal, nice and flat, and all of the sudden out of nowhere, there's this big surge of energy."

"Print that," Ezekiel said, already in motion toward the printer. "Sit tight, Mark, and don't take your eyes off that screen until someone one gives you further instructions. If it spikes again, send an update to Elder Stephen." He snatched up his copy before it could settle into the printer tray, and took off. As he headed for the White Corridor and Elder Stephen's office, he could hear the hero worship spilling out of Claudia. It was as if the woman had never met an angel before.

One inside Elder Stephen's office suite, Stephen's assistant, Jonas, intercepted Ezekiel. After verifying who he was, Jonas escorted him to Stephen in an inner office. Stephen and two other elders were already seated around a small conference table. The room was white on white, and a miniature water fountain added to the ambience with its soft splashing on a credenza behind the door.

Stephen nodded at Ezekiel, and he joined them at the table. While not a mentor—angels, after all, were much more evolved mentally, emotionally, and spiritually than keepers of the Weigh Station— Ezekiel often sought out Stephen when he wanted a different point of view. He was unfamiliar with the others, although he probably knew them on paper. The faces of the three reflected a solemnity that suggested they already knew something of the crisis at hand.

Stephen introduced the other two elders as Barnaby and Patrick and took the printout from him. When Ezekiel opened his mouth to speak, the elder raised a hand and politely stopped him. "Mark and Claudia have already filled us in."

Ezekiel closed his mouth and nodded to the two other elders. They weren't entirely unknown to him. The Angelic Corps jokingly referred to Stephen, Patrick, and Barnaby as the gang of three. If there was a big whoop-de-doo to be settled with the Weigh Station, these men were at the forefront. An angel in need sought out the empathetic and supportive Stephen when a gentle guiding hand was needed, anal and punctilious Patrick when the question required a cut-and-dried factual response, and, when one's wings were on fire and there was no one else to turn to, the stern and glaring, brutally proficient Barnaby.

"Have you ever seen this before?" Ezekiel asked.

"All the time, but never on such a scale," Stephen said, sharing the printout with the others. "When someone dies and a runner picks up their soul, a change in matter occurs. Simultaneously, a teeny burst of thermal energy is released. Infinitesimal. Barely registers a blip, but it's there. But this unremarkable, barely noticeable blip indicates a change in matter—the soul—that compares to a magnitude 7.5 earthquake or an EF-five tornado. It is violent and uncontrolled, and we know of only one way that it occurs."

"Someone has opened one of Pandora's boxes," Barnaby said."

Ezekiel knew the story: a tempted woman unwittingly releasing all the world's ills from one enchanted box—or jar, to be more precise. "Boxes?" he asked.

"That is correct," Stephen said, nodding. "As atonement for her sin, she is tasked with returning every evil to a secure box. A few are associated with human souls." His gaze floated to Patrick, who was tracing a finger across the graph as he reviewed it. "But, of course, it's a bit more complicated than that," Stephen said, wincing.

Ezekiel cocked his head.

"Oh, I don't say that to insult your intelligence, Ezekiel. No, no, no. Let's be clear about that. It's just that we don't have time at the moment. Suffice it to say, this surge in energy is a soul that has been released out into the mortal world without any guidance, or a body subject to the consequences of its actions. A rogue soul. It needs to be rounded up and transported to the afterlife."

"So why am I here?" Ezekiel asked. "Transport doesn't involve the Angelic Corps."

"Well, that's the complicated part. Pandora's grandson, Daimon Bertland, has been collecting portions of souls—dark muses—and hanging on to them instead of turning them over for transport. That violates the agreement with her. He needs—"

"Don't mince words," Barnaby said. "It's a problem only because no wants to deal with it. This nonsense should have been nipped in the bud long ago. If they …"

Stephen stopped him with a flick of his hand. "This is a politically sensitive area, Barnaby. How we got to this point isn't as important as we how deal with it *right now*."

Stephen turned back to Ezekiel. "Unfortunately, it's not something a soul runner can handle. And we foresee other potential difficulties that would prove too much for a soul runner. The Pandora Initiative is under the purview of the Angelic Corps. As our current liaison to the Corps, we need you to go straighten out Bertland and, um, anyone else who might be tangentially involved."

Barnaby coughed.

Ezekiel laughed. "Give me the name, Stephen. As you said, we haven't much time."

"It's a runner, Hamelin Russell," Barnaby said. "The biggest screw-up—"

"Barnaby!" Stephen glared with sharpness that Ezekiel had never seen in the gentle elder. "Ezekiel," he said, moderating his tone. "The spike occurred in a small bayside town along the US Atlantic seaboard—Nevis, Maryland. That's the current location of Hamelin

Russell. It's a curious coincidence. While he may be embroiled in this somehow ..." He cut his eyes at Barnaby. "I don't believe for one picosecond that he's aiding or abetting Bertland in any fashion. So far, he's done an excellent job of adjusting to his relocation. No, I firmly believe the problem is with Pandora's family. It is large and obedient to her, and she tends to form allegiances according to how they will benefit her."

Ezekiel nodded. "Consider it done. I can leave at once."

Barnaby's cough had morphed into a clearing of the throat.

"Excellent," Stephen said. "But there is one thing more. The matter of the soul runner would require a more kid-gloves approach than Mr. Bertland. Have you ever met Mr. Russell?"

Ezekiel shook his head.

"Heard tell of him?"

Ezekiel smiled. "I don't think there's anyone who hasn't heard about his relocation to earth. As I understand it, he's a bit colorful."

Stephen smiled and Barnaby harrumphed, while Patrick continued his study of the graph, making notes along its margin.

"Colorful," Stephen agreed, nodding. "His is a compassionate soul, but he hasn't quite got it right yet. While we don't expect you to uncover anything that would change that impression, we don't want to tolerate any backsliding, either. We want you to serve as Mr. Russell's confessor. Determine what he can add to the story here, and if need be, help him correct any bad habits. Guide him. If you find anything egregious—and I mean *anything*—you take no action but refer it to us."

A messenger of God babysitting when so many more pressing duties needed attention? There were so many ways Ezekiel could bow out of this. His mind sped through them all, searching for the most graceful exit.

"Of course, this has already been cleared," Stephen quickly added. "We didn't want to make assumptions or step on toes. And frankly, managing the activities of Pandora and clan doesn't fall within our mission statement. It's the Corps's responsibility. Our services don't kick in until the end of the process."

"Of course." Ezekiel rued the day he lost at cards to Eli and had to cover his rotation at the Weigh Station. He now found himself dead center in some of the ugliest afterlife politics seen in eons. The Corps felt superior to the Weigh Station, and they frequently proposed it be placed under their jurisdiction rather than have two organizations equivalent in standing. The current pleas had recently hit fever pitch, so it was no surprise that the Corps okayed Ezekiel's participation in mentoring a wayward ex-runner. They would most certainly make political hay of it. Just what Ezekiel would rather avoid: poster-boy status.

"If I may offer a comment?" Ezekiel asked.

"Certainly. The more heads the better."

"These two assignments … You have investigating and reining in Bertland on the one hand"—Ezekiel extended a cupped hand—"and confessing Hamelin on the other." He cupped the other hand. "They seem at odds. Having Russell pour out his soul to me and then turning around to use it in the pursuit of Bertland—and possibly against Russell himself—is sinful, a violation of trust. I will not be party to any effort to deceive Russell. Either I'm a confessor, there to consult and guide, or I'm on a mission to stop Bertland and clean up after him. In good conscience, I can't do both. Why don't you send one of your own to counsel, and leave me free to handle Bertland? That keeps our lines of authority clean."

Stephen smiled. "Wisely put, Ezekiel. Yes, I think we all understand the politics of it. While we prefer to stovepipe our responsibilities whenever possible, it isn't the best approach in this situation. And isn't a successful outcome what we all want in the end? No," he said, shaking his head. "The issues are too intertwined. You have authority to deal with both parties. We don't. Try not to make this situation any more complicated than it needs to be. Don't use what he confesses against him. It's a leaping-off place to help him understand any error in his ways. In cooperating and doing good things, Hamelin will be propelling himself along even faster toward final redemption. Bertland, on the other hand—use any and all means and information to stop him—for good."

Ezekiel nodded slowly to let Stephen know he was considering what he had to say. "Save Russell and destroy Bertland?"

"Exactly."

Ezekiel quickly considered the difficulty and ramifications of walking such a fine line. Oh, it could be done, but was it the most ethical approach to the problem? He looked at Stephen's face, searching for some indication of deceit or darkness. The elder's expression appeared earnest and true. He did the same with Barnaby, and while he sensed an abundance of animosity toward Russell, it was motivated by a desire to uphold the law and not by petty principles. Of Patrick, he gleaned nothing of value. The elder was too introverted and bookish to deal with people issues.

In the end, Ezekiel's gut feeling and opinion didn't matter. This really wasn't a negotiation. His supervisors had already signed off on his participation. It wasn't the plum assignment he might have wished for—not half as showy as Eli preventing the last Pacific earthquake and potential tsunami that would have claimed a million lives. Still, this was a matter of basic law—not showy, yet of enormous impact.

"So be it." he said. "But I'll warn you right now that I will deal as I see fit with circumstances as they arise. And I will not make any false promises to Mr. Russell."

"Agreed," Stephen said, nodding. "Go with wisdom and insight, Ezekiel. Resolve this, and you will have our eternal thanks."

## Chapter Thirteen

# Hunter and Prey

At first light, Hamelin returned to the still-smoking ruins of the United Methodist church. He walked along the odd collection of small shops and the occasional old beach house—now renovated either skyward for a better water view, or out the back because of the narrow lots—and up Bayside Avenue, toward the denser residential section of town.

Stopping at the intersection of Bayside Avenue and Fifth Street to wait for a slow car, he sighed in frustration. *All that is seen and unseen.* Mortals struggled with the second half of the phrase if they gave it any consideration at all. Boogie men? Ghosts? The occult? They considered it the realm of charlatans employing trickery to put one over on them. If only they saw what he did. Or maybe not. The world was frightening enough without introducing the thought of coexisting with beings that you couldn't see or comprehend. Some were harmful, others merely intriguing. A carefully imposed world order assured that mayhem was kept at bay and everyone stayed in their lane, so to speak.

Was he now designated to keep chaos at bay? Hamelin felt like an otherworld enforcer—sentenced to prowl the earth rooting out evil until the afterlife powers-that-be decided he had learned obedience and humility. And probably in that order, although sometimes he wondered. He liked the calm, picturesque beach town of Nevis. If his role were to eradicate evil, would succeeding here mean that at some point he must shove off to somewhere else? He was a migrant by nature, but the thought of permanently leaving this idyllic place was not a welcome one. Then again, nothing would compare to a life in paradise if he toed the line.

Hamelin appraised each property as he passed: inhaling deeply, peering intently, listening carefully. Foot traffic around the small open shops was nonexistent, and the still of morning still hadn't lifted its sleepy veil. The smell of wet ash overpowered the red roses, butterfly bushes, and normally fragrant junipers that lined this street. He doubted that whatever malign entity leveled the church would have gone far. No, it would be lurking close by, perhaps confused—a preferable condition—or maliciously planning another outrageous act to express its anger at being pent up in a box for a century or two. Honestly, he couldn't blame it.

Sudden movement caught his eye. A wispy, diaphanous form darted from the corner of a building to the alley, only to reappear seconds later at the corner of the next building. As it hovered there, it seemed to be teasing him, daring him to engage in its game of hide-and-seek.

"Stop!" Hamelin ordered, pointing a finger in its direction. The creature neither moved nor uttered a response. The window glass in several nearby buildings began rattling, and with a sharp crack, the one nearest the creature shattered, sending shards of glass out onto the sidewalk. And then the next one blew, and then the one after that.

"Stop!" Hamelin repeated, and this time he rushed toward the apparition.

At that moment, three people scrambled out of the middle store. The wisp promptly vanished.

"Sonic boom?" Hamelin said to them, directing his eyes skyward.

He began backing up. He had no wish to explain himself a second time to the police, who would no doubt be arriving shortly.

Unfortunately, the days were gone when he could teleport between the Weigh Station and anywhere else in the universe. So he power-walked back toward the shop, scanning storefronts and rooftops as he went. He observed nothing, but the hair on the back of his neck was at attention the entire way. He sensed the muse's presence, and its negative energy felt like that of a toddler building up steam for a rip-roaring tantrum. Hamelin didn't know whether the dark muse was drawn by his otherworldly connection, or his association with Edgar. He let himself back into the shop, locked the door, and hoped the fuming muse didn't burn it all to the ground.

"What's out there?" asked a woman's voice.

Hamelin whipped around to see Edelin Jacoby as she stepped out from between the stacks. She looked tired and gaunt. "You saved me a search," Hamelin said. "How did you get in here?"

She gestured to the front door. "It was unlocked. I walked right in."

"That's impossible. I know I locked it when I left." He approached, but not closely enough for her to touch him. He wasn't sure yet how to categorize her. Probably human—that was his initial reaction—but given the strange supernatural goings-on in town, he wasn't ready to commit to that.

"Oh, you did. I was watching from across the street. He left it unlocked," she said pointing to the ceiling.

"He's gone?" Hamelin started up the stairs.

"No, stop. He peered out after you left but went right back inside again. He looked scared."

Hamelin descended the stairs. "As he should be. As *you* should be, madam. Why are you here? I would have thought Bertland had talked to you by now. We've reached an accord."

Edelin's eyes fluttered to life. "Praise be," she said. "My prayers are answered. "I never want to see him again. He terrifies me. If I had known then what I know now …" She darted a glance outside and backed up between the stacks again. "I've been hiding out at St. Anthony's. Mass in the morning and confession in the afternoon. As much as he'd like to, I don't think he can touch me right now. My soul is pure. If he has solved his *problem*, maybe he's done with me. If you say you've reached an understanding with him, why were you looking for me?"

"Oh, don't worry, Bertland hasn't forgotten you. I'm sure he'll get back around to you." Hamelin's gaze drifted up the stairs to the second floor.

"Kill him now," she said, following his eyes. "It frees us both. It's your only hope."

"Oh, there's no hope," Hamelin said. "The fool has opened the box and released god knows what kind of energy. It's already claimed its first victim. First Methodist is a total loss. Thank the Almighty there were no parishioners in there. The muse is still here in town, though, bouncing from place to place, energized by its ability to create chaos. I have to catch it, but I don't know how. That's why I wanted to talk to you. You seem to be well informed. What do I need to know that I don't already know?"

"I know how," she whispered, glancing toward the windows again. "Give the box back to me and I'll show you."

Sure, you will, Hamelin thought, but it wouldn't be for his or Edgar's benefit. Her shifty eyes told him he'd be safer driving a load of pipe across a frozen pond. "Ms. Jacoby, do I really look like someone born yesterday? You can't even look me in the face when you offer help." He shook his head. "No, how about I keep the box, we both walk down to the church, and you tell me what to do? That work for you?"

"He'll find me."

Hamelin laughed. "He certainly will, and quite frankly, you will probably get your just deserts, but if your soul is as pure as you seem to think, you'll be okay. You can trust me on that."

"I know you have the power to control it; I can sense it. It will come to you."

"Maybe. But what I sense right now is that your soul is rather far from pure. In fact, it may be as dark as hell could want it. Unless I am sadly mistaken, you aren't one of Pandora's brood. My instincts tell me you aren't immortal, either, but there is something odd about you. Who are you, Edelin? Tell me now, and it will go better for you, for your abuse of souls is a mortal sin. Your judgment will be swift and damning."

"What I am is trapped. I can't just relinquish my stewardship of the muses and walk away until my contract expires at the end of the week. Your buying the shop has muddied the waters. As owner of the shop, you have de facto control, but you aren't yet officially the steward."

"And at week's end?"

"Either Bertland takes direct control again, or he must initiate a new contract with someone. Regardless, he will be free to remove the boxes."

"So all I've done is put Bertland off a few days."

She nodded. "You see how he's tricked you already?" She moved out of the shadows and risked the light. "I've been up front with you."

Hamelin laughed. "No, ma'am. You sold me a business with hidden strings attached."

She grimaced. "I was desperate."

He laughed again. "And you aren't now?"

"Look," she said, her eyes beginning to well up. "I'm trying to do the right thing and you're not even trying to meet me halfway."

"How are you going to do that when you can't even help yourself? You sold the shop, so your judgment is poor, and you seem positive that Bertland is going to wreak destruction on you in the end. What could you possibly offer me?"

"Your instincts are good," Edelin replied. "I exist between two worlds—neither mortal nor immortal. As a caretaker of the boxes, I toil under Pandora's enchantment. Her grandson, Bertland, instructed me in how to do certain things if I ran into problems with the muses. I know how to open the boxes and how to call a muse back to the box. That is why I pose such a peculiar problem for Bertland. I know too much, and a few quiet words from me could short-circuit his work."

"What's stopping you?"

"The fallout would be terrible, and I don't want the responsibility. I'm looking for redemption, and I want to help you. Your poor friend upstairs wants to be whole again and move on to what every other human being expects at the end of life. Stop being cruel!"

Hamelin spent a moment studying her. She seemed sincere, her quest for redemption noble, but he wasn't about to give up control over Edgar's fate to someone who had just found Jesus during the last news cycle. She wouldn't help him without more strings, and that he would not abide. "No."

Her mouth fell open, and her eyes grew wide. "No?" she repeated.

"That's right." He shooed her toward the door. "As I see it, right now I hold all the cards, so I'd be a fool to offer concessions when I have several days left and the upper hand. If I decide on the last day that things are not going to pan out, I'll buzz you."

"Mr. Russell, I'll be dead long before then."

He looked at her and smiled. "There's nothing wrong with being dead, Ms. Jacoby. Some of my best friends are deceased." And with that, he closed and locked the door behind her. She would have to make amends on her own. He had Edgar and a raging muse to worry about.

He stuck his head in on Edgar and him found at his desk, scrawling away. The writer growled in annoyance when he broached conversation, and chased him from the room with his indifference. In other words, Edgar was his chipper, gregarious self, and Hamelin need not worry about him.

Hamelin locked Bertie's front door behind him and headed toward the town green, hoping that the muse would continue its fascination with him and track him there.

# Chapter Fourteen
## Playing the Piper

Edelin was ineffective in getting what she wanted, yet more powerful than she probably realized. If her intuition proved correct, Hamelin held sway over Edgar's dark muse—maybe enough to entice Edgar's muse back into the box. After they unceremoniously bounced him out of the afterlife, Hamelin had thought his runner skills revoked. Before he asked for outside help and made himself beholden to others who might not share his worldview and aspirations, he decided to give his old Pied Piper ways another shot. He took up a position on a bench under one of the massive oaks that stood like sentinels along the perimeter of the town green.

Searching out Edgar's creative influence struck Hamelin as iffy. Better, he thought, to make it come seeking him. Clearly, it was interested enough to taunt him and to follow him back to the shop. What, exactly, did it want from him? Did it realize that he had once been a soul runner? Did Hamelin still retain the touch, the power to transport? Was this what it sought? He suspected that the elders wouldn't leave him defenseless. He knew too much for them to leave one of their own at the mercy of corrupt forces.

He closed his eyes and let his thoughts go, closing out the external world with all its distractions and settling into a quiet, peaceful space within. He floated there a moment, an empty vessel on a placid sea. And then the inside of the vessel began to color and fill—the palest azure, which slowly darkened to a deep navy blue. A single thought occurred, as loud and clear as if someone had spoken in his ear: *How do I kill Daimon Bertland?* The fluid in the vessel began bubbling and boiling as hail rained down on the now-churning sea and shattered on contact into a shout: *Throttle him, cut his heart out, wall him up behind bricks.* The scenarios went on and on, each suggestion more brutal and graphic than the one before it, until the surface of the sea turned crimson, and flames of black raced across its surface and consumed the vessel.

Hamelin suddenly resurfaced from his subconscious. "Got you," he said, trapping Edgar's dark muse in the center of his being. He stood up. Loving couples walked hand in hand, children squealed and chased each other, and exhausted canines slumbered at their masters' feet. He neither saw nor heard hell breaking loose anywhere in town. He fist-pumped the air. *Yes!* Not only did he have the muse contained, his soul-running skills were working fine. He was back, baby!

"Don't worry, Edgar," he whispered to the dark muse within him. "We'll get Bertland, but we're doing it my way." Then he cut the celebration short. No need to shout to the chimneys and invite the Weigh Station to look into what he was doing. He made a break for Bertie's. Oh, how he wished he could still teleport!

Hamelin didn't worry so much about Bertland discovering what he did. After all, capturing Edgar's muse was private soul-running business. By the time Bertland knew, Hamelin's plans would be a fait accompli. He worried more about the monitoring by the Weigh Station. He had kept Edgar off their list of transportees for years, so no problem there, but did the Station keep tabs on Hamelin's current activities? God forgive him, but he was a bit put out with the elders. They should have told him he still had the ability to influence souls.

And what about angels? The flyboys were full of information, although Hamelin suspected it was on a need-to-know basis, just as it was with soul runners. Hamelin thought back to Wallace, the angel who gently nudged him away from taking the second life of the little boy in Mississippi. That day, Wallace was all up in his business. Hamelin decided to keep his motivations pure and transport Edgar in reasonable time. That way, if he happened to encounter another of God's messengers—which was doubtful—the poor, sad flyboy hopefully would be winging it in the dark about Hamelin's activities.

When Hamelin got to the bookstore, Edgar was AWOL. If ever there was an inconvenient transportee, it was Edgar Allan Poe. Hamelin searched upstairs and down, front to back, and out and about on the sidewalk. All he found was himself, standing alone in the middle of the street, dodging cars and wanting to scream *Edgar!* It wasn't like Edgar to wander off; he had been so diligent of late.

Hamelin reentered the shop, weighing the pros and cons of waiting out Edgar versus filling a missing-persons report. *Crotchety old man with nineteenth-century manners who claims to be the great writer Edgar Allan Poe. May be suicidal. Approach with caution, but return immediately.*

Could Edgar have finished his pièce de résistance and headed to the nearest pub to celebrate his impending death? The dark muse confined within Hamelin fluttered with excitement.

Hamelin checked Poe's desk. It had been tidied up, which was out of character: pen capped, stack of manuscript pages stacked with edges flush, chair pushed in, and a check spindle where he kept story ideas. Hamelin flipped the manuscript over and read the last page. *Damn it all.* The story wasn't finished. He sailed the last page back onto the desk, where it landed up against the spindle and the most recent note speared there. He looked at the note more closely and pulled it from the spindle. *Meet me at Leitches Beach as soon as you are able.*

The handwriting looked somewhat familiar, but he couldn't be certain that Edgar wrote it. Was this *to* Edgar, or *from* him? And if it was from Edgar, was it a *let's-screw-with-Hamelin* Edgar? How could Edgar possibly know of Leitches Beach's existence, much less how to get there? The note almost smacked of a kidnapping. Hamelin checked the spike for any other clues, such as a ransom note. Nothing.

Edgar's muse fluttered again. The questions were immaterial. Hamelin couldn't risk having the other half of Mr. Poe misplaced for any reason. He took off for the beach.

# Chapter Fifteen
# The Confessor

Hamelin drove south on Solomons Island Road. Traffic was sparse, and he made good time. The cops loved this stretch of pavement, so he kept up a fast but not excessive pace. The note had no mention of time, and he wondered if Edgar would still be waiting for him. Where once Hamelin showed up whenever the spirit moved him—literally and figuratively—he now made a point of always showing up in a timely fashion. With the exception of activities that intersected with mortals, the afterlife existed in a universe without time constructs. Who really needed hours, minutes, and days when one had all eternity to take care of things?

At the outskirts of Prince Frederick, Hamelin turned right onto Stoakley Road. He followed it past skinny old two-story farmhouses and faded tobacco barns, over Mill Creek, and beyond to Leitches Wharf Road, passing only a big yellow combine running along the shoulder. He turned right onto Leitches and followed it until it ended at the Patuxent River and the remains of an old wharf. He parked where Ramsey Creek dumped into the bay.

Edgar was not in sight. Hamelin had either missed him or arrived too soon. He sat down on a grassy slip to wait, but he had a creeping sense that he was mistaken about the note. This place was isolated and deserted. Edgar wouldn't have come this far. Even if he wanted to, he had no means to get here, and he knew few who would entertain driving him here.

The air shifted—softly, as if stirred by the beating of wings. "Hello, Mr. Russell."

Hamelin turned to see a smiling man standing behind him. His hair was the color of ripened wheat, and it rippled in the breeze. His eyes, a gentle bluish gray, seemed wise and fair and commanded deference. Everything else about him—his build, his clothes, the timbre of his voice—seemed immaterial. He was, by all accounts, beautiful.

Hamelin bowed his head slightly. "Good morning."

"It is. And you—how are you?"

Hamelin started with a rote *fine and you*, reconsidered, and merely nodded.

"A difficult adjustment, I'm sure," the angel said, nodding in return. "I'm Ezekiel, by the way. I'm your spiritual guide."

"You have Mr. Poe?" Hamelin asked, eyes searching the space behind Ezekiel. "I came as soon as I saw his note."

"Sorry for the confusion. The note was mine. Don't worry about Mr. Poe. He is fine. Last I checked, he was sitting on a bench in the town green, watching fishermen." Ezekiel sat down beside him.

"Wait. What? Back up. *Spiritual* guide?"

Ezekiel nodded. "Surely, you don't think they would just toss you back here and not provide any sort of support."

*Well, yes, the thought had occasionally reared its head like a copperhead disturbed from its nap.* "So, should I start packing?" Hamelin asked. "It will be great to see everyone again." He hoped he would receive his just reward. He had tried hard to toe the line and lead an exemplary life. Oh, there were slipups, but he'd given up the instant gratification of going for kielbasa sandwich when he was needed elsewhere. He hadn't failed yet to get his sandwich somewhere further down the line. It was the whole "something-something comes to those who wait" adage. But sending an *angel* to talk to him? This was most unusual. It felt as if oversight had been kicked up a notch. Did the Weigh Station feel that strongly that he needed a supernanny?

Hamelin put on his most easygoing smile as his mind raced to find good possibilities in whatever was about to hit him. Truthfully, his assignment back to the mortal world had put a dent in his self-confidence. Chief Elder Stephen might have called it ego, but Stephen was a man—God bless his soul—who liked to split hairs, and Hamelin didn't think the skill all that helpful at the moment.

Ezekiel didn't look at him but had shifted his gaze out to the river, which was flowing past them at an impressive rate of speed. "You've been doing very well, actually. Everyone's quite proud of you. But you must admit, it's a bit early for packing. How have you been occupying yourself?"

Hamelin hated dealing with angels. There was no room for any wiggle in their most perfect of worlds. He thought for a moment, making sure the question wasn't one of those *Have you stopped beating your wife?* questions. When he was satisfied it wasn't, he said, "If you're waiting for me to tell you how I'm saving the world, *don't*. I'm afraid I'm still trying to settle in." It was one of the sincerest admissions he had ever made, and yet it embarrassed him. He hung his head and studied his hands—hands that could be helpful to so many if he would just get motivated.

"Don't be so hard on yourself. No one expects that of you. It's all about the intent, Hamelin. The things you need to attend to will come, and they'll come naturally."

Hamelin wondered if he was referring to a *specific* intent—like mulligans and complaining centenarians. "I'll keep that in mind," he said, standing up. He hoped Ezekiel would follow suit. No use in the angel making himself comfortable. A chastisement was coming, and the quicker they could be done with it, the better. "All this way, then, just to pat me on the back?"

"Oh, heavens no," Ezekiel said. He leaned back on his elbows and gave no indication he was ready to pick up and move on. "Traveling is as it's always been: here or there in the blink of an eye, beat of a wing. Always on the go. My next stop will be the Eurasian steppe. I'm looking forward to that. It's lovely this time of year. No, Hamelin, you're just a box I had to tick off along with a few other items. You know, duty calls, and all that?" He made a show of putting a check mark on a page in a small notepad he carried with him.

"I suppose," Hamelin said, glancing at his Jaguar. "What can I do for you before you head that way?"

"Oh, no worry. I have some time."

Ezekiel locked eyes with Hamelin, and in his look, Hamelin read something much more complicated than merely going through the motions. "Unfortunately," Hamelin said, "I don't have the luxury, so why don't we get to the real reason for your visit?"

"Oh, I assure you, this is all about you." Ezekiel put away his little red book. "You know, our paths have crossed before. Not that you'd remember, it was so long ago."

Hamelin gave him a hard look. "Sorry. At the Weigh Station?" he asked, picturing one of those boring meetings where the cool kids sat on one side of the conference room and the soul runners on the other.

Ezekiel shook his head. "I was four years, six months, five days, and some hours and minutes thrown in there—the littlest of angels."

When Hamelin didn't respond, Ezekiel chuckled and said, "No worry. I was nothing to write home about, and one of many. Regardless, you were kind to a very bewildered young boy." He waved a hand as if sweeping the subject away. "Anyhow, we're not here to reminisce, are we? I want to give you something to chew on. As I've already told you, you're sailing along at a nice, even pace. No problems there. It's just this hitch that's appeared in one of our monitoring systems—"

"Hitch, or glitch?" Hamelin asked, eyes narrowing, mistrust growing. If they were going to talk graphs and data dumps …

"Well, possibly a glitch. But no worries, I'm sure. Don't fret about me trotting out graphs and piles of computer runs, by the way. It's just this sudden spike in, um, inappropriate energy that some of our monitors picked up. They sent me to kick around and see what's up."

"With me?"

"In the general vicinity of Nevis. You are here, so it is a good place to start. Have you noticed anything unusual in town lately?"

"I still feel as if you're beating around the bush, Ezekiel. If I'm not the one you plan to *kick around*, please come out with it. Exactly what are you concerned about?"

Ezekiel studied him a moment as if trying to decide whether to trust him. He sighed softly and said, "It's Bertland."

"You know about Bertland? He's legit?"

Ezekiel smiled. "Of course. And that he is the current hitch in your side. He's about to go off the deep end to solve his problem with the boxes. In general, we don't care about Pandora's operation. After all, she has certain things to account for; atonement is expected. It seems her descendants are still causing havoc in the world. No matter what they may think, say, or do, they don't decide the rules, and she isn't the final resting place for those boxes. We just go through a little soft-shoe with her—some sort of ancient arrangement I don't know all the ins and outs of. There's a more formal moment of reckoning on the back side of what she does. Anyway," he said, "it all works out. Everybody considers himself important, and there's happy in the ending."

He picked up a piece of driftwood and chucked it out into the water, where it hit with a plunk and a splash. "No, Pandora is all right, but it's her issue we sometimes have difficult moments with."

A chilly breeze suddenly gusted off the water. "*Boxes?* You know about those?" Hamelin asked, side-eyeing Ezekiel as he threw a stick out toward the channel.

"Yes."

Hamelin nodded. If the Weigh Station knew about the boxes, then it was possible they knew about Edgar and his mulligan status. And yet they still weren't revoking Hamelin's stay on earth for a long stay in the hot place? "Edgar ..."

Ezekiel quieted him with a serious look. "For the time being, we'll keep Edgar's situation as a confidence between you and me. The Weigh Station doesn't seem to be aware of his situation. I'm not sure how you've accomplished that, and I don't want to explore it right now. One would think that good judgment would dictate taking him out of the situation entirely."

Hamelin heaved a sigh of frustration. "But he's *so* close."

"As are you, Hamelin. Compassion and freelancing have no place in the existence of a soul runner. Your kind and my kind—we are obedient, loving servants. Period. *Capisce?*"

Hamelin would have sworn it was compassion that softened the look in Ezekiel's eyes. He nodded. "And?"

"It seems you've created a problem with your penchant for, um ...

second chances. We angels have many gifts, but the transportation of souls isn't one of them. It seems your gift to Edgar has complicated our abilities to rein in Pandora et al. When you made Edgar a mullig—"

"S-h-h! Of this we do not speak," Hamelin admonished.

Ezekiel chuckled. "Relax, our conversation is totally private. A benefit of our kind. And look, I'm not here to interfere with what you've done, but when you did it, Edgar's soul—including both light and dark muses—came under your protection and control. It's not my role, or in my power, to interfere with that. I'm not, nor can I ever be, a soul runner. You and I, we're golden delicious and clementines, when it comes down to it." He stopped and chuckled to himself, as if at a private joke hidden in his comparison. Then he grew serious again. "Now, we could pay a visit to the Weigh Station and request another soul runner to gather up all of Edgar, but that would be a little embarrassing."

"Because flyboys don't need help."

Ezekiel's eyes flashed. "Flyboys? Go-and-get-'ems? Really? We could insult each other with childish nicknames until the Second Coming, but it won't get us anywhere. And really, now, we shouldn't stoop beneath our station. What it simmers down to is, you do for us and we do for you. How would you feel about a little assignment that could boost your standing significantly?"

Hamelin studied Ezekiel. He wasn't sure how much of his thoughts this fellow could read. Angels and soul runners might both be loving and obedient servants, but their niches and spheres of influence rarely overlapped. In fact, Hamelin wasn't even a soul runner anymore—at least, not a practicing one. And he had a pretty good idea that love and compassion together were going to do a whole lot more to get him into heaven that sitting on the riverbank bartering with an angel about getting Greek mythological characters to toe the line. "You said that I'm doing okay in Nevis, so I think I'll stick with what works. Let's keep it clean and on the books. You should get another soul runner."

Ezekiel raised an eyebrow. "Are you sure? Because if that's the way it's going to be, it's going to come out that you've been tinkering in no-no land with mull—er, second chances. That won't play well with Elder Stephen and the others. Is that really the way you want it to go down, my friend?"

*My friend?* This was a bamboozle if ever Hamelin heard one. Until now, he'd been indifferent to the flyboys—maybe a little jealous of their obviously higher social standing, but not enough to get in a snit over. But blackmail? That created a new complexity, and one not at all becoming an angel. Perhaps, he was missing something and his new "spiritual adviser" was nothing but a con man. Maybe even a demon in disguise. He watched Ezekiel's gold aura, flashing and dancing in the sunlight, and decided that the vibes of a demon weren't there. "Not really. I assume the little extracurricular involves Bertland. What are you proposing?" Hamelin asked.

Ezekiel smiled. "First, Daimon Bertland is corrupt and must be made to retire; second, Mr. Poe must get his dark muse back; and third, Poe must complete his earthly voyage and his soul must be delivered to its final home."

Hamelin marveled at how detached one could become when referring to people by their last name. "Destroy Mr. Bertland, catch the muse, and terminate Mr. Poe?" That all, Mr. ...?"

"Just *Ezekiel*," the angel replied, eyeing him curiously. "And yes, that about covers it."

Hamelin watched an eagle just as it hit the water and pulled up and away with something in its talons. "I must tell you, I appreciate having a say in this."

"Of course. No one likes being told to do things that push them out of their comfort zone. But ultimately, we're all in this together."

Hamelin stood up. "The answer is no. Edgar needs his muse back so he can finish his story. He's entitled to that. I agree that Daimon Bertland shouldn't be allowed to roam the earth screwing over mortals. But that should already be someone else's responsibility."

When Ezekiel didn't reply, Hamelin said, "Ah. Angels no more perfect than soul runners?"

Ezekiel stood up and faced him. "Only one is perfect. There is a lot of politics going on here, and I wish I could give you the complete picture, Hamelin, but I'm not allowed. You'll have to trust me."

"Ezekiel, those five little words are like a neon sign flashing warning, and you've been throwing up red flags since you got here. The more you say, the less faith I have in you. If you were on the level, you'd already have my caboose before the review board on charges of making Edgar—yes, he has a first name and thoughts and feelings just like a regular guy—for giving him additional time. I'd be history. So what really gives, bro? Because if you're going to try and screw me over, angel or not, I'll throw down with you in a nano." He put his hands on his hips and thrust out his chin.

"Wait!" Ezekiel said, raising his hands in protest. "You've got the wrong idea. I'm not dumping this all on you. I just need your assistance—a wingman, if you will."

"*Wing* man?" Hamelin said, bristling. "Then you've come to the wrong place, sir. Go recruit one from your angel cohort. I never learned to fly." He took off at a brisk pace toward his car, Ezekiel scrambling after him.

"Bad choice of words, Hamelin. I'm sorry. I know our kind can be haughty and exclusive, but I don't buy into all that classism, and I don't think you do, either. We're all equal in God's eyes, right?"

"Sound-biting me, Ezekiel," Hamelin said, not slowing down.

"For God's sake, stop, Hamelin! Please!"

Hamelin whirled around. "Profaning?"

"No," Ezekiel said, catching up with him. "I really meant it. Getting this mess straightened out is a holy quest. And I'm appealing to you to help me pull it off. I've been told by my supervisor to keep this low-key and to work amicably with the Weigh Station. It's a political hot potato, and your assistance would make things so much easier."

Ezekiel stood there with arms outstretched, beseeching Hamelin. A humble angel? Hamelin wondered how long that would last.

"I need time to think," he said. "Meet me here again tomorrow, and I'll give you my answer. You know my mind right now, so maybe you might want to start drafting a contingency plan in case I don't have a change of heart." He beeped his locks and climbed in his car.

That should have been the end of it, but Ezekiel refused to leave the old-fashioned immortal way and simply vanish. He continued to stand his ground—albeit with arms down—imploring Hamelin with thoughts that reached out and played with his emotions.

"Can I drop you somewhere?" Hamelin asked, refusing to be swayed but wondering why he felt the need to be polite.

Ezekiel opened the passenger door and slid in. "Put the lid down? I've never been in a ragtop."

It was all coming back to Hamelin now. The sense of self-entitlement—that was what made angels so intolerable. "Sure," he said, slamming his door. "Where to?"

Ezekiel drew back and cocked his head. "Why, Bertie's, of course. That's ground zero, isn't it?"

Hamelin withdrew his key from the ignition. "Now, hold on. I don't need you babysitting me while you try to guilt-trip me. *Get out!*"

"Hamelin, I can assure you, it's nothing like that. It's more a question of things being somewhat bigger—"

"Than you, an angel, think you can handle," Hamelin interjected. "Uh-uh. As I said previously, get out!

"No," Ezekiel said. He crossed his arms over his chest and stared straight ahead.

"Fine, then." Hamelin huffed out of the Jaguar and tossed the keys at Ezekiel. "If you can figure out the GPS, you're all set." He set off walking for the main road.

Behind him, the car engine revved to life. Hamelin kept walking as he listened to screeching of tires, grinding of gears, and a few beeps of his car horn. When he got the vehicle back, he would trade immediately.

The car roared up beside him. He looked over at Ezekiel, who was wearing a grin from ear to ear. Hamelin kept walking, the car rolling along beside him.

"Come on," Ezekiel said. "No strings, Hamelin. Let's make this baby fly."

# Chapter Sixteen

# Sucked in Anyway

There was something imperfect about Ezekiel, something that screamed, *I'm not really an angel,* and Hamelin liked it. Despite their serious work, a bit of the child lingered in both of them. But despite any lightness they might share, Hamelin still didn't trust him. He climbed in and almost had his seat belt fastened when Ezekiel floored it, pushing Hamelin's head back against the headrest. He could live with that, but it was Ezekiel's rebel yell that scared the living hell out of him. He made Ezekiel pull over so they could put the top down, and then he gave the thumbs-up to let her rip.

Ezekiel learned fast. They hit most of the unbanked bends on the wharf road at hair-raising speed, and Ezekiel still managed to keep it tight on the curves and mostly right of the center stripe. Huntingtown, Sunderland, and Owings blurred past. When they finally parked against the curb in front of Bertie's, Hamelin felt a pang of regret that they had arrived so soon.

Hamelin collected his keys, and Ezekiel followed him into the shop, which was quiet and seemed empty. "Thanks for the ride," Hamelin said. "As you can see, Bertland isn't here. I've had more time to think, and there's no reason for us to put our heads together again tomorrow. My answer is firm, and it's time for you to shuffle off to the steppes."

"Oh, there's no trip to the steppes," Ezekiel said. "I canceled it."

Hamelin studied him a moment. "You're lying."

"Okay, ya got me. No trip to the steppes, but it wasn't a lie. I'm headed to the Peloponnese after this. It was merely a throwaway line to break the ice. I read your personnel file and it said you've been to the steppes several times on assignment. No deceit intended. Okay?" Ezekiel picked up the fat volume of *War and Peace* sitting next to the cash register and flipped it open.

*Sure. Hamelin loves random strangers snooping in his business.* "And who gave you access to that?"

"Elder Stephen suggested it. Look, don't be offended. Haven't you ever reviewed the life of a soul that you were about to pick up?"

"Certainly, but ..." Hamelin stopped himself. He really had no comeback. "Whatever." He took the book from Ezekiel and motioned toward the front door. "Have a nice day."

"So," Ezekiel said, looking around him in the shop. "Rooms upstairs, or should I go find a local B and B?"

"None of the above. Your business is strictly with Bertland. There's a Holiday Inn on the north side. They always have rooms. And you can conference with Bertland there, too."

"Okay," Ezekiel said, nodding. "I can shuffle off, but you know that you and I are not finished, right? I need your insight into Bertland, so I will be back tomorrow. This situation needs to be resolved posthaste. And whether you wish it so or not, you're involved—an invaluable asset in reining in Pandora and her wayward lineage." He gave Hamelin a crisp salute. "See you soon, Mr. Russell."

Ezekiel was halfway to the door when he stopped and turned around. "No, it's more than involvement. You're the *key* to cleaning up this situation. Personal responsibility—that's what is needed here. It never goes well when one tries to play God. If you don't help solve this mess, you're going to rue the day you ever took pity on Edgar Allan Poe. That isn't a threat, just an observation."

All Hamelin's good will vanished. Ezekiel was as arrogant as the rest of the flyboys, and as soon as he cleared the doorway, Hamelin dialed the Holiday Inn and booked all the vacant rooms for the next week. It was more symbolic than anything else—a *Yankee, go home* kind of message. Ezekiel, like the rest of his ilk, could travel back and forth to heaven in less than an eyeblink, outside of the construct of time. He had no need to bed down anywhere in the mortal world. *Don't make me pluck those wings one feather at a time,* Hamelin thought, as he hung up the phone. *We'll see who rues what day.*

He sat down at one of the reading tables and propped his feet up on a chair. Ezekiel was right about one thing: the first step in restoring order was Edgar's muse. Of course, "order" meant something different to each player. Once the muse was reunited with Edgar, Ezekiel would engage the Weigh Station to transport the author, and Bertland would no doubt make a play to enforce his original agreement with Poe. Hamelin didn't trust either Bertland or Ezekiel. The former seemed soulless, and the later was surely looking for self-aggrandizement. Hamelin would move heaven and earth to make sure neither got a crack at Edgar. He could accomplish that only by retaining control of the dark muse. Once Edgar finished his story—and he seemed to be close—Hamelin would reunite him with his dark muse and do the transportation himself. Then the chips could fall wherever they liked.

"Greetings my fine friend!" Edgar said, gliding through the front door with a large, docile black cat in tow. He slammed the door with enough effort to bounce the *closed* sign around so it read *open*. The panicked cat leaped free and disappeared into the stacks.

123

Hamelin gave a silent prayer of thanksgiving. "Where have you been? I was just coming to look for you."

"No need," Edgar said, staying the thought with a raised palm. He took inordinate interest in his hand, waving it around in front of his face as if he were a mime polishing a window. "Never mind," he said. With his left hand, he closed the right into a fist and shoved it into his pants pocket. "I was out shella-shella-shellabrating."

Hamelin rolled his eyes. "You're three sheets to the wind! Where were you? At the Phoenix?"

"No, shir," Edgar said, taking a zigzag route toward the stairs. "Clancy's my boy."

Hamelin made a move to catch his elbow. "Here, let me help—"

Edgar shooed him away. "No need. No need. I'm just off to shlumber away down upon the Shwannee Riv ..." He began to giggle. "I'd like breakfast at seven a.m., please. And don't be late. I have a deadline to meet." He successfully navigated the first step and leaned heavily against the stair railing as his foot floated above the second, searching for firm footing.

"So you'll be done tomorrow?" Hamelin asked hopefully.

"Sausage and toast will be fine," Edgar said. His foot thumped hard on the second step, and somehow, he managed to find the third. "The furry friend will have gin."

Hamelin let him go. He'd have to sleep it off. In a way, it was a shame. The man was pleasant, for a change. Hamelin pulled a chair from the table he had been sitting at, and placed it at the foot of the stairs. Edgar would get out, and Bertland and Ezekiel would get in— over his dead body.

# Chapter Seventeen
## No Place to Hide

Ryan had Maggie Sullivan set up a vigil at the Phoenix. She was about to dig into Wednesday's crab-ball special when her mark walked through the door. Even if she hadn't been there to surveil Jacoby, she could have told Ryan what he wanted to know as the instant she set eyes on the woman. Women were good at sizing each other up. Not for gossip's sake or any other malicious purpose—they just took a lot in with a single glance.

Edelin Jacoby was chicly dressed: well-fitted dark washed jeans, long-sleeved T-shirt stylishly tucked in behind the double "C's" of her Chanel belt buckle, and a leather jacket that hugged her curves like butter on a Parker House Roll. She had it all going on. Her type daunted girls who couldn't quite pull it all together. Maggie got up and moved to the rear of the pub, hovering around the bar top as she waited for Edelin to park herself, which she did at a high top just off the bar.

So what was it that really caught Maggie's eye? From the moment she entered the Phoenix, Edelin wore a tightly drawn facial expression. Her chin dipped ever so slightly as she headed to the tables in back, and her hands were drawn into tight fists. The girl had a problem that weighed heavily, and downing two Long Islands in short order wasn't going to help her with it.

When Edelin's third drink arrived, Maggie pushed past a young stud who also seemed to be sizing Edelin up, and dropped into the empty chair at her table. "Pam!" she said, touching Edelin's forearm in a familiar way.

Edelin pulled away, wide-eyed and trembling.

"Oh, I'm so sorry," Maggie said, springing right back up out of the chair. "I thought you were …"

The tension in Edelin's face eased. She shook her head and laughed nervously.

Maggie removed her drink from the table. "I'm so embarrassed," she said. "You look just like my friend Pam."

"No, I get it."

"It would make me feel a lot better if you'd let me order you another," Maggie said, pointing at Edelin's drink. And then, without waiting for an answer, she hailed Bennie and ordered one more. "There, now I feel better. I'll go wait for the real Pamela, although I think I might have been stood up." She moved off.

Edelin's voice came floating toward Maggie above the hubbub of rattling dishes and whispered conversations. "Edelin. Edelin Jacoby."

Maggie beamed her friendliest smile. "Maggie Sullivan. Nice to meet you."

"Sorry if I seemed rude. I was deep in thought, and you startled me. Would you like to wait for your friend over here?" Her eyes flitted toward the predatory male still at the bar, then back to Maggie.

Maggie took her time answering, her gaze panning slowly toward the pub's front door, and across the room before finally settling on Edelin. "Oh, what the hay. Why not? Looks like my friend is a no-show." She changed tables as Edelin's new drink arrived. "Thanks, Bennie," she said.

"You're a regular?" Edelin asked, watching Bennie head back to the bar.

"Everybody's a regular here. The Phoenix prides itself on being a home away from home. First time?"

Edelin shook her head. "Couple times. It's a nice place. Except for that creep who keeps staring at me like I'm today's special."

Maggie watched the young stud drain his glass and head out. Apparently, he finally got the unwelcoming vibe. "Yeah, it's not really that kind of place, but I guess they're everywhere. Are you new to town, or just passing through?"

"I used to own the bookstore across the street."

"So moving out and up, huh?"

"I wish."

Edelin ran an index finger around the lip of her glass. She wore her heart on her sleeve, and *she was going to tell everything.*

Edelin finally stopped playing with her drink and took a sip. "Have you ever been desperate to cut the cord to something and not been able to do it? Not because of what you yourself could or couldn't do, but because of someone else?"

Maggie thought back to her relationship with her old flame, Hector. Though she thought herself a strong woman, he was the one who had controlled their relationship. "Sure. More than once."

Edelin nodded, finished her first drink, and started in on the second one.

"There's always a way, but you have to work hard for it."

Edelin shook her head. "Not this time."

"So is it a job you need, because I know some people ..."

"It would help only if you knew the new owner of the bookstore. Short of that, I'm screwed."

"Matter of fact, I do! Well, maybe not directly, but I work with someone who is close to the owner. Maybe I could put in a good word. What do you need?"

"Boxes," she said, trying to make a rectangle with fingertips that couldn't quite connect. "Boxes," she repeated, giving up. "They're in there, and I need them back."

"If they're so important, how did you manage to leave them there in the first place?"

"Because I didn't read the fine print. I can't break the contract, and I can't transfer the stewardship."

"Stewardship?"

"Yeah, Edelin the Steward ... *ess*."

"I'll help you find a good lawyer."

"You're so nice, and I don't even know you."

"You don't drink much, do you?"

"Only on birthdays and New Year's. Here's the thing, Maggie. I get 'em back, I get to leave this two-street town. I don't, I'm a dead girl. No nice pants, no nice belt." She looked down at her lower half. She picked up her leather satchel and swung it around. "No more Dooney and Bourke." She put her head down on the table and sobbed.

Maggie caught Ryan's eye staring at them from behind the bar, and gave him a shrug. He returned it.

"It's all right," she said, patting Edelin on the back. "We'll see that it turns out okay. I think your problem is, you don't have anyone to talk to."

"I guess."

"Right. So you're in luck. You've found a friend. And you know what, Edelin?"

"Mmm."

"As your new best friend, I'm telling you that you've had too much liquor and I think you should go home and sleep it off."

Edelin's sobs grew louder. "I don't … have a … home. He took it."

Maggie stopped patting. "Who took it?"

"I can't go back. He'll find me."

"Abusive boyfriend?" Maggie whispered in her ear.

Edelin picked her head up and blew her nose on her napkin. "Abusive," she said, nodding, "But I can't say anymore."

Maggie stood up, pulling on Edelin's arm. "Grab your Dooney and come with me. I'm sure there's a shelter you can stay in. And if we can't find one, you can stay at my place until we get something more permanent."

Edelin gave a bleary-eyed nod and excused herself to salvage some of her dignity—and pretty face—in the ladies' room. Maggie gave Ryan a thumbs-up. A few minutes later, with Edelin still in the bathroom, she wondered whether her assessment might be premature. Ryan tipped his head toward the restrooms, and Maggie got up to see if Edelin had fallen asleep on the can. In she went, and out she came. "She gone," she mouthed to Ryan.

"From a restroom with only one door, and a window the size of a pet door?" Ryan asked, coming over to the table. "Are you sure she went in?" He followed Maggie back to the restroom.

"Ryan, I swear I never took my eyes off her or that door." Maggie pushed the door open to an empty restroom. The stalls were all vacant, and the window was still locked from the inside.

"And look at this." Maggie came out of the last stall, carrying a large leather tote. "It's Edelin's. Something awful is going on here. Nobody leaves behind a four hundred-dollar Dooney and Bourke."

"F-f-our hun …? Bring that to my office where we can dump it out.

Maybe there's a clue in there." Ryan considered the bag a moment; then his eyes shifted to the window. "I wouldn't have thought it possible, but I guess she had her reasons. To be on the safe side, after we're done with the purse I'll call Kurt Walther's Lock and Key and have him install a better lock."

Maggie followed him out. "Let's hope there was a good reason for her to bolt, because the alternative is chilling. She said the person she was running from was going to kill her."

# Chapter Eighteen
# Working the Dark Side

Martin Westwood Cobb sat behind his desk in stocking feet, wiggling his toes and gazing around his office. Takahashi telescope, fine sound system, richly bound books—they were all just as he had left them when he received Elder Stephen's summons to meet in the White Corridor. Soft jazz still gave the room a cozy, familiar feel. This made no sense. He reached for his water glass, but when he tipped it to take a drink, the water dried up in the glass on the way to his lips. He put the glass back down and watched it fill itself with water again. He tried a second time, sloshing the liquid around before lifting the glass to his lips. The result was the same: no drink. He turned the glass upside down and poured water all over the middle of his desk. What good was it? He threw the glass across the room and watched it shatter against the wall.

What was going on? For the millionth time, he relived the recent shocking turn of events in his life. Most cutting was the betrayal of that upstart newbie, Curtis Merriweather, who had turned against him and spilled all sorts of inflammatory nonsense about Martin breaking rules and overstepping his authority. With tears in his eyes, Martin recalled elder Stephen reading Martin's damnation to hell, and Weigh Station officials escorting him out. Why, then, did this look nothing like the hell he had expected to find? He pinched himself and winced. Had there been a last-minute reprieve?

He decided not to question his luck. Someone else would need to clear up the confusion, but he wasn't going to traipse over to the White Corridor and meet with the powers that be in his stocking feet. Where in the hell were his shoes?

He dropped onto all fours and found his penny loafers under his desk. He shoved his right foot into his shoe, realized it was the left shoe, and picked up the other loafer. When he couldn't get his foot into it, he stopped and looked at the pair of shoes. Both were for the left foot. He checked the dates on the dimes he had placed in the slots where pennies normally went. Each was dated *1920*—the beginning of the great Jazz Age. These were his loafers, all right. Well, sort of.

The door opened suddenly, and a fresh-faced, ponytailed young man entered and made himself comfortable on Martin's couch. Although his tuxedo seemed excessively formal, he reminded Martin of any number of newly arrived soul runners: bright-eyed and eager.

"You've sat long enough, and I see you've settled in nicely," the man said, his eyes sweeping the room before settling on Martin. "We can get started."

*Get started? Did they have an appointment?* Martin flipped through the pages of his desk calendar, looking for an appointment, but every day was listed as Monday, May 25, and the only engagements showing were those leading up to his meeting with the elders on that date. Lately, time just seemed to run together. How long had he been here? Hours? Months? Years?

He frowned and said, "You're on my schedule?"

"Oh, no sir, but it's a most important meeting, and you'll be glad you took it."

The man smiled, but there was something off about it, insincerity reflecting in eyes that didn't or couldn't stay engaged with Martin's. The figure of the visitor wavered and then began to pixelate. The image then reformed into a dark-clad man, neither young nor old. No marionette lines, but a forehead grooved with frown lines. Martin felt his heart pumping hard as his blood temperature rose to an uncomfortably high level and then cooled to an icy low that made his legs shake. "Oh, dear God, this isn't the Weigh Station, is it?" he whispered.

The demon shook his head.

"And you're Satan?"

The demon chuckled in a phlegmy, congested way as all pretense of geniality fell away. "Oh, hell no," he said. "Just another demon. I transport soul-runners to Hades. We're not keen on names and individualism down here, but if you must refer to me as something, just call me Bub Number Seven-Point-Five." He paused a moment and then added, "You know, a Beelzebubette?"

Martin began shaking all over. *Hell.* He let the incongruity of a comfortable office existing in the netherworld sink in for a moment. "But the fires ... the burning ..."

"Confused?" Bub said, nodding in a sympathetic way, but the empty, dark look in his eyes suggested anything but consolation. "I understand. It's a common emotional state for newbies. We'll soon whip that out of you."

Martin whimpered, and the demon laughed a second time. "Relax. That was a figure of speech. I haven't whipped anyone in ages. Hell is what you make of it—endless choices. I like you, Martin—so much, in fact, that I'm going to make you a deal. We need your help with something."

"I don't know," Martin said, eyeing him closely. "What could you possibly need from me? And who is *we*?"

"*We*," Bub repeated, opening his hands in an inclusive gesture. "We need your help with someone you know and detest."

"Why would I do that?"

"Not for any noble reason. We are in hell, after all. Revenge is all about the satisfaction of getting even with someone. It's despicable—a perfect activity for hellizens. You're one of the lucky ones because you have something to barter. It's a rare position to be in, Mr. Cobb, and I wouldn't cast it aside lightly."

"Barter?" Martin said, leaning back in his chair with narrowed eyes. "I give you something and I get something in return. What do I get out of this arrangement?"

"Why, all this, of course," Bub said, spreading his arms wide.

"And if I don't?"

Bub jerked a thumb over his shoulder. "*That.*"

Martin got up and opened the office door into a long corridor. The ambient Gregorian chants he had heard at the Weigh Station for eons were gone. In their place, a cacophony of noise assaulted him: grinding, pounding machines, screams of torment, and pleas for mercy filled his ears. The hall smelled of blood and sweat and dead fish.

He slammed the door shut and retreated to his desk. "You seem to have me at a disadvantage."

"That's how it works around here. Your choice."

"Well, I don't see this as being any sort of choice at all."

Bub smiled. "Come, now. You'll enjoy it. It's exactly your kind of thing."

Martin sighed wearily. "All right. So who is it you want me to screw over?"

"It's not my place to say, but you must have been someone

important in life, because there's a big offer for you on the table, and it comes directly from Bub Number Two."

Bub cocked his head sideways and stared, his beady black eyes making Martin feel like a cut of prime rib in a butcher shop. "So what's it going to be, Mr. Cobb? You can keep the office and help me out, or you can take your chances and drift around out *there*." He tipped his head toward the hallway.

Martin flicked his gaze in that direction, then back at Bub. "I guess I'm your man."

"Thought you'd see it that way." Bub got up and headed for the door.

"Is there a required uniform down here?" Martin asked. "Striped pants and shirt? New shoes? I'm afraid something's gone wrong with my shoes."

"Does this look like fashion week? Suck it up, Mr. Cobb, and come with me. We'll be sending you out directly."

Martin studied the mismatched shoes and somehow managed to get them both on. *Suck it up*, he thought in a mocking tone as he limped after Bub. *Can't leave this place soon enough.*

"I heard that," Bub said, waving Martin out into the corridor. "It doesn't do well to mock the demon who feeds you. Now, pick up the pace. We haven't got forever."

Martin walked out the door, into ear-splitting noise and no corridor. In the corridor's place stood a gangplank walkway strung from above by steel cables. It swayed precariously with every step, like some jungle bridge from a Johnny Weissmuller Tarzan movie. Martin held tight to the rope handrail and peered over the edge into a pit so deep he couldn't see the bottom. Heat, smoke, and putrid stench rose from the depths. It reminded him of the engine room of the great ship *Titanic* in a movie he had once seen.

"Hold tight," Bub called over his shoulder. "It's where the despicable go. Falling would be a poor choice."

Bub led him through a dark, hellish landscape with suffering and hopelessness so thick in the air that he could taste the peculiar bitter flavor. The walkway grew progressively narrower and more claustrophobic.

"Not far," Bub said, again as if reading Martin's mind. "In fact, that's him waiting for us."

Martin leaned around Bub and, in the distance, glimpsed a tall figure standing in silhouette against a glow of light. As they drew closer, the passageway widened and brightened. Bub Number 7.5 stopped a few paces from the figure and seemed to await acknowledgment.

The new demon dismissed Bub with a curt word and turned to Martin. "Welcome to hell, Martin Westwood Cobb," he said, offering a handshake. "We're honored to have you."

Martin ignored the extended hand. He, like the rest of the Weigh Station's cadre of soul runners, used handshakes when sealing business deals. He would be doing nothing of the kind with this creature. "Are you Satan?"

"As close as you're going to get anytime soon." The new Bub took off at a leisurely pace in the same direction Martin and Bub had been proceeding, and Martin reluctantly followed. The corridor continued to widen, and the illumination improved, and they walked in silence until they came to a set of metal doors controlled by a security pad. A dark ground fog creeping along the floor piled up against the bottom of the doors and stayed there, throbbing to some unheard beat.

"This," Bub said, indicating the doors with a sweep of a hand, "is an exit from hell."

Martin's heart began to palpitate. "You're letting me go?"

The demon gave him a dry look. "You were a soul runner."

It was more of a statement than a question, but Martin felt inclined to nod his agreement.

"That's what you shall be here, too."

Martin frowned. "I'm pretty sure the Weigh Station isn't going to forego its responsibilities and let your people ferry souls to Hades."

"They don't have to forego anything. Hades has always had the responsibility of transporting all soul runners such as yourself, who have been damned to hell. No more, no less than that. We know our place," he said with a touch of sarcasm.

Martin recoiled as Bub Number Two turned his eyes on him—eyes black as coal, devoid of light or emotion. What unspeakable evil lay behind their dark curtain?

"I usually don't entertain new arrivals," Bub said. "Where they go when they get here, and what miserable activity they're assigned to are of little interest. But you—you, I'm interested in. I need your soul-runner skill set, so I'm giving you a choice."

Bub's tone was flat, but Martin still felt the malevolence. "You want me to bring damned souls to hell?"

"Damned *soul-runner* souls to hell."

"Do I have a choice?" Martin asked.

"Everyone has a choice."

Martin studied the dark-clad demon and thought about everything he'd seen on the way to this meeting. As long as it was God's decision who was damned, what did it matter whether he transported them under instructions from Elder Stephen, or demon Bub? There really was no choice. And he might even be able to throw into the situation a little much-needed humanity. "Okay, you have a manual or something I can reference for guidance?"

Bub showed some teeth, but Martin couldn't call it a smile. "We have no manual. You can wing it." Beckoning Martin to follow him, the demon walked over to the secured doors and punched in a code on the touch pad. The doors opened with a quiet whoosh. "There is a simpler exit you will soon learn. As a soul runner, you may leave at any time, but you must be back by nightfall. If you fail to return ..." Bub shrugged. "Let's just say we're very good at policing our own. Now, off you go. You'll be through your first assignment in no time."

Martin took a deep breath. After the first run, he'd be okay. "All right, I guess. Just point me in the right direction and tell me who to escort."

"Bring me the soul of Hamelin Russell."

# Chapter Nineteen
# When Worlds Collide

Hamelin rolled out of his chair as soon as he saw the lights at the Phoenix come on. He didn't try to account for what he did in the nighttime hours. It seemed his existence just kept moving along. He stretched his arms over his head like a great house cat awaking from a midday snooze in the sun. Which reminded him to search out Edgar's new feline friend before it peed in a box of books. He listened for a moment until he heard Edgar's snoring still raising the shingles, and then headed for the Phoenix to inform Ryan James that Maggie Sullivan's services would not be needed. He had gotten all the information he needed without Edelin Jacoby's help. With the dark muse under his control, and Edgar's manuscript on the verge of completion, Hamelin planned to lie low and be patient—once he got rid of the flyboy, that is.

Two steps out the door, his plans changed. A new note hung from the Bertie's hobbit-hole door: *"Unfinished business. Meet me at Brownie's Beach."* Clearly, Ezekiel aimed to be as big a thorn as Bertland. In a glass-half-full scenario, Ezekiel had decided Hamelin was a hopeless case, and planned to move on and cut his losses. It was a splendid decision. Helping Ezekiel in something questionable wasn't in Hamelin's plans. He didn't need a confessor. "Confessor" was just code for "busybody." If Hamelin truly needed assistance, he would rely on his own self-assessment for correcting his mistakes and moving past them. He figured that was what Elder Stephen would want him to do. Unlike Leitches Wharf, Brownie's Beach was close by, and Hamelin could walk to it along the boardwalk that hugged the public beach.

A few businesses remained along the waterfront, but Nevis had long ago moved past its thriving fishing industry and booming amusement park. The warehouses were few and the brothels gone, as was the pier that once reached hundreds of feet out into the water to accommodate a steamboat landing. He remembered fondly that great white steamboat *Chessie Belle*.

The town of Nevis wasn't a new experience for Hamelin. He'd seen the thriving fishing industry and the amusement park in their heyday, even played pro baseball in the park one glorious afternoon when it first opened in 1901. As he recalled, the experience was cut short by a general brawl that started in the viewing stands and then ran like a wildfire through the entire ballpark. Good times! And then he had visited once more in the 1920s for a transport. At that time, the amusement park was going gangbusters as a summer escape for Washington, DC's, common workingmen, and a winter getaway for the rich and bored. Even then, he could see the town's dependence on the fishery shrinking, and he had enough foresight to sense that the Bayland amusement park wouldn't last forever, either. The magic would slip away, and the place would become one more small town struggling to find a new identity. He had vowed that he wouldn't return unless he had to transport someone. Oddly, his foresight didn't reach far enough to see that not only would he back, but he would actually put down roots here. He didn't fight it. One day, change would come again and he would leave, going with the flow, like water through an ancient river channel, on its journey to the beautiful sea.

At present, the Chesapeake Bay looked ugly—rolling and splashing against the bulkhead as if Poseidon had declared war on Gaia and the shoreline. Hamelin pulled up the hood of his nylon jacket and trudged the last hundred yards of boardwalk with his chin tucked in and a wish that things were different. He missed the luscious garden retreats of the Weigh Station, where one could imagine and behold whatever pleased and soothed the soul: idyllic forests, roaring waterfalls, or scarlet, glowing sunsets. He had paved over his paradise with stupidity and pride. Why had he been so weak? He lost his quiet sigh to the wind and took the stairs from the walkway down to the beach.

One thing that hadn't moved along was the placard of restrictions posted at the bottom of the stairs that went down from the boardwalk to the beach: *Brownie's Beach. No glass, no littering, no dogs.* The first time he'd seen it, the sign was just one more encroachment on his independence—one more voice of authority yelling at him. Now? He looked around at his pristine surroundings: the clean, soft sand; the curved sweep of the cliffs as they rose away from the water; and tall oak trees standing like pinnacles on the crest. While the scene would have been more picturesque at the Weigh Station, it was still magnificent. The beach rules hadn't been so egregious after all.

"Hamelin."

He whirled around to find a dark soul runner standing behind him. He wore black, as they all did. A bit clichéd, but Hamelin couldn't imagine hell being anything but dark and empty—like a black hole where every good thing that defined a human was sucked out until there was nothing left to identify a person as such. Paths of the dark and the light soul runners sometimes crossed—light escorting to both heaven and hell, while dark runners delivered only to hell and under special circumstances—but the two didn't interact. Each kind knew their role and place. Etiquette dictated that each ignore the other, take care of the assignment, and pushing off as quickly as possible without communicating. They were merely transporters, without a say.

Hamelin said nothing and turned to take his leave.

"Hamelin," the runner repeated.

Hamelin stopped. How was it that the dark runner could call him by name? His mind raced back months earlier, to his interaction with a Beelzebubette during the Tippy best-of-bar competition in Nevis. The dark runner had been a troublemaker— gone rogue and bent on dragging an undeserving soul runner to the underworld. And he had almost succeeded in snaring Curtis Merriweather. Had the bubette somehow learned Hamelin's name then? Hamelin knew he should be following protocol, avoiding temptation and moving on, but that voice …

"You have me at a disadvantage, sir," Hamelin said, turning to face the runner. His face blanched, and he took several quick steps backward. "*Martin Cobb?* Dear God! Is it really you?"

"Odd, isn't it?" Martin said. "I guess it's not so different from before. There's no guessing the destination—my charges all go to hell, and God still decides, right?"

Martin looked back at Hamelin again. There was a haunted look in those eyes. Hamelin couldn't begin to fathom …

"How's business?" Martin asked.

"There is no business. I'm no longer a runner."

"Yeah? What is your status, anyway? Mortal? Immortal?"

"I'm sorry, Martin, but I can't talk to you. If I had known the message was from you, I never would have come."

"They tossed you back into this world, and you're still toeing their line and trying to please them? That was always your problem, Hamelin. Just rogue enough to break a few rules, but never enough piss and vinegar to go all out and get the total freedom you really craved."

"Goodbye, Martin." Hamelin headed back toward the beach stairs.

"Wait!" Martin called after him. "I'm sorry. Trust me, I'm sorry for a lot of things."

There it was again: *trust*. Ezekiel and Martin, two bad actors asking him to trust them. It wasn't going to happen. Hamelin reached the stairs and ascended.

"I need your help," Martin called after him. "I'm in involuntary servitude right now. Do you really think I want to be running dark souls? I have no choice. You've got to get me out of there."

Hamelin kept climbing. He heard a muttered curse as Martin kicked his shoes off and also started up the stairs.

"Come on, Hamelin. You're talking to the king of mulligans here. I know what you're juggling right now. Do you really think you can operate with the same latitude you had as a runner? Do you really think you can keep a dark muse for any length of time and not be corrupted by it? It's seeping into your being as we speak."

Hamelin paused at the top of the stairs. He recognized the work of the Great Deceiver. He should walk on, confident in the knowledge that saving Edgar from the obvious mal-intent of Ezekiel and Bertland was the right thing to do. Martin was now in the employ of darkness, and his speech would be full of lies. He would weave a dark thread of deceit through the fabric of truth, and it would seem logical and acceptable. Martin had been judged—and sentenced to hell. Hamelin shook his head.

"No, please," Martin pleaded a second time. "I've come to warn you. You're on his list, and if you don't protect yourself, he's going to make your life hell."

Hamelin turned around and sat on the top step. "A name, Martin?"

Martin looked up at him, and Hamelin could see fear in his eyes. "He doesn't need a name. You know who he is. You embarrassed him, and he's going to return the slight."

"Thanks for the heads-up, but I won't be needing it. The elders created the nonfraternization policy for a good reason: it works. Mind your own business, and everything works out fine. I am sorry you've come to such an end, Martin. Everyone in the Weigh Station was a work in progress, with weaknesses they had to overcome. You had them; I had them. You were much smarter and more politic than I. But you didn't have the sense to sit back and appreciate what you had, and didn't want to plan what would be the best for you in the end, did you? All those gifts … If you had used them for good, you would have been out of the Weigh Station in a New York minute. Instead, you were all about instant gratification. Don't think you'll get much of that where the fires dance. I'm afraid I can't offer anything. This *is* goodbye."

Martin wrung his hands. "Please, Hamelin." He burst into tears and babbled nonsense.

Before Hamelin could finish standing, strong arms yanked him up by the throat and squeezed. As he tumbled into his sub conscience, he thought he heard Martin pleading, "Please don't hurt him," as a languid voice whispered in his ear, "Welcome to the underworld, soul runner."

# Chapter Twenty
## Semblance of Hell

Vanessa Hardy waved at Ryan Thomas as he emerged from the Phoenix, hand in hand with a beautiful brunette and wearing the biggest smile a man could have without being fitted with a straitjacket. With his wife, Marie, now back at his side, he lived in a state of pure bliss. What a strange world it was. She was ecstatic with the way things had ended up.

For a moment, she loitered on the sidewalk outside Barnacle Bertie's, reconsidering her decision. Edgar couldn't possibly be a big grump two days in a row. She took a deep breath, pulled up her big-girl panties, and entered the bookshop. He sat dead ahead at one of the reading tables, head down, probably scowling, and a pen that she could swear was doodling connected ovals across the top of his writing pad.

"Morning, Edgar. I came to check on the book you ordered for me: Wylie's *Fundamentals of Maryland Beekeeping*?"

"Not here yet," he said without looking up. He shook out his writing hand and put pen back to paper.

She looked over at the two unopened shipping boxes stacked next to the counter. "Maybe in there?" she offered.

He grumbled something unintelligible. She decided the last few words encouraged her to have at it so she grabbed a box cutter from a cup full of pencils and highlighters, and slit open the top box. It contained books. When she confirmed that hers wasn't in the first one, she cut open the second box. After plowing through the contents of that one, she found Wylie's on the bottom.

"Got it," she said, waving the book at Edgar.

Edgar gave her a sullen look, then suddenly clutched at his chest and began gasping for air. He staggered toward the counter but found no purchase there. As he grappled with the phone, his knees buckled beneath him and he collapsed to the floor.

*Heart attack,* Vanessa thought, remembering her grandfather's death. With her own cell phone in her car, she grabbed the landline to dial 9-1-1 The phone was dead, the cord ripped from its jack when Edgar fell.

"Bennie," she mumbled. "Be right back, Edgar." She rushed across the street to the Phoenix, flinging the front doors open with enough force to bounce them off the outside of the building. "Nine-one-one, Bennie," she yelled as soon as she cleared the portal. "Call nine-one-one."

"Who. Where?" he asked, already punching numbers on his cell.

"Edgar, in Bertie's. He's on the floor." As she hurried back across the street, the siren on the firehouse three blocks down already wailing.

Ryan sat with his forearms resting on his knees, staring at Edgar as he lay in his bed on the second floor of the bookshop. The writer looked as if he had been lured into a terrifying nightmare. He tossed; he turned; he moaned.

In a brief moment of lucidity, Edgar had refused transport to Calvert Memorial Hospital. Desperate, Vanessa had persuaded Dr.

Champ, the local general practitioner from Upper Marlboro, to pay an unheard-of house call. He dismissed heart issues, pronounced Edgar's vital signs normal, and diagnosed the illness as viral. With Edgar adamant about staying put, the doctor left without prescribing anything except ibuprofen for any pain and fever, bed rest, and observation by family (there were none) and friends (which were few). Shortly after that, Edgar drifted off to sleep and would not be roused.

"Where are you, you irresponsible gallivanter?" Ryan mumbled under his breath.

Vanessa handed him another cool, wet cloth. "What?"

Ryan swapped it out for the one already on Edgar's forehead. "Nothing." *Nothing* that *she* could fix. Only Hamelin—that pesky, good-for-nothing immortal who just seemed unable to stop complicating Ryan's life. Here he sat, in the damnedest of predicaments, nursing the likes of the great Edgar Allan Poe a hundred and seventy-some years after his death. What sin, Ryan wondered, had the man committed that was so egregious that his life should be screwed up like this? *Damn you, Hamelin Russell.* And then Ryan wished he hadn't thought such a thing. He wouldn't wish hell on anyone. Ever. "You haven't seen Hamelin, have you?"

"Not recently," she said. "Hardly at all since you suggested he get a life—preferably one of his own."

Ryan shrugged. "Well, what can I say? He always brings out the worst in me. I don't know which is more annoying: having him here pestering me, or wondering what kind of nonsense he's getting into somewhere else."

"Nevermore, nevermore, nevermore," Poe whispered, pulling the cloth off his fevered face.

"You got that right," Ryan said, slapping it back on with a little more vigor than intended. He adjusted it with a softer touch and said, "As soon as Hamelin gets back."

"What?"

"Nothing, Vanessa. Maybe you should just go. This might be a dreaded lurgy they can't cure. No use everybody getting sick. Tell Bennie I'm across the street, but if he needs anything, they're to call, not visit."

Vanessa shook her head. "Dr. Champ said there was a virus going around and Edgar's *lurgy* would probably run its course in a few days."

Ryan gave her a skeptical look, and she got the message. As she picked up her stuff to go, Ryan said, "I'm expecting some legal papers today. Have Bennie buzz my cell when they come in?"

"Sure thing." Vanessa leaned down and whispered something in Edgar's ear. The corners of his lips turned up in the start of a smile but quickly relaxed again as he started babbling incoherently. Then he let out a scream and again yanked the damp cloth from his head and flung it away.

"Jeez Maries!" Vanessa said, backing away from him.

"*Get thee back into the tempest and the Night's Plutonian shore!*" Edgar yelled, waving his arms at some unseen foe. Ryan latched on to each wrist and gently lowered them back onto the coverlet.

"Okay, I'm out," Vanessa said. "Are you sure he shouldn't be transported?"

Transported, yes, but that was Hamelin's bailiwick. "Nope. It's all right. That's a line from a poem, *The Raven*. He's been quoting his own writing, ranting about death and hell the whole time he's been down."

"*While from a proud tower in the town, Death looks gigantically down,*" Poe intoned.

"The City in the Sea," Ryan said before she could raise the question.

Vanessa walked out and came right back in again. "I don't know whether to be creeped out or feel sorry for the guy. He's out of place and time. Hamelin certainly didn't do him any favors. That's what happens when you try to play God."

"You were better off not knowing. I never should never have discussed Hamelin with you."

"Oh, yes, you should have. Everybody should know not to shake his hand or hug him."

The idea of anyone voluntarily hugging Hamelin made Ryan chuckle. While he could occasionally be entertaining and his guitar-playing was out of this world, there was little endearing about the soul runner. Hamelin's questions, observations, and meddling were a constant annoyance. However, the thought that someone else could be revolted by Hamelin seemed over the top and hurtful. "You know, now that he's stuck back here on earth, he's a shrimp out of water, just like Edgar."

Vanessa nodded. "All I'm saying is, he should come back and make things right."

"Make things *right*?" Ryan repeated. "And does that include taking away Marie's and my second chances at life? You think he should shepherd us on our way into the afterlife because we're freaks of nature just like old Edgar A. Poe here?"

"Oh, hon, you know that's not what I meant at all." Vanessa started across the room, but a quick look from Ryan froze her in place. "I'm sorry. If I had thought it all the way through, I wouldn't have just said what I did." She looked over at the bed. "It's just that he's suffering so much. It seems so wrong. You and Marie are happy, and that seems right."

At this, Edgar sat straight up in bed, pointed a finger at Vanessa, and said, "*There are moments when, even to the sober eye of Reason, the*

LOUISE GORDAY

*world of our sad Humanity may assume the semblance of Hell.*" Then he flopped back down and moaned as if in dreadful pain.

"Oh, there's definitely something wrong," Ryan said, fishing Edgar's head cloth off the floor. "And whatever it is, Mr. Russell is going to have to fix it. Now, scram before there's so much semblance of hell here that we stop speaking to each other."


Ezekiel stood at the bottom of the stairs, listening to the two mortals and the ramblings of Edgar Poe. A dark feeling crept into his heart. He couldn't decide which was worse: the mortal couple's intimate knowledge of Hamelin's business, or Poe's preoccupation with the damned.

He dinged the bell sitting on the checkout counter.

"Not open," yelled a man's voice from upstairs. If it's a delivery, just leave it; if it's a pickup, come back tomorrow."

"And if I'm looking for Mr. Russell?" Ezekiel yelled back. The floorboards creaked above his head.

"I'm Ryan Thomas," said the handsome dark-haired man with a lean, muscular build and a haggard smile. "I own the Phoenix across the street. I'm also a friend of Hamelin's. Who would be asking?"

"His friend Ezekiel."

"Hamelin doesn't have—" Thomas closed his mouth, and Ezekiel could feel the man sizing him up. "I'm sorry, he's indisposed at the moment. If you want to leave a number where he can reach you ..."

"Oh." Ezekiel's gaze drifted to the stairs. "I know just the thing ..." He flitted past before Ryan Thomas had a chance to protest, and hit the top of the stairs three seconds later. Assaulting an angel would have been a painful mistake, and a lesson he would learn the first time.

150

"My dear Mr. Poe," Ezekiel began as he entered the room. He pulled up short at the sight of the man lying in the bed. He went right to the bedside and took his hand. "How long has he been like this?" Ezekiel asked over his shoulder as Ryan Thomas barreled into the room, hostility rolling off him in waves.

"Don't touch him." Thomas pulled Poe's hand free and placed himself between the writer and Ezekiel. "What kind of *friend*?" he asked.

"Not one of *those*," Ezekiel said, elbowing him aside. He took Poe's hand again and smoothed a lock of gray hair from his forehead. "Something is gravely amiss here. I must ask again, where has Hamelin gone?"

"I don't know," Ryan said, moving away. "Poe has been like this since he collapsed yesterday. If he dies, will they know to transport him?"

"Transport him?" Ezekiel asked, eying Ryan with curiosity. He dropped Poe's hand and squared off with Ryan. "What, exactly, do you know about transporting? And how did you learn of it?"

"Hamelin told—"

"Hamelin is as closemouthed and shrewd as they come. Tell me quick, where did you learn it?" Ezekiel seemed suddenly to grow in stature until he towered over the mortal.

Thomas shrank under the intensity of the angel's stare. "Hamelin told me. I swear to God. Edgar is a mulligan, and there is a tug-of-war for the dark muse that inspires his works."

"And?" Ezekiel persisted, continuing to glower.

"Well. There's Pandora's box, and her grandson who goes around stealing parts of writer's souls, but at the moment, I swear I can't put all of that in context." He closed his eyes. "Now, will you please stop staring at me and let me go?"

Ezekiel relaxed his powerful emotional hold. Thomas fell to the floor in a heap, breathing heavily—shaken but unharmed. Ezekiel turned back to Poe.

"Look at me, Mr. Poe."

Poe stirred but continued in a deep, fretful slumber.

"Mr. Poe," Ezekiel persisted. "Wake up and look at me."

Poe's eyes fluttered open. As he focused on Ezekiel, his pinched face relaxed slightly and he grabbed on to Ezekiel's hand as if it were the last life preserver on the *Titanic*. "Save me," he croaked. "I don't belong here."

Ezekiel smiled beatifically, his eyes never leaving Poe's face. After a moment, he patted the writer's hand and gently placed it down on his chest. "Of course," he said. He made the sign of the cross on Poe's forehead and watched as Poe closed his eyes and fell back into deep, more peaceful sleep.

"Of course he doesn't belong here," Ryan Thomas said. "He should have been gone over a century ago." In a barely audible whisper, he asked, "Is he dying?"

Ezekiel turned and looked at him with troubled eyes. "Of course, he shouldn't, but his *here* is not your *here*. He's referring to down *there*." He pointed to the floor.

Thomas frowned. "Downstairs?"

Ezekiel raised both eyebrows and waited.

Ryan Thomas's eyes grew wide. "Oh!" He stared briefly at the floorboards, then asked, "Why did Hamelin take his muse down *there*? Poe didn't seem a bad sort. He certainly hasn't been a bother since he hit town."

*Leave it to a mortal to waste their precious time on earth by asking all sorts of questions.* Ezekiel moved past him and headed for the door.

"Keep him comfortable until I return. Don't move him, and don't let anyone in to see him. Do you understand me?"

"No, I'm not understanding anything."

Ezekiel sighed in exasperation and turned to address him face to face. "In the common vernacular, I think it's what you would call *cutting you out of the loop*. It's not your affair, so take care of those few little things I've asked you to do, and go on about, well, whatever you normally are about."

"Where's Hamelin?"

"Need-to-know."

"Uh," Thomas said, nodding. "You coming back?"

"Certainly."

"Alone?"

"This may be much too complicated to handle alone. And you've raised a good point. If others arrive before I do, just show them up here and go on about—"

"—Whatever I normally am about," Thomas said, finishing the recurring theme. "So help me God, if this is another one of your crazy worldwide afterlife contests ..."

"Mr. Thomas, don't bring God into this. He has people like me to handle these sorts of things while he attends to other issues—delegations of authority and such."

"If you're not a soul runner, Mr. Ezekiel, what are you—an angel?"

Ezekiel ignored the question. It was just another need-to-know. He descended the steps and let his intuition guide him through the stacks, stopping ultimately in the fiction section—author surnames *GaGe*. He removed enough Neil Gaiman and Diana Gabaldon books to reach his hand behind the rest and pulled out Poe's dark-muse box. As he expected, it was empty.

He lifted his eyes toward the ceiling and whispered, "Thy will be done, Lord."

Enlightenment flashed through him like a streak of lightning. "Dear God," he murmured, staggering back into the shelf behind him. "I will try."

He hid the container back on the shelf. It currently served no purpose, but he had no insight into whether it might prove valuable later. Facing a demon in the light of day was more annoying than dangerous, but making a nuisance of oneself in the dark world of the *devil?* He needed a rescue posse, which he would find on Cloud Twelve.

# Chapter Twenty-One
# Underworld Shanghai

Hamelin ran his hand across his clammy forehead. Then his eyes popped open and he looked around. He sat alone in a room that was blast-furnace hot, which was unnerving, on a hard wooden chair that was most uncomfortable. The light was faint, but enough for him to see that there was nothing else in the room except a closed door on the opposite wall. Was he indeed in the naughty place?

He crossed the room and put his hand on the doorknob. The metal was scorching hot, and he promptly released it. Being dead, he felt no physical pain, but the heat answered his question. As best he could determine, while Martin distracted him, a Beelzebubette had latched on to his soul and transported him here. It was a dumb move. Hamelin had been around the universe a few times. Nothing stayed in hell that wasn't divinely ordained to be there. They might make him miserable for a little while, but sooner or later—and, yes, preferably the former—the Weigh Station would realize that they had a man down, and someone would come and rescue him. Hamelin sat down again. He'd heard stories of underworld shanghaiing. They made for great fireside tales after the fact. No, this would all get sorted out eventually. Hopefully before the Bowie Baysox's double-header. He had good seats for that one—right behind home plate.

After Hamelin took a quick inventory of his little hell hole, he inventoried himself: body unspoiled, spirit strong, Poe's dark mojo contained and lurking quietly within him. And there it would stay until Hamelin could get him out of here. He took a long, slow cleansing breath and settled back against the stiff, unforgiving chair, folded his arms across his chest, and slowly released himself into a deep meditation. The air around him warmed and glowed in the soft blue of a contented aura.

The click of the doorknob snapped him back to the moment, and his aura vanished. A bubette entered with Martin trailing meekly behind.

Hamelin focused on Martin, the weakest link in all this. When their eyes met, Martin cast his gaze to the floor and moved out of Hamelin's eyeline, behind the bubette. The bubette stopped several feet inside the door, silent and menacing. The three stood without speaking——energy zipping back and forth between them like electricity. Hamelin felt the bubette prodding at his being, trying to find something to exploit: fear, ignorance, infidelity. Any would do.

Hamelin erupted into peals of laughter, ending the ridiculous preening and probing. "Is this any way to treat a guest?" He glanced around the room and added, "I hope *your* accommodations are nicer than this."

"Did you really expect the Weigh Station, or your little cottage on the shore?" the bubette asked.

"Nah. Don't worry. It'll do in the short term." Hamelin leaned out until he caught Martin's eye again, and winked at him. "Martin I know," Hamelin said, "but the last time we met, I didn't catch *your* name. Will Bub do, or would you prefer something a little more distinguished?"

The bubette shrugged. "It's immaterial. If you employed a little imagination, you could make this place work for you. A desk here, music there," he said, pointing behind Hamelin to a heavy oak executive desk, and then to the farthest wall, upon which now hung half a dozen stringed instruments, including a Rickenbacker twelve-string, a mandolin, and a ukulele. But to each his own." He waved his hand, and it all disappeared—a simple parlor trick made to impress. Then he dropped the civility and his eyes grew dark. "Where's the muse?"

Hamelin's stomach tightened, and he shot a look at Martin, but his eyes were once again directed at the floor. Why hadn't he told the bubette? "Who?" Hamelin asked.

Bub walked behind Hamelin, forcing Hamelin to turn in his chair to keep sight of the demon. He wasn't afraid of the bubette, but he didn't want to be taken unawares a second time, either. Bub sat down in another simple wooden chair that hadn't been there earlier. To Hamelin, it all just felt needy.

"We all have our little tricks up our sleeves," Bub said, causing Hamelin to wonder if he could read his thoughts in this place. He kept his darkest concern pushed down to the place he'd left it a few minutes before.

"I didn't realize one soul runner could transport another soul runner as you did. This *Curtis*—did he survive?"

Hamelin ignored the question.

"I'll take that as a yes. Too bad," the bub said, shaking his head. "That would have made a great conversation starter."

Hamelin offered nothing, instead absorbing himself in the rhymical bouncing of Bub's foot—a trait Hamelin recalled from their initial encounter. The creature was wound tight, with little patience. Hamelin thought it an interesting button he might need to push.

"I seldom have time or patience for such niceties," Bub said. "As I see it, you're in violation of established trade agreements between the Weigh Station and hell. In particular, interfering with the collection and disposal of the contents of Pandora's box—an activity sanctioned for thousands of years. Granted, that's a spit in the ocean of time, but it's been humming along nicely until you came along. Is that the only reason the Weigh Station has you stationed in Nevis?"

Hamelin stood up. "Well, if this line of questioning is the purpose of our little meeting, I'm afraid you're wasting time. I'm not at liberty to discuss Station business. But then, you knew that before you waylaid me—an activity, by the way, which has *never* been sanctioned by *anybody*. So take me back and we'll let bygones be bygones."

There was a soft shuffling of feet from Martin's direction. Hamelin disliked having to divide his attention between the two sides of the room, but he suspected that Martin was an unwilling participant in this strong-arming, so he kept his primary focus on the bubette.

A smile creased Bub's face. "Oh, I don't need to know daily ins and outs. That's what Mr. Cobb is for." He threw a covetous look in Martin's direction. "I ask only because your business is of interest when it interferes with mine."

"Really?" Hamelin asked. "Because my first thought was it's more about face-saving. How hard is it to live down the reputation that you were bested by a lowly soul runner in a pub parking lot in Maryland? As for your Mr. Cobb, how do you know he isn't stringing you along? He was never the trustworthy sort. Isn't that why he ended up here? How can one trust anybody down under?" When he finished, Hamelin crossed his arms across his chest and offered a smile of his own.

Bub's smile vanished. "Where is Poe's muse? It disappeared from

Bertland's radar several hours ago."

*He had been here for several hours, huh?* Hamelin filed the information away for possible future use. "Perhaps his radar is broken. You know, Christmas is just around the corner."

"That holy time of year when mortals stress out, overspend, and would kill one another for that cheap flat screen? Puh-*lease*! You Christians slay me." Bub stood up and snapped his fingers, and the chair vanished. "Poe is still alive, so I know you didn't transport it. My guess? You're shielding his muse somehow, as you did with Curtis, and damn you, if it takes until the arrival of the four horsemen, you're going to stay down here until I find out."

Hamelin laughed. "We both know you have no authority to keep me in Hades. You'll try to make me miserable, hoping I'll scream *uncle* and tell you what you want. But see, here's the thing. The Weigh Station doesn't take kindly to people who don't play nice with their employees. Eventually, they'll send someone to fetch me, and you'll get a slap on the fanny. Then you'll be known as the incompetent bubette who not only got bested by a runner in a car lot, but couldn't even keep him in hell even on a part-time basis. You'll slink back under a dark, smelly rock to lick your wounds and fan your hatred for beings that walk the earth freely and appreciate all the joys God has to offer. What a poor, sad, put-upon boy you'll be. You can sputter and threaten all you want, but I'm in a protected class and there isn't a thing you can do to me."

Hamelin sat back down in his chair, pulled his legs up into a half lotus, and placed his hands palms up in a meditative pose. "Knock yourself out, kiddo. I shall consider it my amusement for the day."

Bub flushed crimson, and his face contorted. He pointed at Martin, who fell to his knees with a yelp of pain. Hamelin tried not to react, but he may have flinched at the swiftness and brutality of Bub's response.

Hamelin leaped from his chair. "Hey, enough of that nonsense. He's not involved in this."

As Martin lay writhing and moaning on the floor, Bub moved his finger until he was pointing at Hamelin. "Unfortunately, not everyone can say the same thing. I think I'll pay a visit to that nice little bayside community of Nevis while you give it all some thought. Come, Martin Cobb."

Martin staggered to his feet, shooting a quick glance at Hamelin as he did. His pinched expression reflected the pain he was still feeling. *Toe the line,* he mouthed, and left. The door slammed shut, plunging the room into darkness once again.

*Whose line?* Hamelin wondered as he watched the once-proud man stumble out the door after Bub like a whipped dog obediently following its abusive master. The bigger question was, *how obedient?* Hamelin didn't want to think about the consequences of Martin revealing to Bub the precious cargo that Hamelin carried into this godforsaken place. Edgar Allan Poe might indeed be destined for an eternity of misery and burning, but so far, the only one who could decide the matter hadn't yet weighed in.

Hamelin resumed his meditative pose. He pushed aside his concern for Edgar, and any feelings of pity he might have felt for Martin, and began to pray for his unsuspecting, unprotected friends in Nevis.

## Chapter Twenty-Two

# Bump and Run

Bub disliked Nevis for all the obvious reasons: it was quaint, had a tight-knit, helpful community, and boasted three, preposterously pompous churches all on the same street. The latter, he speculated, were full of hypocrites.

As he made his way through town, he followed his nose—or, more specifically, the reek of hospitality and happy souls. Nevis was a miasma of goodness, and it nauseated him. He wasn't surprised when his journey led him to the doors of the Phoenix. It was a bubbly hipster pub with a Maryland twist—fish and chips swapped out for crab balls and bay fries. Six of one, half a dozen … People went in dragging baggage and came out unburdened. He despised it.

He'd been here once before—not inside, but in the rear parking lot, trying to get the best of two Weigh Station soul runners duking it out over how to get rid of him. The irony? If they had ignored him, he would have searched out a more interesting arena to create mischief. But once they traded blows, he was all in. Little satisfied him more than instilling terror in a good person by bouncing them down into the underworld for a short, though unsanctioned session in hell. Oh, the abject horror in their doughy, overindulged faces.

Unfortunately, Bub had misjudged the situation, and the joke had been on him. One of the runners, Hamelin Russell, had been more experienced and powerful than he anticipated. Bub had been this close—he unconsciously drew his thumb and forefinger together until they almost touched—when Russell had outsmarted him, subsumed the incapacitated other brawler, and carried him back to the Weigh Station.

Bub wasn't sure how he had managed that—one soul runner taking the essence of another into himself. A nifty trick, but something Bub couldn't do. And honestly, he had tried several times since. As far as he knew, no other soul runner, dark or light, had ever done what Hamelin Russel accomplished.

Bub entered the Phoenix and took a booth by the door. There was no need to squeeze into the center of activities at the bar. He possessed both excellent hearing and speaking skills—the former to eavesdrop and the latter to inflict as much mayhem in as short a time as possible. Martin Cobb had never been here, but with a little encouragement, Bub had squeezed enough information from him to know what made this place hum.

The tubby bartender was Bennie Bertollini, an insufferably happy reliever of parched throats and whatever else ailed you. Bub's eyes settled for a moment on the collection of shot glasses arranged on a shelf behind the bar. Just as Mr. Cobb had predicted, one of them commemorated Bennie's winning of the soul runners' best-of-bar competition. For now, Cobb's information had panned out. That was good—for Cobb. Bub briefly considered toppling the shelf and its contents and then decided not to become sidetracked. He had a more important mission.

Then there was Bennie's boss, Ryan Thomas. Bub surmised that he was the tall, slim man gliding between tables serving up faux niceties and encouraging people to drink up. Bub concentrated on him. According to Cobb, Thomas was Hamelin's Achilles' heel.

"May I get you something?"

"Coffee, black," Bub replied to the baby-faced waiter grinning at him. Bub wondered whether the youngster was serving liquor and whether they had ever bothered to card him. Bub raised a pair of fingers, indicating two cups. Somewhere in his wanderings, he had learned that such an order indicated one wanted to be left alone to sip one's beverage and contemplate life. He couldn't case the joint if plagued with constant interruptions.

He leaned toward the solo drinker at the next table. "Hey, you. Smoke?" he asked, pointing to the pack of cigarettes in the man's pocket. It came out as more of a demand than a request. Without commenting, the smoker tapped him out one and went back to his drinking.

Bub inhaled deeply and exhaled slowly. He hadn't had one of these in years. *Years.* Hell permitted no self-indulgence, and soul-runner duties left no time. If it wasn't dragging mortally sinning soul runners down into the bosom of the realm of eternal fire, it was plenty of this, that, or the next thing. Bub checked his thoughts. He might not have local ears eavesdropping, but his boss, Big Bub, certainly did. He stubbed out the cigarette.

The Phoenix was a low-key place: steady foot traffic in and out, murmured conversations, and the quiet clinking of glassware. Bub watched Ryan Thomas slap Bertollini on the back and peck the cheek of a beautiful brunette reading a newspaper at the end of the bar. Then he scooped up some folders and loose-leaf pages lying near her and headed for the door. Bub followed him out.

Thomas turned left and continued down the sidewalk at a leisurely pace. He must be staying local, Bub thought, watching him bypass the alley leading to the parking lot. As they passed Wagnon's Cleaners and Pam's Hallmark card shop, Bub stayed close. The next block had a whole series of shops that Thomas could duck into.

Thomas turned left again at the next street. An overhead black iron sign advertised Duckett Law Office. Bub guessed it was Thomas's destination. Foot traffic? None. Traffic easing by? Check. Bub picked up his pace. In a blur, he came up behind Thomas, and as he drew abreast, he put a shoulder into the pub owner. Thomas sailed out into the street. Bub sensed death pause as if making its choice to settle in or move on.

Screams pierced the air, and brakes squealed. Bub rushed to Thomas's aid. The car had nailed him dead center grill and knocked him up onto the hood, where he now lay groaning, eyes closed. Others soon flocked close, offering assistance and gawking. PUB OWNER KILLED BY AUTO IN FREAK DOWNTOWN ACCIDENT. Wouldn't that be a hoot when it hit the papers? Bub couldn't wait to share a copy of the *Evening Star* with Hamelin Russell.

"EMT. Back up. Let me through. Please, coming through."

Bub found himself edged aside by a bespectacled man in jeans and a gray T-shirt. The self-proclaimed emergency management technician began talking softly to Thomas and going through a ritual of checking vital signs and diagnosing trauma. In the distance, a siren sounded and seemed to move toward them. Bub slunk off and took up a position on the sidewalk. He watched as more EMTs emerged from an ambulance and begin working on Thomas. The scent of death vanished. Damn these quick first responders! Didn't they have something better to do?

Bub moved on, too. Death would have been nice, but this was

something he could work with, spin if he needed to—a good start that would certainly rattle his haughty little guest.

Hamelin sat locked in his cell, the feeble light of his aura fading to gray and unable to illuminate the darkness. How long had he been in this dreary place where time had no meaning? Soul runners never considered time, but those joyous days were over. He wasn't a runner anymore, and quite frankly, he had no idea how the Weigh Station now categorized him. Mortal? Immortal? Self-doubt poured into every crack in his weakened being. Maybe Hades *was* his final judgment.

He put his head in his hands and tried to pray, but his thoughts kept bouncing around. No, not damnation—not yet, anyway. Ezekiel had said the movers and shakers at the Station were pleased with his progress. Hamelin needn't panic. Someone would discover his whereabouts and rescue him. He could beat this, *would* beat this. Being dragged to hell like this went against God's natural order. And so his thoughts went, 'round and 'round.

Hamelin got up to circumnavigate the room again. He counted his steps—thirty-two—and the door was still locked. He returned to his chair, which he had developed a new appreciation for. Without it, he would have been obliged to choose between standing—doable, but not comfortable—and sitting on a filthy floor that crawled with tiny, hideous, unthinkable things.

He felt Edgar's muse whimpering, and the rest of his soul in the realm of the living, answering with its own suffering call as the two parts connected virtually across time and space. What would happen if Hamelin were forced to give up Edgar's dark muse? Could Poe fight off the desperation and melancholy? Hamelin shuddered at the thought of Poe, bedridden and caught between the living and the dead, wasting away in Nevis.

When the bubette returned, Hamelin hoped he would come alone. Martin was the wild card in all of this—a trump card if Bub used it efficiently. If Martin had remained in the Station long enough to hear how Hamelin had absorbed Curtis's soul to return him to the Weigh Station; then he knew that Hamelin was capable of hiding Edgar's muse in the same way.

What would it take to get Martin to give up that kind of information? A position of devilish authority? That would certainly appeal to him. He was a social and corporate ladder climber from the get-go. But surely, he was smart enough to realize that the devil and his crew sealed all their deals with lies. They would never deliver what they promised. That left the affliction of severe and endless mental and corporal punishment. Hamelin wasn't sure how well Martin could withstand that kind of pressure. For Edgar's sake, Martin didn't need to hold out forever—just until the good guys swooped in on their white chariots and plucked Hamelin out of this miserable place. They would come. They always came. Or so he'd heard.

He rocked back in his chair. Did he, in fact, *know* that they always found people like him? His status wasn't that of your typical immortal, mortal, or whatever the hell he was. There might be a chance of falling between the cracks—just like all the mulligans he had created. Hadn't he found a loophole to make them do just that? He cradled his head in his hands. Wouldn't that be karmic bitch.

The doorknob clicked and he sat upright again. Bub came alone this time.

"Who is this Ryan Thomas?" the demon asked.

Prickles ran up Hamelin's arms. "Sounds like a mortal. Why?"

Bub held up a copy of the *Nevis Evening Star* newspaper, which was radiating an eerie green in the blackness. The headline on an article on the lower left caught Hamelin's eye: POPULAR PUB OWNER INJURED IN AUTO ACCIDENT.

Hamelin snatched the paper out of his hand and skimmed the story while trying to keep the alarm out of his face. "Well," he said, handing it back. "Sounds like he's a popular pub owner. Are all your quizzes this easy?"

"Yes, a close call for the mortal." The newspaper ignited in the demon's hand and disintegrated into a puff of smoke.

"Abracadabra," Hamelin muttered under his breath. "There a point to all this, Bub? Because you are kind of cutting into my meditation time."

"It could have been worse."

"What's the matter—get scared?"

No," Bub said, shaking his head. "Pragmatic. Too much of a fuss, and I get chastised and wrist-slapped. But there's wiggle room for a little playing."

"Scared," Hamelin repeated. "So hell does have a few rules. Messing with mortals is a no-no? Good to know."

"Left you a copy," Bub said, pointing to a folded newspaper on a new side table sitting to Hamelin's left. "To glean the more salient points you missed the first time around. Cobb tells me that you frequented the pub. I'm going to rip it down one brick at a time. Starting with the first person who walks out the front door at noon today."

Hamelin's mind darted back to images of Bennie and his main squeeze, Jean; Ryan Thomas's mother, Vanessa, and his ladylove, Marie, and countless other kind, unnameable faces he had seen breaking bread and sharing drinks at the Phoenix. "Leave those people alone. You know I can't discuss my business with you."

"Give me the dark muse and I'll let you go. Let *all* those people go. I know you have it, because it's become terribly quiet in Nevis. If the muse were still about, the town would be a whirlwind of destruction and chaos."

"Besides the havoc that you're creating."

Bub sat down in a chair that suddenly materialized behind him. The bit was growing tiresome, Hamelin decided. He should just add some permanent furniture and quit the showboating.

"Look, Hamelin Russell. No need to be dismissive. I do what demons do. Just as you and your kind laze around all day singing songs of praise to a deity who allows his children in the world to suffer. We are alike in that we both ferry souls to their appropriate rewards, but the similarity stops right there."

"It's called free will, and everyone has a choice."

"No," Bub said, shaking his head. "It's the nature of the beast. Just look at Mr. Poe's dark muse. One could no more change that than one could ..." He paused a moment, searching for the right words. "... than one could teach a bird to swim and a snail to fly. Evil is hardwired."

Bub leaned back in his chair, and even in the dimness Hamelin could read the smirk on his face.

"That's laughable," Hamelin said. "And merely an excuse so you don't have to take personal ownership of all the vile and grubby things you've accomplished in your existence. I have no doubt that at one time you were good. God's plan is good and infallible."

Bub got up, and the chair vanished. "Talking to you is useless. It's the muse or your friends. Let me know." He didn't bother with the door but disappeared in a huff and a poof of smoke. Hamelin wondered whether his hardwiring had short-circuited.

He picked up the newspaper and, in the faint glow of his aura, read the article again. He hadn't missed anything the first go-round; his speed-reading skills were impeccable. He couldn't take what the bubette did and said at face value. He lied; he twisted; he deceived. So, was the article real? Were any of the news events real?

One by one, he skimmed through the articles, letters to the editor, even the ads. And one by one, he sensed that the information presented was—allowing for some journalistic bias, of course—factual and logical. There were no talking horses, lovers fornicating in public places, or public hangings that might delight a denizen of the underworld but be totally out of place to nonhellizens. To his sorrow, his friend Ryan Thomas had stumbled—or, more likely, been pushed—from a Nevis sidewalk into the path of a car. Blessedly, the automobile had been creeping along, and Thomas's injuries were not life-threatening. Praise be to God.

Hamelin tossed the paper onto the table. He wasn't going to give up the muse. That violated every tenet of a soul runner's code. Even though that was no longer his calling, it was a noble cause and he would not desert it. He got down on his knees and steepled his hands. The demonic shenanigans had to stop before someone died. As he bowed his head, the oppressive gloom surrounding him began to shift and lift, and unseen creatures scurried for the corners as his aura began to grow and pulse.

# Chapter Twenty-Three
# Flyboys

Ezekiel exited at the first Weigh Station teleportal. Mortals thought of the great beyond as a realm forever separated from their world, but he liked to think of the infinity of such entrances and exits as akin to subway tunnels. They were constantly humming with the comings and goings of immortals doing God's work. To the average Weigh Station citizen, the portal-to-portal transportation system traveled in two directions: toward earth and back again to the Station. But in fact, it ran in many directions, on many different planes of existence. After all, God's universe was boundless.

The portal dumped Ezekiel off in the middle of the White Corridor, the section of the Station that housed upper management and coordinated all the activities of the Soul Runner Corps. Elder Stephen had an office here, and Ezekiel prayed that he could find him quickly.

Luck was with him. Dead ahead stood Elder Stephen, quietly gazing out one of the enormous bay windows, at some sector of the cosmos. "Elder Stephen," Ezekiel called. "I need your assistance."

The silver-haired old man, unstooped by age, turned slowly toward him and smiled. "And so you shall have it." He embraced Ezekiel as if he were the Prodigal Son. "How goes the task?"

"Not well, I'm afraid, sir. It's Hamelin Russell," Ezekiel began as he drew Stephen into a more private nook.

Stephen's expression tightened. "What now?"

"Oh, he's been doing exceptionally well," Ezekiel said, bringing delight back into Stephen's expression. "It's just that I can't find him, and I fear the worst."

"The worst in your mind being ...?"

"I think he's in hell, sir."

Stephen's facial expression remained unchanged, but he took Ezekiel by the elbow and hurried him down the hallway. "Call a meeting of the elders," he said as if talking to himself. "Now." Half a dozen doors down, he pushed Ezekiel into an empty conference room and closed the door behind them. "Again, Ezekiel. Leave nothing out."

Ezekiel related Hamelin's association with Edgar Allan Poe, and the writer's mulligan status, as well as Pandora's grandson and his quest to retrieve Poe's dark muse. "I am sorry to dump all this on you," he said after laying it all out. "I normally complete my tasks without assistance, but in this case, even with the help of the Corps of the Twelfth ..."

"No," Stephen said, placing a hand on Ezekiel's shoulder. "Don't assume you've *dumped* anything on me. When I gave you this assignment, I told you I wanted to be kept in the loop. Venturing alone into hell without a plan and without backup firmly in place would be foolhardy. Good judgment, as well as all our operating procedures, dictates that problems are never to be handled in such a way. No, you did exactly what's expected of you. And trust me, I know far more about what goes on here than they give me credit for."

That elicited a smile from Ezekiel. The only thing Stephen might not have received credit for was an exquisite wry sense of humor, and the angel loved him all the more for it. "So you know where Hamelin is?"

"With all these soul runners flitting about?" Stephen said, gesturing with a hand. "I'm an administrator, not a GPS. The Pandora story has been going on for eons, and obviously, it's not going away anytime soon—at least, to my way of thinking. I leave that in the Lord's hands. But here's the thing. They can have a crack at the dying, but interfering with a soul of the living is an egregious violation of our agreement."

"But you could say the violations began with Hamelin Russell creating a mull—er, second-chancer."

Ezekiel heard voices coming down the corridor. Stephen apparently heard them, too. He started for the head of the table. "Mulligans," the elder said, shaking his head. "I had such high hopes for that man."

"But the mulligan isn't a recent one," Ezekiel said, reading Stephen's mind, which slammed shut like a bank vault as soon as Ezekiel made his observation.

Ezekiel hung his head. "I didn't mean to intrude, Stephen, but that was a pretty loud thought. He's been on the straight and narrow since he left here."

"We'll address that later. Let's find him first." He started to sit down, paused, and then added, "And we can begin by leaving the bit about mulligans out of the immediate narrative."

The conversation shifted as the door opened and the top brass from the Station began trailing in. There were twelve in all. Ezekiel had dealt with a few of them before, but over nothing as troubling as a soul runner lost in hell.

Ezekiel took a seat at the far end of the table and again related the turn of events, starting with his appointment as Hamelin's confessor, through his discovery of Edgar Poe lying near death and at hell's door in the little bookshop in Nevis. Those around the table (all men—a glaring problem of gender inequality that no one ever seemed to want to address) ceased their fidgeting with paper, pens, and various widgets as the enormity of the situation registered in dropped jaws, hands to foreheads, and quiet pleas of "God help us."

When Ezekiel finished, dead silence filled the room. He looked to Stephen for guidance, but the elder, with head bowed deep in thought, kept his peace.

Finally, Barnaby broke the uncomfortable silence, his gravelly voice booming in the small, quiet room. "How can you be so certain Hamelin is in the netherworld?" he said, fixing Ezekiel with his laser-like stare, "Perhaps he's off galivanting again."

"Hamelin was Poe's protector, Ezekiel said. "I saw the work of the devil in Poe's eyes and heard it in his suffering. There is no doubt. Hamelin is one of us, a dedicated servant of the Lord. The question should be, how are we going to help him?"

"*Was*. Was one of us," Barnaby countered. "No longer."

The dynamic in the room shifted as all twelve began talking at once. Precious time ticked away as some advocated a wait-and-see approach, others doubted Ezekiel's assessment of Poe, and a third advocated kicking the whole situation over to the Clouds and the Angelic Corps, who were "responsible for anything related to Pandora."

Ezekiel sat listening and steaming at their talk-and-do-nothing attitudes. As they continued bickering and posturing, he realized that, like the soul runners who were working at the Weigh Station while awaiting their final judgment, these men, too, were here to improve their spirituality before judgment. In times of crisis, they were woefully inefficient—bureaucrats to the end.

Ezekiel got up and walked out. The time for arguing and jockeying for position was over. He needed action *now,* and clearly, only the Clouds could provide that. He found the nearest portal, left the

Station, and headed for Cloud Twelve. His fellow angels there would not be afraid to enter the depths of hell with him.

Unlike the inhabitants of the Weigh Station, *average* would never be an accurate term for describing the Angelic Corps. They were powerful, they were lovely, and they were active soldiers in God's plan. Ezekiel's comrades-in-arms operated out of what was affectionately called Cloud Twelve. It was a nickname, of course—the full name was much too long and cumbersome for everyday use. All the angelic operation centers were nicknamed in similar fashion. The naming had nothing to do with condensed water vapor. Rather, it referenced the simple stories that mortals told their children to help them understand an afterlife none of them could begin to imagine. Cloud Twelve's members eventually shortened their name to *the 12th.*

Although hardworking and obedient, they were young angels (relatively speaking), and a cocky, cliquey bunch. Those who had a problem with it were drummed out to other clouds. The older, more seasoned members of the Corps left them alone. With experience came wisdom, and with just a smidge of oversight and an occasional guiding hand, the exuberant young rowdies would one day turn out just fine. For Ezekiel, time here was rapidly coming to an end. He had proved himself capable and mature and had already been notified that he would be reassigned to Cloud 6 after he completed things with Russell. He kept this knowledge to himself, however. He would deal with the emotional fallout from his friends when the time came. And so, to this group Ezekiel brought his dilemma. To an angel, the five squadron members would rally behind him.

He found them sitting at a round table near one of the many fountains that graced this city of peaceful light and gentle music. It was a table of equals with no official leader, although Eli had the most sway by virtue of his direct and decisive manner. When Ezekiel convinced him, the rest would fall in line.

The 12th were letting it all hang out: disturbingly loud talking and laughter; disheveled, drooping wings, and a bit of alcohol. All tomfoolery ceased as he approached the table. It wasn't because they thought they should straighten up and fly right. Rather, it was the pause before they all ganged up on him to razz him for some minor or invented transgression.

Ezekiel stopped at the table and waited. And they in turn waited with cocked heads, raised eyebrows, and bated breath. Did his trouble show so clearly?

Eli, the nearest angel, of light brown hair, deep-set eyes, and a strong jawline, spoke first. "Who died?"

The other four angels laughed and bantered.

Ezekiel stood quietly, letting them get it out of their systems. Eventually, they paused and considered his still-sober manner.

"Sorry," Eli said, "but hey, you *do* look like your grandmother died."

Ezekiel shoved Eli's feet out of the chair he had propped them up on, and sat down. "Who's out of rotation right now?"

"All of us." It was Matthew, the mildest of the group, but with build that would discourage most others from testing his good humor.

Ezekiel nodded. "I need a search party to take back to earth. Two days max, their time. Can I count on you?"

Five chairs simultaneously scooted back from the table. "Let's go," they said in unison.

"What are we hunting for?" Eli asked as he gathered several things from the table.

"A soul runner is missing," Ezekiel said. "We need to go to hell and pull him out."

Four of the five sat down. Only Eli remained standing. "Who's the runner?"

"Hamelin Russell."

"Oh, I've partied with that dude," said one of the four. "Too bad. Great guy, but a bit crazy." He shuffled the deck of cards in front of him and began dealing out six hands.

Ephraim, standing next to him with a blond Mohawk, added his two cents. "Might want to sit down, Eli. He's the runner they bounced back to earth for a little more soul-searching."

"Too much soul *switching* is what I heard," Miguel said as he dealt the last card and turned the top card up on the rest of the deck.

"I know who he is," Eli said. "Unless he's been officially condemned, he needs to come out. How did he get there, Ezekiel?"

"He accidently got mixed up with one of Pandora's crew. If you ignore the fact that the kerfuffle happened over an old mulligan that Russell created, it really wasn't his fault."

"Booyah!" Miguel said, pointing at Ezekiel. "Just what I said. It's too messy to get involved." He initiated a game of one by taking the upturned card and discarding another.

Rhini didn't join in the conversation or the cards but sat twirling the ends of her long auburn tresses as her big, violet doe eyes studied Ezekiel. Ezekiel wasn't surprised. Rhini generally kept her own counsel. She would eventually share her opinion privately with Ezekiel or through Eli. She was grounded, as thoughtful as she was comely, and the group's best asset after Ezekiel and Eli. As Ezekiel assessed her, she was currently on the fence.

Eli was quiet and thoughtful for a moment and then nodded as if his mind were made up. "So we'll need to bring him out *and* clean up the mulligan."

"No, we don't," Ephraim said. "Mulligans, soul runners—that's Weigh Station business."

"*Former* soul runner," Miguel corrected.

"It's still the Weigh Station's responsibility."

Ezekiel shook his head. "No—at least, not right now. I've got marching orders to clean things up, and it doesn't initially include the Station."

"Official?" Eli asked.

"From the top," Ezekiel said. "Go in, get the runner and the muse he's rescued from Pandora's grandkid, and then address the mulligan."

"Who is the mulligan?" Rhini asked.

"Edgar Allan Poe."

"Excellent taste," she said, a smile crossing her lips."

"Dude hid a mulligan for, what, a hundred and seventy years? *Wow! Eso es una locura.*" Miguel let out a long, low whistle, folded his cards, and took his place beside Eli. "Respect, man," he said, and struck his fist against his chest. "Let's go get him."

The others murmured their agreement, and so, to Ezekiel's utter surprise, it was Miguel and not Eli who rallied the squad on Hamelin's behalf.

Eli was first to the portal. "Meet me at …" He stopped and turned to Ezekiel. "Where the hell *are* we going first?"

A sinking feeling hit Ezekiel. They hadn't left yet, and Eli was already taking charge. He tried to tamp down feelings unworthy of his status. Eli hadn't done it on purpose. It just seemed that Eli couldn't control his larger-than-life persona. It was just there *all the time.*

"Not yet," Ezekiel said. "There's a little speck of a town called Nevis. We can hammer out the finer details there before we go down under. Meet me in front of a watering hole called the Phoenix."

Eli looked at the others. "Well, you heard him. Let's go!"

# Chapter Twenty-Four
# In a Bad Place

Hamelin drew his hand back and admired the image. The face was a bit rough, he thought, running his forefinger along the upper edge, but he could already see the glow of the golden aura haloing the blessed infant's head. He entertained no illusion that when completed, it would rival his greatest masterpiece, the *Madonna and Child* that had been wrongly attributed to his mentor, Berlinghiero. Once upon an eon ago, that memory would have sent him into a whirlwind of anger and resentment. No more. Life was too short for such negativity, and too long to waste not creating something new and wonderful.

Pleased, he dipped the tip of his jerry-rigged paint brush—a pencil from his pocket, and thin wood strips carefully shaved from his chair leg—into the gray paint he had created from water and ash, and set back to work on the Madonna.

The spacious, comfy office where Martin had so recently taken solace now felt as much a prison as Hamelin Russell's cramped, dark hell hole. The metal frame that once held a picture of his promotion letter to a supervisory position at the Weigh Station had succumbed to the heat and now lay in a puddle of molten aluminum that bubbled and popped on his desk. His favorite books—Michael Connelly's *The Poet*, *The Glass Key* by Dashiell Hammett, and Patricia Highsmith's *The Talented Mr. Ripley*—now lay tumbled on the floor, collateral damage from a wooden shelf that refused to stay fastened to the wall.

He studied the couch and chairs in his conversation area, where he had once held sway over countless impressionable newbie soul runners at the Weigh Station. He didn't doubt that the fabric and cushion foam would be the next to go. He decided to take charge and dispense with it before that happened. He shoved it all into a pile against the wall. And then he began to pace back and forth, forth and back, until he could swear he saw the beginnings of a worn path beneath his feet. With each turn, he whispered, *Dear God, I am heartily sorry for having offended thee, and I detest all my sins, because I dread the loss of heaven and the pains of hell.* What a fool he had been—heaven within his grasp, and he had traded it all away in whims and fancies. It struck him that if he paced long enough, his feet might wear a trench deep enough to reach somewhere else. China? Or perhaps heaven, with a quick test for admittance by Saint Peter at the shining gates into the blessed realm of eternal joy and love. He would repent until God forgave him.

Suddenly, he stopped. He hated Bub, hated the transporting trips Bub was forcing him to make—delivering to hell the poor soul runners who came so close to heaven but fell short in the end. He hated Bub with a fury unlike any he had ever felt, and it was growing by the day. No, not by the day, for increments of time didn't exist here—just endless existence without breaking for food or sleep or personal interaction of any kind. When he first arrived, Martin had slept. And he assumed each period was equivalent to a single night. But now there was no sleep, and the calendar on his desk was as worthless as the choir concert tickets he had stapled to the month of July.

Martin gazed about the rest of the room. He envisioned all these prized possessions becoming irrelevant—the telescope that had no sky to view, and even the comfortable leather desk chair that was now too hot to sit on. The sage who said you couldn't take it with you obviously knew whereof he spoke.

The door creaked, and Martin whipped his head around. Bub entered like a dark, rain-laden cloud.

"Sit," the demon ordered with the flick of his hand. "You're not happy."

Martin hesitated, unsure what had precipitated this sudden concern for his well-being. Demons never cared. He shook his head.

"I need information."

A trade? Info for something to improve his situation? Martin silenced that thought. Never trust a bubette. Besides, giving him confidential soul-running information might arm him with powerful information he could use against other soul runners—innocent ones like Hamelin. The vinyl record on his turntable skipped, destroying a delightful clarinet passage in Brubeck's "In Your Own Sweet Way."

"Such as?"

"Why did the Weigh Station kick Hamelin Russell out?"

Tricky one. "He was never on time," Martin answered. "Nobody ever knew where he was." And it was the partially the truth. The rest of the story—mulligans—would never cross his lips. He pressed them firmly together and waited to see if that would satisfy Bub.

As Bub mulled the answer, his black tongue slide around his lips without moistening them. Heat parched everything in this place.

"Lying," Bub said after a moment, "which doesn't play well in this universe, either." Martin listened as the needle on his turntable screeched across the surface of the record. A *pop* followed, and he watched his stereo burst into flames. Then his mind flashed to Hamelin imprisoned in his small, filthy cell. He sighed in frustration and guilt. "For making mulligans."

Bub frowned. "Speak plainly, Cobb."

Martin's heart pounded, and his throat tightened. "Instead of transporting souls of the deceased, Hamelin allowed them to float into the body of another at the same moment of death."

Bub's eyebrows shot up. "And they survived to live on in this new body?" he asked.

Martin nodded. "It's not that difficult once you know the ins and outs."

"This is what he did to Curtis Merriweather?"

"No, Curtis was a temporary thing." Martin's mismatched shoes began to squeeze his toes, and he longed to get them off.

Bub closed his eyes, and Martin could see him beginning to work the information to his advantage. Martin was a cooked goose now; he'd gone too far. After this betrayal, there was no chance God would forgive him. The Weigh Station wouldn't take him back, and Bub would pick his mind like a vulture.

"And all soul runners do this?"

"Can but wouldn't dare. It's not some—"

"And it can be taught." Bub opened his beady eyes. They were hyperfocused on Martin. All the puzzle pieces had fallen into place.

Martin hung his head. "Yes. It's not hard once you understand what you're doing. The skill is in the recordkeeping so the higher-ups don't catch you at it."

Bub nodded. "Teach it to me."

"What?" Martin stood slack-jawed. "I, uh, really couldn't do that."

Bub grabbed Martin by the placket of his shirt and pulled him close. "Show me."

Did Bub envision a rebirth for Hitler, Genghis Khan, and Vlad the Impaler? "Of course, you can't bring anyone back who has already had final judgment. It only works on the newly dead, at the moment of death."

Bub released him. "Are you sure?" He directed Martin to his desk chair. "Sit and tell me exactly how I make these mulligans."

Martin began to shake. "I would love to do that, but I swore an oath that I cannot break."

"And I will swear an oath at you that you will wish you never heard."

"I can't." The words were no sooner out of his mouth than Martin felt the first three fingers on his right hand hyperextending. He dropped to the floor, moaning and clutching at his hand. "All right, all right. Please, my fingers."

His fingers relaxed, but the throbbing pain remained. Martin stayed on the floor. "First, you close your eyes and clear your mind," he said. Then, step by step, he explained the entire process.

When Bub left, Martin wept. The power of hell would create an army of demonic mulligans and unleash them to destroy world order. It would happen so quietly and so fast that the Station gatekeepers would not realize what hit them. And there wasn't a single thing Martin could do to stop it.


Bub paused outside Hamelin Russell's cell. The soul runner should be distraught enough to hand over the information he needed. The notion did disappoint him a bit. He really got off on a bit of suffering. The comeuppance he got from Mr. Russell in their parking lot encounter still stung. Russell should feel the sting for a little while, too. If left up to his own devices, Bub would make it so, but unfortunately, the big bub was involved, so Bub had to be quick and efficient and settle for less. He'd have to find someone else to torment—like Martin Cobb. When soul runners legitimately ended up down here, the demons showed no mercy. Before long, Cobb would wish he had straightened up in life and delivered by the book.

Bub twisted the doorknob and entered.

"Holy shi ..." Bub took a step back. Colored lights filled the cell, dancing and pulsating to the beat of salsa music. At the far side of the room, Hamelin sat cross-legged on the floor, writing something. When he lifted his head, Bub saw in his eyes serenity and something else that set his teeth on edge: defiance.

Hamelin put down his improvised writing instrument, and like an orchestra conductor, silenced the music with a slash of his hand. "Drink?" he asked, holding up a cup. "Oh, sorry. Not a drinker, as I recall. Smoking is your vice, isn't it?" He suddenly held a lit cigarette and offered it.

Bub walked over and studied the painting on the floor. Then, with his foot, he smeared the face away. "Apparently you don't value the right things. I'm going to give you a choice: the bartender, the wife, or the mother?"

"The *wife?*" Hamelin asked with a bit of puzzlement. It slipped out before he thought about how it sounded.

"Excellent choice. She dies at noon."

"No wait," Hamelin said, scrambling up. "That was a question, not an answer to your question."

"My bad," Bub said. He walked out and the door automatically closed behind him with a boom and a click of the lock.

"No, wait!" Hamelin cried again. Bub didn't answer. Hamelin pawed uselessly at the doorknob.

"Not Marie, not Marie," he whispered, falling to his knees. Feelings that he would never admit began flooding over him. He bowed his head in disgust at his betrayal of Ryan Thomas's friendship. *Thou shall not covet thy neighbor's wife.* He couldn't help the way he felt about Marie, but he had never acted on those feelings. Hadn't he reunited both lovers in the end? Why, he could have given Ryan up to Martin Cobb and still protected her, but he refused to do so. He had loved her ever since he first met her in the Phoenix. And now he was sending her to her grave. Somehow, someone would come and put an end to this nightmare.

He returned to his ruined drawing and wiped the floor as clean as he could. Then he picked up his brush again and started a silent, reverent conversation about serving others. Oh, how he wished he hadn't dismissed Ezekiel so easily. A flyboy right about now would be an answer to his prayers.

# Chapter Twenty-Five
# All the Kings Men

When Ezekiel arrived in Nevis, he found Eli standing on the sidewalk outside the Phoenix, one thumb pressed to his lower lip, and a preoccupied look on his face. Eli was already three steps ahead of him in planning. Rhini was a short distance down the street, either studying the architecture of the Smithville United Methodist Church or watching a conspiracy of ravens grumbling on the roof overhanging the front doors. Ezekiel knew better than to assume that she was loafing. Her brain never shut off, either.

Ezekiel acknowledged her and approached Eli. "I didn't mean for you to figure it all out by yourself."

Eli's look of seriousness fell away. "Since when?"

"Since never. At least wait until we're all here. Where is everybody else?"

"We're early. I need inside," Eli said, and they entered the bookstore.

No one was downstairs, and Eli ascended to the second-floor bedroom. At Poe's bedside sat a woman Ezekiel knew to be Vanessa Hardy. The bar owner, Ryan Thomas, was elsewhere.

"Wh-who are you?" Vanessa asked rising abruptly. The plate that had been in her lap hit the floor and shattered. Then she caught sight of Ezekiel. "What's going on?" she asked him.

"Don't be afraid," Ezekiel said. "We're all friends of Hamelin. Where is Ryan Thomas?"

She gave Eli a second look, but he was already at Poe's side, holding his hand and whispering to him. "At home. Should I call him?"

"No, please don't. We'll only be a minute. If you would wait at the bottom of the stairs ..." Ezekiel watched her hesitate, torn between arguing and trusting them. He wrapped an arm around her and guided her to the door. "Go. It will be okay." When she acquiesced, Ezekiel joined Eli.

"Mulligans. Most unfortunate," Eli said, shaking his head. "What senseless suffering."

"Can the muse be pulled back from Hades?" Ezekiel asked him.

"No. It's in the soul runner's control, and there it will stay until he comes back or relinquishes it. What a fool Hamelin Russell is."

"What would possess him to take it to hell?"

"The trip was not of his volition. There is treachery and collusion at work. The damned cannot be trusted." Eli stood another moment, looking at Poe, then said, "I'm afraid Hamelin can't be left to his own devices. You have to report him. They never should have sent him back. A final judgment is due." He looked at Ezekiel. "Or would you prefer I do it? As his confessor, I thought you would prefer ..."

"Stephen already knows about the mulligan. His counsel was to keep it quiet for the moment."

Eli shook his head. "You need to make it clear to everyone, including our people. *Now*, Ezekiel."

Ezekiel nodded. As much as he hated to do it, Eli's judgment was sound.

"Let me by." It was Ryan Thomas's voice, from the first floor.

"I have it," Ezekiel said, staying Eli with an upraised hand. "I'll be right back."

Halfway down the stairs, he blocked the bar owner's ascent and began backing him down the steps with a menacing look. It wouldn't have been a difficult task for anyone. The mortal moved as if every muscle in his body ached, and one arm was immobilized in a sling.

"Ryan Thomas," Ezekiel said. "I know what you are, but right now I don't want to deal with all the trouble that introduces. Trust me, if Eli meets you and becomes less focused on Poe, he will think differently. Go back across the street and stay uninvolved."

"Vanessa," Ryan said, turning to his mother. "Let's go. They can handle this." She nodded and they left without delay.

Ezekiel rejoined Eli, who was looking out the bedroom window. "Let me tell you what I think," Ezekiel said. "Then you can add in your own thoughts. The ferryman can carry three at most in his boat. You and I can cross, enter the gates, and escort Russell out. Rhini, Miguel, and Ephraim should stay on this side of the river. If we run into difficulty, they can cross together. Matthew hangs back here to send word should something need our immediate attention."

"Exactly. In and out with no complications. Then we put our feet up and enjoy a cold one, eh?"

Ezekiel laughed at Eli's nonchalance. Once his path was clear and his mind made, Eli could chill with the best of them. "No complications. You're on."

By the time they reached street level, Miguel had joined Rhini. "The rest should be along shortly," he said. "Like now," he added, nodding at Ephraim and Matthew as they rounded the corner of the church.

"Ezekiel," Miguel asked, throwing Ephraim a knowing look, "are we going to roar in, or did you have something a bit more subtle?"

"Roar in?" Ephraim said. "You're mistaking Ezekiel for Eli. It's all about subtlety, right, Ezekiel?"

"Okay, here's the plan," Eli said, speaking before Ezekiel could open his mouth. He repeated Ezekiel's plan word for word, throwing in additional details here and there. Eli had been to hell, and the devil *was* in the finer details, but it still didn't excuse Eli for seizing the lead and bulldozing ahead.

"Ezekiel, do you have anything to add?" Eli asked.

Ezekiel brought to mind Poe in his bed and Hamelin in his hellish resting place—the real victims in all of this—and put aside his rising annoyance. Reaching into his pocket, he pulled out a handful of gold coins. "Take one," he said, sharing with everyone. "It will take one to bribe the ferryman and cross over the Styx, and one to get back. Those of you not crossing shouldn't need the coin, but whatever you do, don't misplace it. The ferryman accepts no other currency. I will keep the ones for the return trip."

"So, you've been there before?" Miguel asked, pushing the coin deep down into his vest pocket.

Ezekiel shook his head. "Eli has."

Eli nodded. "Once we cross the water, there will be a single guarded iron gate. They will challenge us. Don't engage. They have no power to stop us. Once we're inside the gate, it will be clear where the soul runner is. Quick in and quick out. Do all of you hear me?"

When they all nodded, Eli turned to Ezekiel. "All I got. Just don't a want a mix-up and have someone get left behind."

"We got it," Miguel said. "Nobody relishes the thought of having to go back a second time."

"And Poe?" Matthew asked, making himself comfortable on one of the sidewalk benches. "When all the king's men have him back put together again, who ends his life and escorts him to wherever final judgment dictates? I wouldn't count on this Hamelin fellow. He seems incapable."

"And it wouldn't make sense," Miguel said, "to have him escort Poe right back to hell, if that's how it shakes out. Who's making the transport request to the Weigh Station? Eli? Ezekiel?"

"I will," Ezekiel said. His fear about Eli butting in again was unfounded, for Eli said nothing and seemed suddenly preoccupied with the Phoenix across the street. Ezekiel prayed Ryan Thomas realized the jeopardy he was in, and had gone home for the day, but he doubted it. Somehow, the man struck him as the live-free-or-die type. Eli could certainly accommodate the latter.

"Eli," Ezekiel, said, bumping Eli's shoulder. "Did you catch that? I'll contact the Station about picking up Poe."

Eli's intense concentration snapped, and his attention shifted to Ezekiel. "No, I'll do it. Who owns—?"

"No. Already settled," Ezekiel said. "I'll arrange it. Now, come on. We'll celebrate later." He nudged Eli in the direction of the nearest portal and sighed with relief when Eli reconnected with their mission and entered the portal first. Hopefully, when they were done, Eli would find bigger fish to fry than the bar owner, who was quietly and productively living out his second chance.

## Chapter Twenty-Six
# The Mighty Styx

Ezekiel had never been to Hades or even the River Styx, which one must cross to get there. Ancients whispered that the river could be found in the Aroania Mountains, in the Peloponnese in southern Greece. They also cautioned that its black, poisonous waters posed a deadly challenge that few would risk even if they found it. Of course, the route was known to working immortals, although none traversed it except runners ferrying souls to Hades, and a few other messengers and *attachés* sent there on special, confidential missions. Eli was the only angel Ezekiel knew who had ventured there, but Eli would speak little of it.

Ezekiel, Eli, Miguel, and Rhini stood at the boundary between the land of the living and the realm of the eternally damned and watched the dark, silent River Styx flow by. The boundary was as quiet as death itself. Whether or not the ancient Greeks believed the story of Achilles' heel or Alexander the Great's death by poison, Ezekiel knew that the river's power to mute, kill, or uphold a man to his sworn oath was the stuff of tall tales. Angels showed a healthy respect for evil, but they did not fear the waters of the Styx.

As they waited for Charon, the ferryman, to return and carry them across in his boat, the 12th Corps settled final mission logistics in hushed but self-confident tones. As long as they followed their plan, they would be fast, they would be efficient, they would be successful.

Charon soon appeared, crossing toward them as soundlessly as the Styx itself. He leaped up on the small wooden dock like a nimble old mountain goat and approached them carrying the long, gnarled staff that he used to propel his boat across the river. He wore a cloak of dark color—black or perhaps navy—and its large hood obscured his face. When he reached the end of the dock, he said nothing but stuck out a skeletal hand and wiggled his fingers. Ezekiel and Eli paid him while Rhini, Miguel, and Ephraim moved away and sat on a fallen log near the shore.

Charon led Ezekiel and Eli back to his boat and shoved off promptly. Right before they disappeared into the mist, Ezekiel looked into the eyes of the three companions left behind, and registered the concern he saw there. He felt the same but hoped he conveyed a sense of calm and strength. He and Eli were on a righteous quest, and they would not be denied.

The door to Hamelin's cell ground open. "Martin," Hamelin said, watching the former soul runner slip inside and close the door firmly behind him.

"I'll be quick," Martin said, hovering near the door. "You need to get out. *Now.* I don't know how much longer I can hold out on your, you know." He gestured to Hamelin's midsection.

"What have you told him?" Hamelin asked, eyes narrowing.

"Nothing, I swear—at least, nothing about that. But other things, things I'm not proud of … It's time to get you out of here, and I have a way." He held up a gold coin between two fingers. "Every time I need to collect a soul, I get two, to cross the Styx: one to leave and one to return." He dropped his voice to a whisper. "I found an extra one wedged in the bottom of ferryman's boat."

"And in return?"

"Put in a good word for me."

Hamelin looked at the sad, defeated man who had caused him so much grief in the Weigh Station—who would have sent him hurtling to the underworld just to ensure his own success—and all Hamelin felt was pity. The man was clearly delusional, but if he could facilitate Hamelin's escape, others could sort it all out later.

"You've received final judgment," Hamelin said. "What could I possibly say that would change that?"

"Just tell the truth. That I protected a runner—"

"Former soul runner."

"—and the soul of an unjudged mortal from the clutches of the underworld. How are my actions so different from what earned you clemency at the Weigh Station? You saved Curtis, and I'm saving you *and* him," he said, lifting his chin in defiance.

Hamelin cocked an eyebrow. This place was warping Martin's judgment. True, Martin had been selfless in preventing the suffering of an innocent fellow soul runner, but the other "good deed" had been a purely self-serving act to escape the eternal torment of hell.

"You're allowed to move about at will?" Hamelin asked.

Martin's gaze went south. "I'm still running souls from the Station to here. I have a pending assignment."

"I'm sorry," Hamelin said, averting his own eyes. "And no judgment on my part. I guess you probably don't have a choice, do you?"

"Let's just say it's the least of a few evils, and drop it, okay?"

"Sure." Sadness swept over Hamelin as he thought of another fallen soul runner coming to join Martin in this godforsaken place. He wondered whether he knew the runner. He pushed the thought and feeling aside. He couldn't control the fate of others, not even Martin. What would be, would be. "Then I will put my trust in you, Martin Cobb. Just tell me when I can go."

"*Now.* Before he comes back."

Hamelin swept a hand toward the door. "After you."

They crept from the room and bolted down the gangplank walkway. After that, the flight became a blur of flaming-hot and freezing-cold corridors—all filled with suffering that assaulted the ears, burned the nose, and sought to crush every good thought and hope Hamelin possessed. They crossed tenuous hanging bridges of plank and rope that swayed precariously hundreds of feet above pits of sulfurous, belching lava; squeezed through narrow, dank passageways that dripped putrid slime; and, most terrifying of all, sprinted across open caverns that offered no protection from inquisitive eyes. And everywhere, the stench of misery and death clung to them like a second skin. Martin threw an occasional look back to make sure Hamelin was following, but mostly each remained in his own private bubble.

Hamelin's heart momentarily sank when they approached an imposing set of steel security doors, but Martin suddenly veered left and entered a nearby tunnel instead. The warren of passageways continued. Hamelin closed the distance between himself and Martin, wondering all the while whether Martin could truly be acting on his own. Why so noble? If he couldn't be trusted on his best days in a wonderous place like the Weigh Station, how could Hamelin rely on him here, in the hideous depths of this Gehenna. Hell, it seemed, would amplify a person's bad qualities, not replace them with good ones. Perhaps Martin operated at the bubette's direction—one more machination of the demon's twisted mind—and they had no chance of crossing the Styx.

At last, one of the passageways began to climb, the air freshened, and the stifling heat of the passageway eased to something more bearable. They emerged from the warren of suffering and filth to find themselves at the mouth of a cave. Beyond it flowed a dark, wide, silent river. A high wrought-iron fence running along the shore appeared to be all that stood between them and the water. Hamelin had never been on this side of the Styx before. He always made his deliveries to the ferryman, who rowed them across the river in a small boat. Even now, Hamelin could see him lurking on the near shore, ready to take him across should he possess the required fee. Hamelin believed the fence to be more of a psychological barrier than anything else. Even if one could navigate the maze of tunnels, no one sentenced to hell would ever manage to get out merely by climbing a metal fence.

Some hundred feet beyond the cave rose black iron gates, manned by a pair of guards whose bodies confused the eyes as they shifted and blurred under black cloaks that hung to the tops of their heavy boots. As Martin and Hamelin drew near, they snapped to attention, barring egress through the gate with their long, sharp pikes. Hamelin saw no faces—only blackness beneath hoods pulled low and tight.

"Crossing," Martin said to the guards, and he waved a gold ferryman's coin at them. They bowed, pushed open the gates, and went back to whatever they were doing. Hamelin stepped through while Martin stood for a moment, deep in thought.

"I'm sorry to see it end like this," Hamelin said. "I never wanted to see you punished for our disagreements at the Weigh Station. I promised I'd put in a good word for you, and I'll keep that promise. I'll also keep you in my prayers, Martin. Take care."

Martin didn't respond but stood motionless, his face contorted in what Hamelin could only describe as pain. "Martin?"

"Take me with you," Martin whispered.

Hamelin heaved a painful sigh. Somewhere deep inside, he had expected a pathos-laced plea for rescue. "You know I can't. Soul runners—even former ones—do not reward or condemn. You're already serving your judgment. I am powerless."

Martin's eyes filled with tears. "Take me with you," he whispered again, his eyes darting toward the guards. "Take me back, or I'll tell the guards to detain you. Please don't force me to do that. You know I don't want that, but I will if I have to. Maybe when it's clear that I helped you and Mr. P ... Maybe there will be a change of heart and I'll receive the forgiveness I need to leave this place forever. Who says it can't happen? Please. Please don't leave me here."

Hamelin looked toward the boatman and, to his surprise, found that he was gone. Had they lost their chance to cross? "Where did Charon go?" he asked.

"To the other side for a pickup," Martin said. "Don't worry. When given coin, he is unable to deny passage. So, what's it to be, Hamelin?"

Outside hell's gate, Hamelin felt the calling of Poe's dark muse, and the writer's wounded soul in Nevis: their pleas to be reunited and to receive accounting for their earthly time. It gutted him. He could refuse Martin and wait to be rescued, in which case everyone would continue to suffer, or he could transport Martin across and restore Poe to wholeness in the land of the living. In the former scenario, he stood to be rewarded for his personal sacrifice, and disciplined for perpetuating Poe's mortal suffering. In the latter case, he would reap the terrible consequences of his gross violation of transportation directives, and in the end, God would certainly cast Martin back into the fiery pits anyway. Hamelin would get the shaft no matter what he decided. And truth be told, he would be getting his just deserts. In this whole sordid tale that had suddenly spun out of control, Poe was the only true victim. Hamelin looked at the desperation in Martin's eyes. Oh, how he wished he had never mulliganed Edgar Allan Poe! "Call the boatman," Hamelin said to him.

"Thank you—"

"Don't you dare," Hamelin said, stepping away from him. "You deserve whatever is meted out to you. Now, get that ferry back across the water before I change my mind."

Charon reappeared before Martin could comply, the boat gliding out of the mist as if pulled by some powerful unseen force. The ferryman was not alone. To his utter joy, Hamelin noted the two flyboys he ferried. When the boat grounded itself halfway onto the shore, Ezekiel and the other angel hopped out.

The guards, clearly unaccustomed to such a showing of angelic force, backed off and watched with some wringing of hands and looking to the boatman for assistance. Charon stayed in the boat, seemingly unperturbed by his latest passengers. After all, they had paid him in coin of the realm.

"You are safe?" Ezekiel said, coming straight to Hamelin.

Hamelin nodded.

"I won't ask how you managed to get yourself on this side of the gate," Eli said. "Suffice it to say, this makes things much easier, and we will talk later. No need to create an incident. Get in the boat *now*." He took Hamelin by the elbow and propelled him back toward the boat.

When Martin made a move to follow, Ezekiel whirled on him, the air around him shimmering with bright yellow light that radiated off him in great waves. The guards fell to their knees with fearful cries.

"Even here in this place, I will warn you only once, Martin Cobb. Stay back, or I will smite you."

Martin shrank back. "You can't kill a dead man, flyboy. Hamelin, you promised."

"What's going on?" Ezekiel asked as he and Eli turned their puzzled faces to Hamelin.

"Unfinished business," Hamelin said. He pulled loose from Eli and paced back to Martin.

"What would Jesus do?" Martin whispered.

"He would not have extorted me in the first place," Hamelin replied. "You aren't coming, Martin. You have been condemned and will serve where God has willed it. Now, if you fly—er, *gentlemen*— will get us out of here, I would be very much obliged."

"They've already reported your ill behavior," Martin said. "Bringing Poe's unjudged soul into Hades will damn you."

The confidence in Martin's voice worried Hamelin. "*I* didn't bring anything. You do recall your complicity in my forcible abduction?"

"And then there's you agreeing to bring me, one of the condemned, out with you. That will also make you burn."

Hamelin shook his head in disgust. "I leave that to God to understand." With that, he turned and walked away.

Ezekiel shoved Hamelin into the boat. Eli flashed a handful of coins at Charon, and the ferryman pushed off from the riverbank with surprising alacrity.

"Please," Martin shrieked, running toward them. "I have payment to cross. I just need protection."

With the angels now offshore, the guards seized Martin by the arms and dragged him back toward the dark gates.

"I'm allowed out," Martin screamed. "I have an assignment to transport someone. See? I bear the ferryman's coin," he said, showing them his gold.

As he struggled to free himself, he dropped the coin, and the guards trampled it underfoot. They tossed him back through the gate and pulled the gate shut with a clang, but Martin wasn't finished. He thrust both arms through the iron grillwork and screamed, "I haven't been completely honest with you."

It struck Hamelin as the truest words Martin had ever spoken. Martin Cobb was where he should be. He would never change.

"Hamelin, tell them I'm sorry. I didn't have a choice."

And as the boat shot across the water, Martin lobbed a final parting shot. The words fragmented and bounced as they hit the thickening mist that threatened to swallow up everything around it. "Beware the new mulligan! ... soul runner ... I was ... transport ... was you!"

Ezekiel turned to look at Hamelin. "Mulligans? What is he talking about?"

"Anything that might make us turn around," Hamelin said, praying to God that was the case. "As the Lord is my witness, I told them nothing about soul running or mulligans."

And then the mist on the water swallowed them. Hamelin clutched the boat's gunwales to maintain a sense of orientation in the impenetrable fog, and Martin's pleas were lost to the depths of hell.

# Chapter Twenty-Seven
## Descension Within the Ranks

As the ferry approached the opposite shore, sunlight sifted through the fog and began to burn it away. Hamelin didn't recognize the three angels waiting on the shore, their auras shining like silver beacons of hope. When Charon docked the boat, Hamelin hopped out, Martin's last words still echoing in his head. In a flash, the boat disappeared back into the river mist.

Eli hopped out right behind him. His wings were tucked in, but Hamelin could sense them momentarily bursting forth, along with the wrath that simmered beneath. Eli's eyes were burning, and the terrible sight of him triggered the old runner adage "A mad angel is a bad angel."

"What did you promise him?" Eli asked, his voice booming with anger well beyond anything Hamelin would define as merely *bad*.

Hamelin knew he should cast his gaze to the ground, express deference, and say he didn't promise anything, but being pushed around by a flyboy didn't sit well with his sense of dignity. Besides, until he knew what, exactly, Martin had been alluding to, the best defense was a good offense. He sidestepped the looming angel and bore down on Ezekiel. "How about you tell me what's going on here. I've been to hell and back—kidnapped, threatened, and blackmailed—and now I find out I've been convicted of some sort of trumped-up charges? How about a little filling in, *confessor?*"

"Whoa," Ezekiel said, raising his hands and taking a step backward. In the blink of an eye, the three new angels were at his back, staring Hamelin down. "Do you suppose everyone could cool it until we're sure we're all listening to the same Scripture?" Ezekiel's eyes flicked toward the mist, where the ferryman had just disappeared, then back to Eli and Hamelin. "And this is neither the time nor the place. I say we take it back to town and discuss."

Hamelin and Eli exchanged heated glances before nodding in agreement.

The trip back to Nevis was a silent one, and when they all settled on the sand at Brownie's Beach—the angels on one side and Hamelin facing them—the tension showed no sign of easing. The gentle wash of the bay on the shore accentuated the silence.

Ezekiel and Eli exchanged a few private words, and then Ezekiel took the lead, saying, "We have seen Poe. From his ramblings, we determined that you had descended into the darkness."

"How is he?" Hamelin asked. "He's still in Nevis? We should do this later. I need to see him."

"He was in dire straits," Ezekiel said. "But I have been advised that he is now much improved—as soon as you crossed the Styx, I think. And yes, the sooner things are put to rights, the better. Are we correct that you currently have his dark muse in your possession?"

Hamelin nodded. "I trapped it out on the town green, and when I went to return it to Bertland's box, I was lured away by a cryptic note from Martin. I didn't know it was his, but … As I dealt with him, the bubette surprised me from behind. The next thing I knew, I was in Hades."

"Any previous interactions with the demon?" Eli asked as he drew a picture in the sand with his finger. He was wound tighter than an eight-day clock.

"Yes," Hamelin said.

A murmur ran through the little knot of angels.

"He was the same bub who confronted Curtis Merriweather and me months ago here in Nevis. I frustrated his plan to drag Curtis to hell and have a little fun with him. I believe this latest clash was an attempt to even the score with me."

"And there was no provocation on your part?" Ezekiel asked.

"Absolutely none," Hamelin said, shaking his head. "During my incarceration, Bub visited me several times, trying to learn more about Weigh Station business. I told him nothing. During one of those visits, he brought Martin Cobb along with him."

"For the purpose of ...?" Ezekiel asked, crossing his arms and canting his head slightly.

"Leverage, I suppose. Cobb was being terribly mistreated. Bub probably thought I would give him the information he wanted, in to order to spare Cobb. He also threatened my friends here in Nevis."

"And you gave him ...?"

"Nothing. I gave him *noth-ing*." Hamelin sought support in the faces of the other angels. Four neutral expressions stared back at him. "Look," he said. "I can't emphasize enough that Cobb let me know, in subtle ways, that I shouldn't knuckle under. And in the end—at great personal risk, I might add—he sneaked in to see me, with an offer to help me escape. It was he who led me out of hell."

"To get himself out," Eli said, taking a moment from his sand picture to glare.

Hamelin nodded. "Yes, he had an ulterior motive in setting me free.

Regardless of motivation, though, here I am—*free*."

"Hmm," Eli said as he resumed his drawing. "I've never heard of a runner delivering souls *from* hell. Must have missed that memo."

"Enough," Ezekiel said.

Hamelin knew that if he locked eyes with Eli, he would want to pound the crap out of the smart-mouthed angel. He would come out on the short end, of course, but he'd get a few satisfying licks in before Eli got the best of him. But Hamelin listened to his better judgment. Eyes fastened on Ezekiel, he said, "Martin knew I was carrying Poe's muse. Any experienced soul runner would. He could have informed Bub and no doubt made things a lot easier for himself, but he knew that keeping silent was the honorable thing to do. He was fighting for his dignity. It wasn't until we arrived at the guardhouse that he grew desperate and demanded I take him across the Styx."

Eli stopped his digging. "You really think that was spur-of-the-moment?"

Hamelin took a moment to consider. "I wanted to believe that, yes. Regardless, I refused him. It wasn't until he threatened to tell Bub about Poe that I felt I had no choice. I had *no choice*, Eli."

Hamelin's gaze slid from Eli to Ezekiel. "What, exactly, is my standing in the community? If what I have done violates some directive, tell me quickly so we can put an end to all this. I've got to get back to town to make sure people are okay."

Ezekiel stood up, and the others followed suit. "I feel better after hearing the specifics, Hamelin. It appears you've been a victim of circumstance, and I don't know what else you could have done given those circumstances. You've successfully protected your charge, and I can find no deceit in anything you have related to us. It's upsetting that you have been left here on earth without protection of any sort while you're still carrying quite a bit of baggage from your previous position. You and I will need to talk privately about how best to address that problem." He turned to Eli. "Are you satisfied?"

Eli spent a moment taking Hamelin's measure. The eyes were still burning, but Hamelin wasn't sure whether they reflected anger, or the angel's earnest attempt to know what made him tick. Quick to anger, flyboys were not to be fooled with, but by the same token, they were also quick to move on. Finally, his expression softened and he said, "Let's get back to Poe and make him whole again."

Hamelin would have preferred to deal with Poe alone, but the flyboys had decided otherwise. His second choice would have been to have only Ezekiel tagging along, but apparently, for all Eli's facial expressions, Hamelin still wasn't in Eli's good graces. Eli announced that he would come, too. No one voiced an objection or, apparently, heard Hamelin's silent plea to back off.

The rest of the nanny-squad—that was how Hamelin thought of them now—agreed to amuse themselves on the town green, so at least they wouldn't inspire an impromptu Jesus-freaks' parade down Main Street. That was good. Hamelin had to live in the community long after the flyboys winged off to somewhere shinier.

Hamelin, Ezekiel, and Eli found Poe in the easy chair in his bedroom, halfway through a Paul Bunyanesque breakfast of scrambled eggs, bacon, fried potatoes, biscuits, fried apples, and coffee. As soon as Poe saw them, he put down his coffee mug and greeted them with a cocky smile. "About time," he said.

Vanessa took one look at Hamelin and his entourage and scooted out the door. In her haste, she slammed it behind her with a bang that rattled the still life hanging on the wall.

"You look better than last we saw you," Ezekiel said, approaching

Poe. "I'm Ezekiel, by the way. You were somewhat non compos mentis the first time we met. This is Eli and, of course, Mr. Russell."

Poe pointed a bony finger at Hamelin. "He stays. The rest of you can get out."

Ezekiel opened his mouth to speak, and Poe yelled, "Out, I say! Have you no manners?"

Hamelin looked at Ezekiel and Eli and tilted his head toward the stairs. "Do you really think I'm going to spirit him out the window? Stay at the top of the landing if you must."

Eli and Ezekiel exchanged a look and left without protest.

"Bite off more than you could chew, did you?" Poe said when they left. "I'm really not worth all this trouble."

"You know what's happened?" Hamelin said, pulling up the other chair.

"That part of me took a quick side trip to hell?" Poe turned to gaze out the window. The strong morning sun lit up his face in soft golden light. He closed his eyes and seemed to savor it. "How could one *not* know?"

"I am sorry. I didn't intend to take a side journey. But it's all good now. I've got your muse, and if you're ready, I can give it to you now and you can finish your writing."

Poe's eyes popped open. "Hell, no."

"Huh?"

"Who are those smug bastards out there, anyway? More troublemakers like you? Angels, maybe? Who needs 'em? You're all like vultures waiting for a meal. At least the ravens have the courtesy to wait outside on the rooftop across the street. What kind of life do you think I'm living? I spend all my waking hours in this pit. If those winged creatures out there have their way, that pendulum is going to come swinging down sooner rather than later. Then they'll have their way and me, too, by God."

Hamelin felt his eyes tearing up. Responsibility for Poe's misery weighed heavily on him. "Would you like me to preempt that? Because I can, but it's going to cost me."

"*Hmpf.* As it should. This is all your fault. Yes, preempt away. Send me off to greater glory right now." Poe walked over to his bed, carefully smoothed the sheet and quilt before tucking himself in, and bounced his head up and down on the pillow until he was positioned just right. "Proceed, Mr. Russell," he hissed.

Hamelin joined him at the bedside. As he looked at Poe, he saw not the great writer, but another of his transportees, Malcolm Derby. Derby, a grocer of simple means in the little soot-covered mill town of McKeesport, Pennsylvania, had been delighted to see Hamelin, and very receptive to closing out his life's account. But taking his spirit had been a mistake, just as this would be. Other than by suicide with all its horrid ramifications, no one got to call their own final hour. Hamelin had ignored his misgivings in the Derby debacle, but he wouldn't do so now. It wasn't Edgar's time, just as it hadn't been Malcolm's. Hamelin felt it in every fiber of his being.

He sat down on the edge of the bed but refrained from touching Poe. "You've misunderstood me, Edgar. I meant that we don't have to let those two angels out there decide. *We* can make the call."

Poe responded with a growl and turned on his side to face the wall.

"Just listen. I'm going to give you your muse back. I suspect that once you have that, you'll feel entirely different about finishing your grand opus. The juices will flow, and I won't be able to pull you away from that desk over there."

Poe responded by pulling the sheet over his head.

"Damn it, listen to me! You're Edgar Allan Poe, and I won't let you leave this earth cowering in a bed. Now, get out of there and take care of your business. I'll protect you from those SOB's until you finish it. Now. Get. Up!" Hamelin stood up and pulled Poe's covers from the bed, grabbed him by the shoulders, and yanked him upright.

Poe's eyes were wide, filled with both surprise and fear.

"I'm returning your muse," Hamelin said. "Close your eyes, and you won't feel a thing."

Poe complied, shuddered, and then opened them again just as the door burst open and both angels rushed in.

"Stay!" Hamelin said, holding up a palm at them. "It's done, and here is how it's going to go. Edgar Poe has his mojo back and a job to do. When he finishes that," he said, gesturing toward Poe's manuscript lying open on the desk, "I will transport him as required."

In two strides, Eli had Poe by the arm and yanked him to his feet. "You'll do it now," he thundered at Hamelin. "Stop playing games and sidestepping your responsibilities."

Hamelin stepped back out of arm's reach and folded his arms across his chest. Eli could be on him in a flash, but Hamelin had to send some body language of his own. "No," he said. "I'll do it *then*. I have already charged him as my transportee. You have no jurisdiction here, so let him go. Now, *flyboy!*"

Eli turned Poe loose and trained all his towering rage at Hamelin. Hamelin heard the fabric of Eli's shirt tearing as emerging angel wings threatened to shred it. "You can't do that. You're no longer a runner."

"Yes, apparently, I *am*, and apparently, I *can*," Hamelin said, momentarily engrossed in Eli's struggle to contain both his anger and his wings. "It seems, once a runner, always a runner. My little side trip to the dark place proved that. When this is all said and done, I will accept the consequences for my actions both past and present. Until then, stand down and don't interfere with Weigh Station business." He turned to Ezekiel and said, "I believe we need to have our *talk*, confessor. How about you get your pal here to cool off and tuck his wings back in while we go take a walk along the beach?"

Ezekiel put his hands on Eli's chest. "Please step away. We have too many other concerns—Bertland, for instance—without feuding amongst ourselves. Why don't you join the others and discuss what we're going to do about Pandora's unruly brood?"

Anger still flared in Eli's eyes, and for a moment, Hamelin thought a few feathers might fly. If he weren't already dancing precariously along the edge of the angel's flaming sword, he could go for that. These flyboys always acted as if butter wouldn't melt in their mouths. Truth be told, they had their dust-ups but generally kept them private and apologized quickly. How he wished his runner friend, Luke, could see this.

Eli didn't utter a sound, but some sort of silent communication passed between him and Ezekiel. After a moment or so, Eli nodded. His expression became neutral again, and he rolled one shoulder back, then the other—no doubt retracting his great whites.

"We can talk when the two of you are done," Eli said, and he walked away from the group without giving Hamelin so much as a *this isn't finished* look. The back of his polo shirt was shredded.

# Chapter Twenty-Eight
# Negotiating Barrels

Hamelin and Ezekiel cut through a series of alleyways to the beach. In Nevis's heyday in the early twentieth century, this area hummed with vacationers and a bustling commercial waterfront. Now, a century later, there were few hints at what used to be so grand. First, the fishing industry collapsed, and then, without any breakwaters to slow erosion, hundred-year storms and nor'easters shifted and swept away most of the beautiful sand that had once lined this section of shoreline. And finally, when the Chesapeake Bay Bridge connected the western and eastern shores of Maryland in the 1950s, beachgoers forsook bay beaches for those of the Atlantic. Nevis's glory days were over. The town trucked in a new layer of sand annually to cover the rocky patches and reclaim the beachfront. It felt soft as it shifted beneath Hamelin's feet. But this time next year, the reclamation process would start all over again.

As they passed through the alley next to Sharper's Florists, Hamelin was struck with guilt, and his eyes went south. It was in this very alley that he had once planned to remove Ryan Thomas's mulligan status. Even when he tried to do the right thing, he hurt people. Only their friendship had kept Hamelin from revoking the life card of the best friend he ever had.

It was still early in the day, and few people walked the beach. Confessor and confessant faced off a few hundred feet past Sharper's and the modern-day band shell. When they halted, there was no gazing out across the sparkling water, no tossing of driftwood or skipping of stones. Ezekiel turned toward Hamelin and squared his shoulders. His demeanor was calm, but he got right to it. Hamelin would not have expected anything less. It was so with most angels unless they were pushed to their absolute limit. Hotheaded Eli was the exception to that rule. Ezekiel surely felt put out finding himself in the middle of the Hamelin-Eli tug-of-war. That was okay. Hamelin was fed up with the lot of them. He could handle things alone from here on out.

"You know that Poe can't stay," Ezekiel said.

Hamelin nodded. "Not permanently. Even Edgar doesn't want that."

"Let's not play games, Mr. Russell. None of us have the authority to grant him more time. You need to transport him *immediately*. His continued existence on earth is causing nothing but problems."

"I think if you check the soul runners' transportation roster in Appendix C of the runners manual, "Pickups and Drop-offs," you'll find that Edgar has a pickup date of two weeks from today. Unless, of course, they've moved that roster since I've been away. But somehow, I doubt that. Pretty sure the Station has better things to do than play alphabet soup with the appendixes."

Ezekiel blew out a long, slow breath. "I understand you think you have us over a barrel—"

"I don't *think* that at all."

"Okay, so you have us over a barrel. But please understand, you're not hurting us. In two weeks, Mr. Poe will be exactly where he should be. He's not so much the concern. It's *you*. You just can't accept authority, and you're digging for yourself a spiritual hole so deep that you're eventually going to reach the other side, and it's going to be a whole lot hotter than Death Valley. Is that really what you want? You've gotten a bare taste of what hell is like, although I can assure you, that while the bubette's hands were tied this time, he'll have free rein over your misery if you're condemned."

Hamelin shook his head. "I made a pact with Edgar. The honorable thing to do is see it through."

Ezekiel threw his hands up. "It was an unholy pact, Russell!" You don't have ... have *never* had the authority to set dates."

"And neither do you."

Ezekiel turned away, and Hamelin could almost hear him counting to ten. Angels were interesting creatures when riled, and they could get quite exercised. Songs and stories mostly depicted them as gentle and mild, but they also could be terrifyingly powerful. Their saving grace was their intellect and their self-control—no sudden smiting out of spite or fear. They knew much and feared nothing. Ezekiel would make a good decision, but was it one Hamelin could live with? *Wise and patient Ezekiel, please don't go to the Weigh Station for another runner*, Hamelin silently prayed.

Ezekiel turned back around again as if nothing had ruffled his feathers. "You're right, Hamelin. Angels don't have that authority. In a fortnight, this will all be behind us, and as much as I'd like to let this slide, I can't. My role here is clear. They sent me to verify that you were succeeding where they placed you, and to offer any guidance should you need it. I'm sorry, Hamelin. Just as I have to report our rescue mission, I have to report your activities with Poe to the Weigh Station and my superiors—the *whole* story to everyone. If only you had followed your manual. If only you had transported him once you looked him up again. If only, if only ..."

"But I didn't *know* I could transport him," Hamelin said. "It wasn't until I caught his muse out on the green that I realized I still had the skill set."

"Then you should have called for someone to pick him up."

"And how was I to do that when they have essentially washed their hands of me? You've said that yourself."

"That still doesn't excuse you for not coming clean about mulliganizing Poe. In formal proceedings, you've been asked more than once whether there were any outstanding performance issues that needed addressing. And every time, you've lied about it."

Hamelin shook his head. "I didn't lie. Honestly, I had completely forgotten about Poe. Think about it. Why wouldn't I have transported him immediately when Martin started giving me a hard time at the Weigh Station last year? Before Martin completely went off the rails and was condemned? The answer is simple. Because my encounter with him was long ago. And also, I have attention deficient. It's all there in my personnel jacket."

Ezekiel gave him a sour look. "Rubbish! There is no sense of time for a soul runner. And I've heard all about your ADD."

Hamelin sighed theatrically. Ezekiel was a much harder sell than Elder Stephen. "You people are impossibly righteous."

Hamelin scanned the beach. Coming toward them were a man and a woman toting beach chairs, an umbrella, and two complaining children—an excellent audience for his purposes. He stretched his arms out from his sides and said to Ezekiel, "Judge me. Come on, look deep into my soul and tell me I'm lying." He closed his eyes.

"Cease this!" hissed Ezekiel. "We have witnesses!"

Hamelin kept his eyes closed and waited. And waited. Finally, he opened one eye and found Ezekiel staring thoughtfully at him.

"Put your arms down," Ezekiel said. "You know it's not my position to judge."

Hamelin closed his eye, squeezed both eyes tighter, and remained as he was. "Poppycock! Stop playing word games with me. It's called insight. Do it, *flyboy!*"

"Open your eyes!"

"No! Not until—"

"You're not lying."

Hamelin opened both eyes. "Told you." He took a moment to smile at the two children as they passed by giggling and pointing. "And in hindsight, Ezekiel, I admit I made a mistake mulliganizing Poe. I should have let him be. But as they say, if wishes were horses, beggars would ride. No," Hamelin said, shaking his head, "I exercised no deceit, only shoddy recordkeeping."

"Ha!" Ezekiel said, shaking his head. "Let's not take it that far. I sense you still have many secrets, Hamelin Russell, but right now I have my hands full with Pandora. Pray that you can resolve the other ones without making yourself a permanent fixture in Beelzebub country. Come on. The others are waiting." He took off toward the road and the florist shop.

"So we're going with the two weeks?" Hamelin called after him.

"No. The chips are going to lie where they fall, but I'll try to do a little damage control on your behalf."

"Generous," Hamelin said. "That does raise the question of what kind of damage you've already done that requires control. What did Martin mean when he said that I was the runner he was tasked with transporting to hell?"

Ezekiel made an abrupt U-turn and came back. "Yeah, speaking of, let's go back to several things Martin said. Starting with his admonition to watch mulligans. What is that all about?"

"I asked first," Hamelin said.

"There's been no talk of bringing you up on charges or having you receive final judgment."

Hamelin didn't expect an angel ever to have a tell, but there was something about Ezekiel's demeanor that wasn't selling what he was saying. "And?" Hamelin asked.

The answer came out in a rush. "I had to tell Stephen about your history with Poe."

"For heaven's sake," Hamelin said, pacing away.

"It couldn't be helped. But he acted as if he didn't want to touch the issue with a ten-foot pole. It's my higher command who doesn't know."

Hamelin brightened. "Really? Because if I had to do it over again, I certainly wouldn't." He raised his right hand and said, "And that's the gospel truth."

Ezekiel nodded and gave him a hint of a smile. "Then don't fret over it, Hamelin. Now back to my question. What did Martin mean about watching mulligans?"

Angels never lied, but their honeyed tongues could compete with the best. Hamelin bet he would have to fret about it later. "Yeah, the mulligan thing could be bad. Bub had a keen interest in knowing how I was able to transport Curtis Merriweather back to the Weigh Station when his soul went into free fall."

Fire leaped into Ezekiel's eyes.

"Now, you relax!" Hamelin quickly added. "I didn't tell him anything, but Martin did. The bubette tortured the information out of him. My guess is that Bub will try to create some mulligans of his own—all bad actors with rap sheets that would curl your wings."

Ezekiel's head tipped back as if he were beseeching the heavens. "Bertland and Bub—trouble on both fronts." The head came right back down again. "Unless … There's nothing else I should know, is there?"

Hamelin's gaze wandered to Sharper's Florists. Ryan Thomas was a model citizen, hurting no one. He turned his attention back to Ezekiel. "Nothing." There were some secrets he would never give up.

Ezekiel nodded. "Come, then. Let's rejoin the others. The quicker we nip this in the bud, the sooner we all rest easier."

"Still keeping with Poe's two-week time frame," Hamelin reminded him. "Poe's no longer an issue, right?"

"As long as you keep up your end of the bargain, apparently not, Hamelin. Right now I think we have much bigger problems to confront."

They found Ezekiel's cohort on the town green. Eli was leaning against a century-old oak, Rhini was nearby, petting one of the normally skittish gray squirrels, and the others were gathered in earnest discussion at one of the wooden benches that ringed the open space. Hamelin admired this idyllic spot straight out of a Norman Rockwell painting. Birds sang, the leaves of the giant oak stirred gently in the breeze; and strolling couples and tag-playing children and solitary dog-walkers crisscrossed the lush tree-lined space without giving the flyboys a second glance. If they only knew the problem at hand and the evil that walked among them.

The flyboys stopped everything and focused on Hamelin with cautious eyes. Eli pushed away from the tree, and Hamelin thought he looked considerably calmer, their earlier dust-up now in the past but by no means forgotten. Ezekiel launched right in without giving the hot head time to direct the conversation.

"Bertland and his boxes," Ezekiel said. "How do we shut that down?"

"We just go in and get them," Miguel said, getting up from the bench. "He's no match for us."

Ephraim and Matthew closed ranks with him, murmuring their assent. Most everyone at the Station had heard stories of the trio's exploits. Hamelin suspected the strong, steady hands of Ezekiel and Eli were often all that kept them from permanent suspension and perpetual rehabilitation. Hamelin found their devil-may-care attitude appealing. He might have been a much better angel than soul runner. Unfortunately, that would never be his lot.

"Yes," Eli said, nodding in agreement. "That would work here, but what about all the other little stashes of boxes that we *don't* know about?"

"Exactly," Ezekiel said. "What about the others? Thoughts, Rhini?"

She sent the squirrel off and got up from the ground with the grace of a ballerina. "The problem isn't just Bertland. It's all of Pandora's progeny. We need to destroy them all. And then we bring in enough senior soul runners to track down the muses. They should be able to do that. It's second nature. What do you think, Hamelin?"

It was the first time she had spoken directly to him. Hamelin looked at her, standing with the sun and shadows dappling her long hair, and saw not only a beautiful woman, but also the powerful avenging might of God. He found it hard to reconcile the two. He found her exciting, and despite his years of celibacy, feelings of desire began creeping out from somewhere deep inside. It would be counterproductive to become enchanted by her. He shifted his gaze to Ezekiel. "It would take many runners, but yes, it wouldn't be hard. Do we know how many grandchildren there are and where they work from? Maybe the rest of them are on the up-and-up."

"They all operate under agreement with some heavenly office," she said. "It shouldn't be too hard to figure out."

At that moment, a bright blue Frisbee came sailing into the midst of the group. Miguel snatched it mid flight and flipped it back out toward a teenage boy wearing a backward baseball cap. The boy yelled a *thanks, dude* and resumed playing ultimate Frisbee with two others.

When the boys had moved on, Eli said, "Rhini and I can seek out the information." He looked at her for affirmation, and she nodded. "And authorization to deal with them as appropriate."

"That leaves the Weigh Station," Ezekiel said. "I'll line up runners there … and a few other dangling issues." He shot Hamelin a glance but didn't elaborate.

"Which we still need to discuss," Eli said.

"And we will, but later," Ezekiel said. "You go take care of your end. I'll arrange a meeting with Elder Stephen, and everyone else see if you can discover where Bertland is holed up. Don't confront him; just keep an eye on him."

"And the third issue?" Rhini asked. "How should we address the bub?"

Ezekiel smiled. "Yes, *him*. You all know the issue, then?" he asked checking the faces of the others. "What do we do now that down under knows how to go about creating mulligans?"

"Go in and incinerate him in his own fire. Problem solved," Miguel said, snapping his fingers.

"We can't just Rambo our way in there," Rhini said. "That will create even more uproar. We need a well thought-out plan—and higher-level clearance."

"Yes," Ezekiel said, nodding. "But we must be fast about it, or we'll be cleaning up the mischief by an army of ex soul runners with allegiance to a very dark master, and a bone to pick with the Weigh Station and anyone who isn't damned."

When Rhini spoke again, her power radiated from an aura of bright orange that flickered in tips of golden hue. She was both magnificent and terrifying. "Eli and I will seek permission and guidance when we find out the location of the offspring."

"Settled, then," Miguel said. "You and Eli to Cloud One, Ezekiel at the Station, Mathew, Ephraim, and I hunting down Bertland. *Te veremos pronto.*"

"There's still one more issue," Eli said. He nodded at Hamelin. "What about him?"

"Don't worry about me," Hamelin answered. "I'll be with Poe."

Hamelin didn't wait for further discussion. He left them to their business. He had friends to check on, and a prima donna writer to hover over.

# Chapter Twenty-Nine
# Wives, Waifs, and Welfare Checks

Hamelin skidded to a halt between Bertie's and the Phoenix, conflicted about who to check on first. His head said right toward Bertie's, but his heart said the Phoenix, to his left. He let compassion win out and swung left. If something terrible had happened to his best friend or Marie, he would never forgive himself.

Dead ahead sat Ryan, at the bar, talking to Bennie. Relief swept over Hamelin as he took in the scrape on Ryan's face and the sling on his left arm. He had anticipated much worse. Their eyes met, and Hamelin burst into a smile.

Ryan slid off his stool. "Hamelin! Where in God's name have you been? I've had Maggie sitting here every night waiting for Edelin, and you scamper off like it's a holiday."

Hamelin's smile vanished. "And?"

"Nothing."

"Where's Marie?" he asked, eyes searching.

"At home in bed," Ryan said.

Hamelin's stomach lurched. "How bad? What can I do?"

"There's nothing anyone can do. It will just take time. That's just the way morning sickness works. Even the pictures on canned goods make her sick."

Hamelin crossed himself and said a silent prayer of thanks. "Pregnant? I am glad for you. Tell her to stay home."

"Yeah, well, as soon as I can get rid of the cast," he said, waving his arm around, "I'll be much more supportive. Now, tell me about Edgar."

"What happened to you?"

"It was the wildest thing. I accidently bumped shoulders with someone on the sidewalk, and the next thing I knew, I was riding the hood of a Toyota Corolla. Bystanders said I was lucky to have broken just my wrist."

"Who'd you bump?" Hamelin asked eyeing him cautiously.

Ryan shrugged. "Not a clue. It was a bump-and-run."

"Well, accidents do happen," Hamelin said. "One can never be too cautious these days. Tell Marie to stay at home until she delivers. Now, if you'll excuse me, I've got to check on Edgar."

Ryan put his hands on his hips and cocked his head at Hamelin. "Really?"

Hamelin rolled his eyes. "Although it isn't my first language, I speak English very well. Skip the histrionics, and say it straight."

"Edgar's fine, damn it. But you picked a fine time to leave me, Russell. Are those men coming in and out of Bertie's who I think they are? They've banned me and told me to stay over here. Kinda like the directive you just gave me about Marie. Don't think I didn't notice that. I'm okay with being bossed around by good people who know what's what, but I need to know who the good guys are."

Ryan clearly needed more information if he was to make safe choices. "Chips and salsa," Hamelin said to a passing waitress, and he sat down at a nearby table. "You may have five minutes of my full attention; then I really must cross the street. If you're guessing angels, then yes, they are exactly what you think they are. Good guys up until you cross them. If you're doing what they asked, you're gold."

"Where did they take you?"

"Oh, not them. It was someone else."

The waitress brought Hamelin his order, and he dug right in. "You really don't want to know, so don't pursue it. Just do what you're told, and things will be fine. For a change of pace, this doesn't involve you." He looked at Ryan's sling and considered saying something else, but shoved a chip in his mouth instead.

Ryan looked at his arm and then back at Hamelin again. "Oh, God. I knew having you hanging around would be a mistake. Someone tried to *bump me off*, didn't they? Do I need to go home and protect my wife?"

"Absolutely. Order some General Tso's chicken and work on some puzzles together. This storm will pass." Hamelin wolfed down several more chips.

"And Edgar—he's the cause of this. Will I see him again?"

"He's not the cause per se, but everything revolves around him. As soon as you let me go, he'll be in good hands. Don't give him a second thought. By the time you come out of your self-isolation, yes, he'll be gone. It's for the best and he's all for it."

"You'll transport him."

"Someone else. I'm no longer in the biz, remember?" Hamelin looked away. Yeah, so that was a little white fib, but if Ryan knew that Hamelin could still meddle as much as he did before, it would probably unbraid him. No use introducing more stress into the poor man's life. Hamelin pushed the half-eaten bowl of salsa away and wiped his fingers on his shirt. "Have you seen Bertland or Edelin?"

"Just Edelin. She crawled out my restroom window and I haven't seen her since. Should I call you, or do I avoid them, too?"

"Crawled out?" Hamelin repeated. "Well, I don't see how you could possibly run into them if you're at home where I told you to go. If, perchance, you should happen to run into them, don't go anywhere with either of them. I don't expect to see them hanging around, but these are desperate people who won't take no for an answer."

"*They* kidnapped you?"

"Bertland and someone else, if you must know." Hamelin lifted an order of french fries from the tray of a waitress as she walked by.

Ryan watched him shove three fries into his mouth. "Since when did you become a chowhound?"

"I've had a trying day," Hamelin said, his mouth full of fries.

"Well, don't do that again. It's bad for business. Now tell me who else?"

"Can I arrange to have meals sent over to Bertie's every day for the next couple of weeks?" Hamelin said, dousing his ill-gotten gain with ketchup. "He will be keeping his nose to the grindstone, and I could be in and out."

Ryan ground his teeth together. "Bertland and who else didn't feed you while they had you?"

"Never you mind. You can deliver the food? I can pay handsomely."

"You know it's not the money. It's fine as long as you don't bring back any more stray sheep. Any other crazy mull—"

"Shush! The answer is no, I won't. And stop asking about things you don't really need or want to know about." Hamelin shoved the remainder of his fries at him and stood up. "There is one other thing. If you should need them, all my important legal papers are in the top drawer of the desk in my den. If anything strange happens, everything I own goes to you."

A deep crease formed on Ryan's forehead, and he said, "Be serious. Who do you think is coming for you?"

"I am being serious. Let's see: infuriated angels, representatives of the Weigh Station, possibly a few hellizens." Hamelin checked off the parties with his fingers. "And not necessarily in that order. There. Now do you have enough information to calm your nightmares? As I said, go home to your wife. You waited long enough to find that woman. Why aren't you spending more time with her?"

Ryan snorted. "You know nothing about women or marriage."

"Who told you that?"

Ryan's eyes grew wide. "Wh-who ... You're *married*? They allow that at the Weigh Station?"

"Don't run off with anyone," Hamelin said, stabbing a finger at him. He extracted a particularly long French fry from the pile still on the plate and walked toward the bar. "Mr. Bertollini, I'm still waiting for that invitation to an open-mike night."

Bennie's face lit up like a Christmas tree, birthday candles, and sparklers on the Fourth of July. "You got it, Mr. Russell. I'll get back to you later this week. And thanks, man. The patrons will love it! Heck, *I'll* love it even more." He reached out to shake Hamelin's hand.

Hamelin gave him a sheepish look. "Sorry, man, tendinitis. Good thing I play left-handed." He gave Bennie a wink and left before Ryan could start up a conversation again.

Bertie's was open for business, but there were no patrons. There never seemed to be any customers. He wondered whether the shop had run in the black when Edelin owned it. Somehow, he doubted it. It didn't need to generate money; it just had to house Bertland's little trophies.

He was about to pull down the shade and lock the door when he heard what sounded like a landslide of stacked books, and the pounding of feet. As a flash of red darted past him, he reached out with cat-like reflexes, grabbed a handful of material, and slammed the wearer of the shirt up against the door.

The kid couldn't have been more than twelve years old—all pimples and braces and goggle-eyes. Hamelin could have kicked his caboose out the door, but of much more immediate concern was the small black box the boy clutched to his chest.

Hamelin yanked it out of his grasp. "Where were you going with this? Who sent you?"

The boy began to shake, and his eyes went wide. Hamelin looked out the door and saw another boy hiding behind the large mailbox on the far sidewalk, his hand clutching what looked like a plastic trash bag. As soon as Hamelin made him, the accomplice took off.

"Don't move," Hamelin said to his little thief. "I know where you live." He let go of him and took after the second.

The little imp was quick, but Hamelin quicker. "Drop the bag," Hamelin yelled as he closed the distance between them.

"*Unlock. Openclose!*" the urchin yelled. Then he dropped the bag and headed toward the town green, which was populated with enough people to make grabbing and interrogating a child somewhat awkward. Hamelin let him go.

Hamelin descended on the bag as if it were the last meal of a condemned man. It wasn't plastic at all, but heavy cloth that looked like burlap but felt much softer. He sensed its enchantment immediately. He opened it and found dark wispy tendrils rising and swirling from the three wooden boxes inside. Dark muses. He closed his eyes and willed them to enter within him, much as he had done with Poe's muse and with Curtis's soul before that. He had never transported more than one soul at once. Was it even possible?

All three muses obeyed at once, hitting him with enough force to drive him to his knees. His insides swirled, and the outside world pivoted as he fell prostrate on the sidewalk. He pulled the unopened fourth box tightly to his chest and blacked out.

# Chapter Thirty
# Mitigating Risk

Ezekiel made his way down the White Corridor, greeting each Weigh Station manager with a nod but no smile. He loved this place, the sense of order, the dedication. Any other time, he would tarry a while. But not today. They were already waiting for him. He passed several open doorways—all peaceful havens of pickle-finished white conference furniture and thick, white looped carpet—until he found the right one. The twelve elders were already seated: Stephen at the head of the table, Barnaby and Patrick at either elbow, and the rest packed on both sides of the long table. Ezekiel recognized a few faces. He asked everyone to excuse his lateness and took a seat opposite Stephen.

Stephen nodded to him and launched right into the gist of the matter before them. "We meet with a heavy heart, dear friends. I'm afraid the trust we placed on another has been violated. I think it's only fair that we hear firsthand what the true circumstances of this case are. For the sake of brevity and efficiency, we'll put pomp aside. Patrick here will record our minutes, and all else in the meeting will be governed by common courtesy and thoughtful discourse. Ezekiel," he said, "would you care to give us a rundown and your impressions?"

The dynamics in the room changed as eyes and bodies turned to Ezekiel. In their expressions, he read the deference always given for his kind, and grave concern. He started with a sedate, measured account of all that had occurred in Hamelin's sphere of influence: the mulliganizing of Edgar Allan Poe's soul, Bertland's responsibilities and activities, and Martin Cobb and the whole obscene business in hell. When he finished, there was not a sound, a shift, or a fidget in the room. Some sat with their eyes closed, others remained staring at him, but to a man, they were actively churning over his recitation.

Cranky, conservative Barnaby stirred first. "I see no problem," he said, breaking the silence. "Hamelin Russell sat here in this very room and assured us"—here he side-eyed Stephen—"that he had confessed all his violations committed as a soul runner. Stood at that very window over there, searched his black soul, and swore that we knew all his transgressions."

Ezekiel's gaze wandered to the window in question. The Station was full of these windows, all showing different outside views. This particular one gave a panoramic vista of eternal night. Broad sweeps of glittering stars and spinning galaxies filled the portal, and the gorgeous Engraved Hourglass Nebulae hung dead center. Even though Ezekiel could multitask and heard every word, he brought his eyes back to Barnaby. It would be rude to appear disinterested. Bless the man, how he rambled!

"The man lies at will, without fear of consequence," Barnaby continued. "He has violated policy, and he should get no more chances. Final judgment, I say." He slammed his ancient fist down on the table. It made a feeble thumping sound, but his point was clear.

"Yes, yes, Barnaby," Stephen said, while shaking his head. "The memories of our counseling session are fresh, but I would never recommend final judgment without giving someone a chance to rebut our accusations. Seeing as how Hamelin is not here now, we will not be going that route. At any rate, things are not as straightforward as they would seem. I've been upstairs—"

"*Up* up?" Patrick said.

"No, of course not," Stephen said. "It's not *that* important in the scheme of things. I spoke with Chief of Staff Salvio in Weigh Station Ops. Don't get me wrong. It's not that they are unconcerned. But it seems they're more inclined to approach this with a hands-off policy."

"They see redemption in the soul runner's actions," an elder in the middle of the group said.

"That's my take on it," Stephen said. "They seem quite impressed with Mr. Russell's sense of compassion."

To Barnaby's left, a silver-haired slip of a man with a long, crooked nose pushed up in his seat. His name was Timothy, and Ezekiel knew him only by face. "I'm with Barnaby. Mr. Russell does an adroit job of dancing along the edge. Unfortunately, he's elbowing everyone else off into the volcano as he goes."

Several others in the group agreed.

"The biggest hang-up," said someone across the table, "is, once a runner, always a runner. He can do whatever any other runner can do. One can't simply throw him back out into the world and permit him free use of his skills."

"True," Stephen said. "But he's under the impression he no longer has those skills."

"Then what is the risk assessment, and how do we mitigate risk?" asked the elder to Stephen's right. "What if he discovers he hasn't lost his touch?"

Seemingly content to let the conversation play out, Stephen sat in silence as comments and unanswered questions began ping-ponging back and forth across the table.

Timothy spoke again. "We could bring him back here and not give him anything to do—a sort of house arrest."

"The sorry soul," Barnaby muttered.

Stephen cut his eyes at him and cleared his throat. The kibbitzing ceased. Barnaby began examining his cuticles.

"Ezekiel," Stephen said. "We all value your opinion. Based on your experience with the situation, you may have the best discernment. What would you suggest our course of action be?"

Ezekiel, who had also been quietly observing the back-and-forth at the table, acknowledged Stephen's invitation with a smile. "As someone who's literally been to hell and back, I think Hamelin has been punished enough. I discern a deep remorse in him. He regrets getting involved with Poe, and he understands the hardship it has created for others. In all fairness to him, however, he was dumped back into a life without any kind of support system. Money, yes, but that's hardly adequate given all the threats and temptations lurking in the modern world. Hamelin is a complicated individual, and to make any sense out of what he did, you need to understanding what makes him tick. He's a frustrated artist—"

A *humpf* came from Barnaby's direction. Ezekiel gave him a hard stare, but the elder was wise enough to keep his eyes down.

Ezekiel continued. "He has one of the most artistic souls I've ever encountered. Frustrated in life by a domineering stepfather who robbed him of destiny as one of the greatest painters of the late Middle Ages— brilliant brushstrokes and a genius's eye. He has carried that need to be creative into the afterlife, and when given the chance, he bends over backward to help creative souls. I honestly believe he thought he was helping Poe by letting his soul skip into another body."

"But *why?*" Stephen asked.

"So Poe could finish his magnum opus—something Hamelin didn't have in his own life. It gives a vicarious sense of completion."

"And would Poe have?"

Ezekiel shrugged. "I can't answer that, but Hamelin was there, and he evidently thought so. 'A loss to the world, and the waste of a great gift from God.' That's how Hamelin put it. Hamelin is more than eager to transport Mr. Poe to the afterlife when he is finished. He asks for two weeks' time. That's all."

"So he directed you to advocate for him," Barnaby said.

"Sir," Ezekiel said, drawing himself up, "only God directs me."

"Yes, of course," Stephen said. "Barnaby's words were hastily chosen. I don't think he meant to sound as he did."

Stephen waited for Ezekiel to accept the explanation with a nod and continued. "So you're suggesting we let Mr. Poe finish this crowning achievement and then have Russell transport him. And that Russell will stand down until that time, and do it without further frustration at the agreed time?"

"That is correct."

Stephen placed a hand to his forehead and massaged above one eyebrow as he considered the suggestion. "But surely Mister Russell understands that there will be a full accounting at the end of all this?"

"Most assuredly," Ezekiel said, nodding. "He knows he erred."

"Then unless I hear any solid arguments against it, we'll follow Ezekiel's suggestion. Then Hamelin must report here, and I expect that you, Ezekiel, will provide escort." He surveyed the group. "Any nays?"

Ezekiel watched Barnaby, who had already made plain his opinion. But this time, the old curmudgeon kept his mouth shut—willing, no doubt, to let this skirmish go and then fight more vigorously when Hamelin was summoned to appear before them. This was but a single battle, after all, not the war.

"So be it," Stephen said. "That would bring us to our second piece of business: Bertland."

"Pardon me, Stephen," Ezekiel said, "But there is one more troubling issue: the unfortunate situation of Martin Cobb."

"Don't even suggest we go in and bring him out," Barnaby said.

"Oh, no, sir," Ezekiel said. "He's been judged, and there he'll stay. But as someone said earlier, once a runner always a runner. He is now transporting to Hades the souls of condemned soul runners."

"There's nothing we can do about that," Stephen said. "The function has been assigned to hell. It's codified under Section DSR Twenty-Two Forty. It's not unreasonable to assume they would use former Station runners."

"Yes, but a problem occurs when those runners disclose to their handlers how to create mulligans."

A collective gasp rose from the assemblage.

"That introduces a whole new problem." Ezekiel related Cobb's behavior at the River Styx, the last words Cobb hurled at them, and the likelihood that he had been pressured to reveal runner trade secrets regarding mulligans.

"*Beware the new mulligan?*" Stephen repeated. "Hell intends to create mulligans of its own?" He turned to Patrick. "Is this even possible?"

Patrick put down his pen. "Yes," he said. "Light runners, dark runners—all soul runners have the same skills. Only the populations they minister to are different. Provided a soul hasn't received final judgment, it can be mulliganized, and any runner can do it. Even light soul runners can be mulligans. They are peculiar in nature—no longer mortal, but existing in a suspended state, awaiting their final judgment. A soul transfer is quite possible." Patrick picked his pen back up and began to scribble again, then paused and added, "But all this takes practice, and we've prevented its use by putting the fear of damnation in every soul runner's head." There was an assurance in his voice that discouraged any further discussion on the matter.

"Dear God," Stephen said. His face went pale and the rest of the table erupted into a heated free-for-all.

Ezekiel stood up. "Silence!" he said, smacking the table with his palm. "Not all is lost. To resolve this, we need several things. First, dark runners should be banned entirely from transporting souls. Rescind DSR Twenty-Two Forty and task only light runners with transporting the souls of fallen runners to hell. Light runners already transport nonrunner souls there. It may be painful to drop a compatriot at the dark iron gate, but we must keep faith that they can do this. As long as demons are allowed to roam the earth, no dying mortal's soul is safe. Ban them to their godforsaken realm, to torment the earth no more."

Ezekiel looked around the room to see if he had them on board. They were pensive, but he saw no anger or disagreement in their faces. He continued. "Second, although I don't see why the loophole that allows creation of a mulligan and absorption of souls could ever have been allowed to occur, it's apparently there for all runners to use. That must be rectified immediately. Stop it immediately!" Ezekiel said, pounding his fist on the table.

"I'll leave it up to the policy people how to accomplish that," he continued, "but it must all start in motion here, with you. *Today.* Because if you content yourselves to sit on your hands and argue about it, hell will start churning out its own army of mulligan troublemakers—a terrible army that swears allegiance to evil and darkness." He sat down again.

"All who would vote nay?" Stephen asked, looking at his peers. No one objected. "As soon as we adjourn, then," he said, nodding.

Timothy raised a tentative hand. "Yes, Stephen, and if I may question something else. As I understand it, a mulligan is created at the point of death and before final judgment. But with the exception of a mulliganized soul runner, none of these other mulligans could create a mulligan. Is that correct? They are simply mortals. So while hell could create an army, they would all be human foot soldiers, so to speak."

Stephen nodded.

"Then who of our soul runners," Timothy asked, "is experienced enough to make mulligans, yet willing to flirt with damnation? Isn't that who will create hell's army?

Stephen and Barnaby exchanged glances.

"Mr. Russell—"

"Barnaby!"

"Don't beat around the bush, Stephen! Russell would be next," Barnaby said. "Isn't that rich? How do we know he hasn't already cut a deal with the devil? He gives them the how-to and they promise him a new life as a mulligan. He could be out there right now, selecting another body."

The suggestion hung out there a moment, and once again the room filled with a dozen voices talking at once.

"There is Martin Cobb," Ezekiel said. "But he aided Hamelin's escape. I doubt the devil will ever trust him enough to let him walk the earth again."

"Enough," Stephen said, tapping the table three times with his hand. "This is most inappropriate. No one sitting here should be bandying about names that only the Holy Father, in his most gracious mercy, has the right to judge. There will be no further discussion. I will take this upstairs." He turned to Barnaby, eyes blazing and said, "We will speak later."

Stephen looked at Patrick and said, "Begin a new page here, if you will." Then he turned his attention back to the group. "Because time is fleeting, let's move on to Bertland. Ezekiel and I have already discussed Pandora at some length. The agreement with her and her grandchildren is a given and out of our hands. That rests with your side of the house, Ezekiel. However, the custodial care of souls isn't. That's us, and we can't have her grandson Daimon Bertland harvesting and holding dark muses ... fragmenting souls ..." He looked at Ezekiel. "Do we even have a clear picture of how extensive and far-flung his little depositories are?"

Ezekiel shook his head.

"And I would assume we have no idea of the size of the collection, either?"

"None, sir."

"Hmm. No matter. All will have to go. There must be an immediate reunion of muses and souls, and then transportation. And this must never be allowed to happen again. Dear Father," Stephen said with a sigh. "I hate to even imagine what her other children are up to. Where is the oversight in all this?"

"Maintaining the agreement is not part of my duties," Ezekiel said, "but anecdotally, I see scant evidence of oversight by the Clouds. Bertland's collecting activities completely violate the rights of the individuals affected." He handed a scrolled paper to the elder on his right and gestured that it be passed around the table to Stephen. "I stopped at the Clouds before I came here. This document is from our chief of staff, authorizing the Station to conduct on-site reviews of all the activities of Pandora's grandchildren, take any and all action to collect and transport all overdue souls, and report back to Cloud One on what you have found. The Clouds don't have the authority to transport, but if needed, the Twelfth and others are at your disposal to facilitate this endeavor in any way needed."

Stephen unrolled the document and scanned it. Then he reached past Barnaby and passed it to Timothy, asking, "How difficult will it be to deploy a group of soul runners? How long?"

Timothy perused the scroll. "A little shuffling of assignments? Perhaps a little stretching of delivery retrieval times? Not long. It can be done. We'll have to pick up our pace a bit, but considering that it's the end of the performance cycle, I'm sure there are several runners who will be looking to pick up their game."

Tittering broke the solemnity of the gathering.

Stephen nodded, a slight grin on his face for the first time in the meeting. "We'll need a point guard on this, Timothy. Thoughts?"

"Francis?" Timothy offered.

"Luke."

All eyes turned to Patrick, who until now had offered no opinion. He raised his eyebrows, seemingly shocked at all the attention one word got him. "Luke," he repeated. "He's Hamelin Russell's best friend. It seems to me we will do best if we work together. Hamelin trusts Luke, and there won't be any cross-purposes. They'll communicate well, and it will save needless hassling. We should pick our battles."

"And you think Luke will be able to transport Hamelin to his destination should the need arise?"

Patrick considered it a moment. "Yes. He is obedient in all things."

"Luke it is," Stephen said. He turned to Ezekiel. "Do we know where Bertland is?"

"Eli and others were searching for him when I left them. If we can't find him, we'll use Hamelin to draw him out."

"And he's willing to do that?"

"Absolutely," Ezekiel said. "Hamelin is on board. He doesn't like the situation any more than the rest of us."

Ezekiel stood up. "I think we've covered everything. I need to return to Nevis. When will you send Luke?"

"He'll not be long behind you," Timothy said. "Let's finish this quickly so we can move on to more rewarding things."

"Amen," said Barnaby. "And please make it clear to Mr. Russell that as soon as that happens, he will be reporting to me."

Ezekiel took his leave and ducked out the first available portal. The Weigh Station's decisions were guidance, not orders. The Clouds issued his marching orders, and when he completed them, he would decide how to direct Hamelin. He wasn't convinced that justice would be served by dishing the wayward soul runner up with an apple in his mouth to an intractable elder who had already decided he belonged in hell. Now, if he could just keep the impulsive but honorable soul runner out of trouble long enough to make things work out for everybody …

# Chapter Thirty-One
# Boxing in the Boxer

Try as he might, Hamelin could not open his eyes, nor could he get up from the sidewalk. He remained with his face firmly planted in a spray of fine grit and a wad of Juicy Fruit chewing gum. A series of colorful flashes illuminated the darkness behind his eyes—all strobing to the beat of three different voices spouting narrative, dialogue, and maniacal laughter. He was a walking—er, resting—audio book.

"Quiet!" he yelled, although he wasn't quite sure whether he had actually voiced the command, or merely thought it. The response, however, was immediate silence. He had no idea whose dark muses he had just put in their places, but they at least had the capacity and good manners to take direction.

Hamelin started his self-inventory: heart fine, all ten toes wiggleable, hearing fine. Everything fine, fine, fine, fine, fine. He wasn't in some sort of free fall, just preoccupied and lost in his own subconscious. "Some assistance, please?" he yelled. His lips were sticking badly to the pavement, so that even if he had uttered that out loud, his enunciation was terrible.

And then he heard whispering. Not the diabolical planning and scheming of the dark literary muses within him, but the halting, shocked voices of preteen boys. Two of them. Why, the little thieving rapscallions had come back to gloat at his misfortune.

"*Mum mum mum mum,*" Hamelin said, trying to put the full weight of his powers behind the words.

There were giggles, a few snickers, and then "What?"

"*Mum mum mum mum,*" Hamelin repeated. For heaven's sake, even he couldn't understand that. Which was good because he was reorienting himself with reality, but horrible because this gibberish would get him nowhere.

And then the muses began again, grumbling about their lack of space and the bad lighting, and bemoaning the ensuing writer's block that was apparently beginning to run rampant.

"Shut up," Hamelin said.

More giggling. The toe of a shoe jiggled his side, then a hand closed around the box that he was still holding, and tugged.

Hamelin rolled over, pulling the box free. Before him stood the two boys he had confronted earlier. "Don't move!" he growled. The two remained rooted in place, demonstrating that Hamelin still had *it*. "Well, don't just stand there. Help me up!"

The boys scurried to either side of him, grabbed an arm and hoisted him to his feet. Then they backed off but didn't flee. Hamelin swayed a moment until he had his sea legs. Then he asked, "Did Mr. Bertland send you?"

They nodded in unison.

"How much did he pay you to steal the boxes?"

Boy number one, the taller of the two, pulled a hundred-dollar bill out of his jeans pocket and showed it off. The other just stood there nodding, his brown eyes wide with fear.

Hamelin pulled a C-note out of his own pocket and offered it to him. Boy number one stood frozen in place, his hundred-dollar bill flopping limply off his fingers.

Boy number two, shorter but thicker, snatched it up. "You want us to go steal from Mr. Bertland?"

Hamelin eyed him curiously. "And what might Mr. Bertland have that I would covet?" he asked, narrowing his eyes.

"B-b-boxes?"

"Yeah, boxes," the taller boy chimed in, securing Bertland's payment back in his pocket. He side-eyed his compatriot for moral support and then said," Just tell us how many you want. Then we can let bygones be bygones, right?"

*Bygones be bygones?* Where had Bertland found these promising little criminals? Hamelin reached in his pocket a second time and pulled out two twenties. It was all he had, but a quick trip to his bottomless Weigh Stationfed bank account could fix that. Where the Station got the dough was a mystery to him. He sometimes wondered if it was home-printed, but ultimately, as long as the ATM dispensed what he needed, the money's origin was immaterial.

He held up the additional money. "This if you tell me where Bertland is and where he keeps the boxes." Hamelin's vision began to dance, and there were large blank spots where the children should be. He grabbed onto the shorter boy for support. He could feel the little guy trembling. "Sorry, I'm still wobbly. How does that sound?"

"Too good," said the first. "You're not going to kill him, or anything, are you? Because we don't roll like that."

*Not yet, anyway.* "Of course not. You watch too much cable TV. All you have to do is let me put eyes on this guy, and then you guys and I are good. And then I want you two to run far away from Bertland and any of his associates, and don't go back. He's a bad sort, and you'll live to regret the moment you ever met him. You didn't sign anything, did you?"

The boys looked at each other and shook their heads.

"Good." Hamelin studied them further. Sure, they wanted the money, but they seemed too scared and too conflicted to take it. He shook the two bills. "Ten more seconds. Deal or not?"

"You got it, mister," said the first. "The sooner we go, the quicker we can leave this all behind." He reached out and eased the money out of Hamelin's grasp and took off running up the street, his friend close behind.

"Hey wait," Hamelin said, feeling a bit sluggish. "I'm hurt here."

The little thieves slowed to a fast walk. Hamelin had to pick up the pace, but it wasn't easy hauling a band of arguing, fractious authors with him. He staggered along behind and prayed no copper would arrest him for public intoxication. It would be a first for the teetotaling immortal. How did he get himself into these things? He had been but a flight of stairs away from checking on Edgar and maybe even sending him on his final journey. Why had karma turned against him?

The little delinquents held to their word. They took him straight to tree-lined, residential Eighth Street and pointed out a small 1940s beach bungalow with a white picket fence around the yard. He paid them the money he promised, and by the wide-eyed look still on their faces, Hamelin knew they wanted no further dealings with Bertland— or with him, either, for that matter. They raced off to grift someone new.

Bertland wasn't sitting on the porch steps waiting for him, but Hamelin knew he had holed himself up inside. He sensed the man's troubled, deceitful aura. Bertland was an abomination to all that Hamelin stood for. The muses had to be freed now, and Hamelin had to kick a little butt to ensure that Bertland didn't try to screw with him again.

Hamelin didn't fear Bertland, but he did have a problem. Unlike the flyboys, who could come and go at will, walk through walls, ascend mountains in the flash of a wish, and travel forward in time (though not back), Hamelin possessed no special abilities enabling him to storm Bertland's bastion and take the boxes he possessed. Whatever arrangement Pandora's crew had with the Weigh Station prevented Hamelin from outright claiming and transporting the partial souls as he would a regular soul. He could enter when invited but was helpless to initiate the action. Bertland would certainly never entertain the thought ... Or would he?

Hamelin hopped the broad front porch steps two at a time, grabbed the tarnished metal crab that served as a door knocker, and rapped twice. When no one answered, he knocked again.

The little curtain that covered one of the sidelights parted, and Bertland's face appeared. "What?" he said through the glass.

"Bertland. We need to talk."

The curtain fell back in place. "Go away!"

"Let me in," Hamelin said, rattling the doorknob. "Circumstances have changed. I can't keep Edgar safe any longer. I'd like to strike a new deal with you."

The response was total silence. Okay, it was a tough sell, but surely Bertland must know trouble was afoot. "Bertland?"

Finally, Bertland asked, "What kind of deal?"

"A face-to-face one. Let me in. You're making me feel like a beggar in the night."

"I don't care how you feel."

"I'm sure you don't care that I just spent an unlawful amount of time in hell, where I was forced to shield the object of your obsession from the devil's coven. But you should care about the response precipitated by that, and the chain reaction that's going to sweep you away like a spring flood." Hamelin pounded on the door again. "Open up!"

"No funny stuff?"

Whoa! Bertland's confidence and swagger gone? "No. And I expect reciprocity."

"All right." The lock clicked, and the door cracked open.

When Hamelin entered, Bertland had retreated to the fireplace on the far side of the living room. "We already have an agreement. When Edgar fails, the muse reverts to me."

Hamelin parked himself on the floral print sofa that looked as if it had been found in a 1970s dumpster dive. The rest of the scant furniture was a hodgepodge of boho meets cheap beach. "And I'm still good with that, but it seems that other forces—higher forces—are not. Ever deal with the flyboys?"

"I knew this was going to be a waste," Bertland said with a huff and a roll of his eyes. "I don't listen to music. Get to the point or leave."

Hamelin chuckled. "Not the Beach Boys. *Fly*boys."

Bertland's brows remained knitted.

"Angels?" Hamelin offered. Bertland's countenance darkened. "They're going to come for you. Just as you were telling me, I don't care how you feel, but I do care what happens to Edgar. My promise to him predates ours. And in recognition of that, I want to propose something. It will mainly benefit me, which makes sense because I currently have the upper hand, but it will also make your existence somewhat easier."

"Go on," Bertland said, eyeing him cautiously.

"Give me the dark-muse boxes you have here. I'll get them transported, and then maybe the boys will let you be. Of course, that would be predicated upon your promise to be more prompt in your deliveries from now on."

"I don't have any boxes here. With the exception of Poe, I am current in the transportation department." Bertland smiled. "He's always been a favorite of mine. Haven't you ever had one?"

Hamelin's lip curled in revulsion. "No. That is hideously self-centered."

"Sure you have. You're quite chummy with Poe." Bertland ran his hand along the fireplace mantel, flicking the dust from his fingers when he reached the end. "By the way, tell me what it is that makes him have that effect on people?"

A ripple of shame rolled over Hamelin. He was exactly that way with Edgar. The man could have been in eternal repose nearly two centuries before if Hamelin hadn't demanded something from him. He swung his feet off the couch and stood up. "Maybe. But the difference between you and me is that I am trying to make amends and send him on his way. You will never do that unless people make you. I'm appreciating something he could achieve, something people could enjoy. You just want to possess him because he's gifted, but without any intention of letting him *use* his gift. That's much worse."

Bertland shrugged. "Potato, potahto."

"You don't have time for this, Bertland. The flyboys are no doubt mobilizing their forces outside as we speak. When good people like me are forced to spend time in Hades—and one of their own, at that—do you really think the boys are going to cut you any slack? You're history, man. *Ancient* history. An anachronism. You really think it takes centuries to atone for Pandora's sin? Get real. You're dunzo."

Bertland took a quick look left, toward the hallway that probably led to the bedrooms. "You can have Poe and I'll keep the rest."

"No! The gig's up."

Suddenly, Bertland darted from the fireplace into the adjoining dining area and through an archway on the opposite side. Hamelin took off after him, but all he found through the archway was an empty kitchen and a locked back door. He made a quick sweep of the rest of the house—a tiny bathroom and three small bedrooms—and found them empty. Bertland had accessed a travel portal of his own making.

Hamelin returned to the living room. He wouldn't chase Bertland. The miscreant was other people's problem now. Instead, Hamelin followed his soul-runner instincts. He pulled down the retractable steps from the ceiling in the hallway and found two of Bertland's boxes nestled in an old coat in the attic. Bertland might be cutting his losses here in Nevis, but there was no question he had more dark muses hidden across the globe. Who could even begin to guess the number? But that was not Hamelin's concern, either. The Weigh Station would handle it.

He returned to the couch and arranged the boxes—the two new ones and the empties the kids had stolen—before him on the coffee table. Several minutes later, he had returned all the free muses to their appropriate boxes. Then he closed his eyes and cleared his mind of thought and clutter. When he felt himself floating and his aura strong and pulsing, he called softly, "Luke? If you can hear me, I have a transport issue … Luke?"

Not a ripple or undulation disturbed his ocean of silence. "Luke," he began again. "I ha—"

"I heard you the first time," Luke said. "This is most inappropriate. To whom may I direct your call?"

"No, Luke, wait! Don't blow me off. This is a legitimate request for assistance. I have souls that need transporting. Can you come get them?"

"What?"

"Souls. Come get them."

"I'm not following you. They should already be scheduled for pickup by another runner. But then, I don't need to tell you that. Give me the names and I'll give the transporter a heads-up."

"I don't know who they are, but they've already been picked up once—at least, most of them have," Hamelin said, shaking one of the boxes.

Luke let out a weary sigh. "Go through channels, Hamelin. I'm not touching that with an eighty-foot crucifix."

"No, wait! It's Pandora's group. You must have heard rumors about her offspring by now, that one of them has veered off script?"

"Silly rumors for the bored mind."

"Only they aren't. And look, I haven't got time here to explain it all. If you don't want to come get them yourself, use those IT skills you have and add them to somebody else's pickup schedule."

"Going now, Hamelin." The voice was clipped.

"Do it now and I'll let you have Edgar Allan Poe."

"Oh, I love him!" Luke gushed. And then "Nice try, bro. They transported him over a hundred years ago. What not-in-God's-name are you doing down there?"

"No-o-o. Actually, there's a long story connected to Poe, too. But now isn't the time. Let's just say he's alive and well, and he's finishing up the greatest—"

"I'm sorry," Luke said. "The number you have reached is no longer in service. Please try again."

"*Per l'amor del cielo*, Mr. Amergetti! Cease your nonsense and listen to me. This is no longer my responsibility. I'm going to leave these little wood boxes filled with partial souls unattended on the coffee table here, and whatever happens, *happens*. You know, as in 'excrement happens'? And then it's all on you. You're an official representative of the Weigh Station. If you want to ignore me, then go ahead. But you'd better decide what you'll say when they call you on the carpet for refusal to transport."

"What do you mean, *boxes?*"

Hamelin smirked. He could picture Luke with his eyes narrowed and his head cocked just so. Luke was hooked. Now all Hamelin had to do was reel him in. "There is an official deal with Pandora and her grandchildren. Pandora's grandson, Bertland, is responsible for collecting and removing from the world the dark muses of authors, but he's failing to turn them over to runners like he's supposed to. I have six of those muses right here."

Luke didn't respond. Maybe Hamelin had reeled too fast. "*Capisce?* I'll let you have them cheap if you take them today. And as soon as Edgar is done with his opus, you get the honors for him, too. I need an answer now, though, or I have to go to the next runner on my list. Do you really want to listen to someone else brag about transporting the great Edgar Allan Poe?"

"Pshaw! You don't have enough friends to make half a list."

"Charlotte might do it for me. I was the only friend she had when Martin started bullying her. Yeah, I'd bet my guitar that she'll jump at the chance. Thanks, Luke. I'll call her."

"Hold on."

A deep growl filled Hamelin's ears.

"I can never tell when you're fabricating," Luke said. "But Poe? Think of the conversations I could have."

"Oh, he's quite the conversationalist," Hamelin lied. "And I'm giving you the straight skinny on the boxes. You are just going to have to trust me. Have I ever led you astray before?"

"Buda in 1686; a quick pop in for a bite to eat in Tiananmen Square 1989; oh, and those two sisters in Metz back in 1539." Luke rattled them off without missing a beat. "I could go on *ad infinitum*."

"All ancient history. And no, Metz wasn't a mistake, just a little difficult. You know I take transportation seriously. What other motive would I have for contacting you? You have no conception of what it's like here or what I've been through—not the half of it."

"Not true, Hamelin. I was keeping pretty tight eyeballs on you until they caught me. You make it sound like I don't ... Oh, never mind."

"Care? I'm touched, dude, but as I said, no time. The flyboys will be here any minute, and then you won't get a crack at it."

"*Flyboys?* Really? If you had included that up front, I wouldn't have wasted all this time with you."

"Please?"

An uncomfortable silence hung in the air between them.

"Luke?"

"Hang, on," Luke said in a whisper. Or maybe his hand was covering his mouth. "Timothy is here to speak with me, and he looks like he won't be put off. I'll be there as soon as I'm finished with him. You know how I detest those posers."


When Ezekiel rejoined his friends in Nevis, it was as if the whole group had been transported lock, stock, and no alcohol from Cloud Twelve to the idyllic bayside town. They were tailgating it on Eighth Street, where Bertland was apparently hiding.

"Where?" Ezekiel asked, flipping the straw boater off Miguel's head in passing.

Eli lifted his chin toward the end of the block. "Third house from the end."

Ezekiel hopped up on the red Silverado's tailgate and crept behind the cab window next to Eli for a better look. "Thanks for clearing the Clouds authorization," he said. "The Station is sending another soul runner to assist Russell until Poe is finished. The new one will transport Poe, and Russell will be recalled to the Weigh Station."

Eli nodded. "Free reign to take care of the Pandora problem."

"Take 'em out?" Miguel asked, brushing off his hat and putting it back on.

"Whatever it takes," Ezekiel said. "If they come willing, there might be amends and new, stricter controls, but I'm more inclined to believe their cheek is so offensive, they'll be shut down permanently."

"I wonder where demigods go when that happens," Miguel mused.

"Wherever God wants them," Eli said. "Let's go before word leaks out."

"And where is Hamelin?" Ezekiel asked.

"AWOL," Eli said. "Not to be trusted. We shouldn't have let him wander off. Being here was more important than tracking him down. Rhini is at the bookstore with Poe. If Hamelin returns there, she'll read him the riot act."

They couldn't get a bead on exactly where in the house Bertland was. Given his odd immortal status, they chalked it up to some sort of natural cloaking surrounding the house. It wasn't a big problem, and it certainly wouldn't keep them out. They planned around it and divvied up the parts of the house: Miguel and Matthew on the back stoop, Ephraim out front, and Ezekiel and Eli inside.

Suddenly, Eli whipped around to look at the house again.

"Yeah," Ezekiel said, mirroring Eli's action. "What was that?"

"Showtime!" Eli said.

An instant later, Ezekiel and Eli stood in the center of the living room. Bertland was nowhere to be found, and Hamelin was on the couch with his feet up, watching *The Price Is Right*.

Hamelin clicked off the television. "You've missed him. He darted into the kitchen and then, *poof,* he was gone. Back to Grandmummy, I would suspect. He had two boxes hidden in the attic. They've already been transported to their proper final destination. Now, if you will excuse me, I must ensure that Edgar has his nose to the parchment." He hopped up and head for the door.

The flyboys took the news about Bertland surprisingly well. It was Hamelin who received the brunt of their displeasure. As he tried to glide past them, Eli blocked his path.

Hamelin halted, drew himself up, and looked the angel in the eye. "At your peril, flyboy. Not even you may interfere with a soul runner's obligations. Stand aside."

Eli stood firm as an aura of bright golden light began to form around him, brightening in increasing, blinding intensity. Hamelin likewise maintained his stance, projecting his own aura of scarlet. It throbbed and licked at the air as it crept precariously close to Eli's golden corona.

There they stood like two peacocks, their displays growing more intense with each passing second. The wood doorjamb gave a loud *crack,* and its white paint bubbled and began to run down the horizontal surface.

"Enough," Ezekiel said, passing a hand between their faces. It cut off their aggressive displays like shutting off the fuel to a blowtorch, and their auras simmered down to a dull glow.

"Frankly," Ezekiel said, "I find you both a bit childish. Eli, we have better things to do than preen and posture." He turned to Hamelin.

"The power surge we felt outside—it was a runner. Who transported?" Ezekiel asked.

"Luke," Hamelin said. "Here and back. No need to trust my word— you can check."

"No need," Ezekiel said. "Go handle Poe, the soul you are charged with. Rhini is there. Try not to rile her too much."

Eli stepped back and, Hamelin stepped quickly past and out the front door.

Hamelin shook the encounter off and hoofed it back to Bertie's. He really didn't have time for a pissing contest with a hotheaded messenger of God, but he'd never live it down if his coworkers at the Station should find out he backed down from an invitation to throw down with a flyboy. Never mind that Eli could slice and dice him. It was the principle of the thing.

# Chapter Thirty-Two
# New World Order

Bertland closed his eyes to the rush of air in his face. When he opened them again, he stood outside a sprawling villa built of finely cut pink stone. Its red tile roof glistened from an earlier rain, and the sweet smell of hyacinth wafted from the central courtyard. Through one of the villa's archways, he saw Pandora pacing and fretting. She wore a laurel wreath on her head, and her dark hair hung loosely to the shoulder of her chiton, whose blue silk rippled like water when she moved. She had an allure that enticed men to fight for her and over her. At the moment, she was not happy, and she would make sure no one else was, either. Bertland hesitated, debating whether to leave and muddle through on his own, or stay and beg for help. He started up the steps toward her.

"Grandmother," he called, trying to infuse the word with warmth. There was no loving bond between Pandora and him, or between Pandora and any other of her grandchildren—just blind obedience. Bertland doubted there was a single grandchild among the lot who hadn't, at some point, contemplated parricide. If he acted on his urge, he would join good company. His ancient Greek forebears had practically made an art of it. The only thing that stopped him was the realization that the power vacuum would soon be filled by a cousin he hated even more. So he suffered in silence and accepted his lot.

Pandora halted abruptly and lifted her dark-brown eyes to him, nailing him in place with a look that challenged his worthiness to enter under her roof.

"Where is Edelin Jacoby?" he asked, half expecting her to be waiting patiently at table for him.

Pandora waved toward one of the villa's great arched windows. "Feeding the birds."

Bertland's brows shot up. His grandmother was still very much old-school. "Birds?" he asked, not liking the sudden shine in Pandora's eyes. "Dear Zeus. Not next to Prometheus, I hope." He had brought Edelin here to teach her a lesson, not to have her liver pecked out. He rushed to the window as Pandora erupted into peals of laughter. Edelin was sitting among the day lilies with two of Bertland's sisters, feeding white geese from a bucket. Her shoulders drooped, and her head was down. He felt a wave of pity and vowed to take her back home—provided she promise never to cross him again.

He turned back to Pandora and uttered the words he had sworn would never cross his lips. "I need Daemopoulos." It was a preemptive action. While she bore no maternal feelings for her grandchildren, Daemopoulos had her respect, and she never failed to insert him into the life of every child who struggled or failed. At least now, Bertland thought, there would be no lecture on all his cousin's wondrous attributes.

"As I expected," she said, turning to sit on the dais behind her. "Daemopoulos is currently out cleaning up other messes. Tell me what you've failed to accomplish, but make it quick. I'm expecting someone."

Bertland heard footsteps, and the gossamer curtains to the right of the dais fluttered and were swept aside by the demon who had been present the last time Bertland was here. Without so much as a glance at Bertland, he asked Pandora, "Coming?"

"In a moment. I have business first."

"If you need assistance ..." the bubette said, ascending the platform. "It will cost you, of course."

"No."

The bubette took a place behind her. "Fine, but not too long. I, too, have appointments."

"Don't deal with him," Bertland said, coming closer. "He has no honor."

Pandora looked at the demon and laughed. "I'm not interested in honor right now."

Apparently unoffended, the bubette ignored Bertland completely and smiled at her. It was as fake as a bronze drachma.

"I don't understand why you are having problems," she said to Bertland. "You had clear instructions. Collect and deliver the muses according to a specific time frame."

"Not so different from you, Grandmother. You had but one prohibition: not to open the jar." He shrugged. "Sometimes we are weak. Mistakes happen."

He watched her eyes darken as fury twisted her face. "Daemopoulos doesn't make mistakes. I'll summon him, but you've left quite an *imbroglio*. And hiding here isn't going to make it all go away. You may have slipped the angels and the runner once, but they're still coming for you. What are you going to do?"

Bertland took a chair at a side table laden with food for a dozen people—heaping bowls of figs and grapes and oranges, platters of roasted game, salted fish, and a great wheel of yellow cheese. Bertland suddenly realized how famished he felt. He cut off a large slice of cheese and added it and ripe black olives to his plate. "I can't stand against that many. I'd be forced to give them what they want. I'm just letting you know so you can warn the rest of the family and give them a chance to transfer anyone or anything they are holding contrary to established agreements."

Pandora shook her head. "You're a covetous fool, Bertland. No one but you holds. Make a deal with them and cut our losses."

"What kind of deal?" he asked, watching the bubette massage his grandmother's shoulders.

Pandora shooed the devilish hands away and stood up. "We let them know we are sorry for our laxness and any misunderstanding we may have created. And we pledge a solemn vow not to do it again. The soul runner has been complicit in preventing Edgar Allan Poe's soul from being judged. If the Clouds and the Weigh Station are willing to bring him up on appropriate charges, I would consider that fair. And, of course, you'll be relieved of your duties. That will probably take care of things."

Bertland's plate hit the floor with a crash. "Me?" he asked. You're sacrificing *me*?"

"We're all sacrificing," she said, sweeping down the steps. "Now," she said to the bubette who still stood behind her chair, and she disappeared behind the curtain.

"Is this still, perchance Hamelin Russell?" the bubette asked.

Bertland nodded.

"So he wasn't returned to the Weigh Station," Bub said, more to himself than to anyone else.

"No, no, no! You don't see any punishment on their side, but when it comes to me ..." Bertland stopped as he noticed the bubette inching past the curtain. "Yes, he's still active. I had a dust-up with him right before I came here. He took two of the dark muses I was ready to transfer."

The bubette put a finger to his lips. "Give me ten minutes, and I'll help you with your problem." And with that, he followed Pandora out, turning to wink at Bertland before he, too, disappeared behind the curtain.

Pandora was a cheap whore, and the bubette a prowling opportunist. Soon, if not already, she would be with child, and Bertland shuddered at the thought of the demonic brood that their coupling might bring about. Disgusted, he took his leave and went off to negotiate before he wound up with a new dad who would insist on far worse things than a romp with his grandmother, and the seizure of Bertland's most precious possessions.

Pandora stood in the middle of her great hall, looking regal in her silk robe. God's messengers were coming, and she could not stop them. When they materialized before her eyes and approached without weapons or fanfare, she sensed their unassailable authority. They were lovely. And deadly.

"Bertland is not here," she said, coming forward to greet them. "But I can tell you where to find him."

The one with wheat-colored hair and noble carriage stepped forward and said, "I am Ezekiel, and we come on behalf of the Clouds. We know where he is. Where are your other grandchildren, and their children?"

She looked toward one of the archways and pictured her family quietly reading, enjoying music, and the children playing. She lifted her chin. Then she said a prayer of thanks to her Gods and drew upon the gift of Hermes. She looked at them again, tarrying on the face of each until she felt sure they saw her as the perfect woman: beautiful, caring, and unarmed. "But surely, you will not enter my house unbidden?"

Ezekiel smiled benevolently, but she sensed that he would not be swayed by anything she might do or say. He unrolled the scroll in his hand and offered it to her, but when she refused it, he walked over to a nearby column and plastered it against the stone.

"Inasmuch as we have uncovered grievous violations of your long-standing agreement with the Clouds, all authority vested in you to collect and transport dark muses, as well as all other activities associated with your atonement, shall cease immediately. All previous agreements are null and void. In addition, all individuals associated with said collection shall be transported immediately to their adjudged place of final repose. You may continue to reside here for the remainder of a mortal life, at which point you, too, will be judged and transported to your eternal rest. You shall conceive no more children. Let it be declared that henceforth, the house of Pandora will exist no more."

It was as if the angel had struck Pandora with his sword. Her hand when to her heart, and she whispered, "Conceive no more?"

"Absolutely not."

"Is that really necessary?" she asked, dabbing with the back of her hand at the tear trickling down her cheek. "I love my family. Bertland, and Bertland alone, is to blame. All the rest have toed the line. Punish him and leave the rest of us to carry on. I will personally guarantee that all the accords are followed. I have yet to atone for all the suffering I have caused the world."

Pandora stood silently as Ezekiel studied her up and down and then took in their surroundings, his gaze tarrying a moment on the banquet table heaped with the bounty of a generous earth. Then he looked her in the eye and said, "It is too late."

He stepped away from her. "Eli, Miguel, and Rhini," he said, pointing to where Pandora's brood resided. "Matthew, Ephraim, the rest."

Pandora wept freely now—no crocodile tears, these—her face buried in her arms as she sat alone at the table set for a dozen as the angels swept through her palace with a terrible vengeance. They overturned tables, pulled the torches from their wall sconces and set everything ablaze. And when nothing was left, they escorted Pandora out to the entrance of her now-ruined villa and left her there. They disappeared as quickly as they had arrived, taking her beautiful granddaughters, grandsons, and little ones with them.

Pandora sat on the bench outside the villa, her family gone and her residence a burnt-out shell. Smelling of smoke, she shook in fear, and her belly cramped as pillars crumbled, her wild birds cried, and steam rose from her once-glorious courtyard fountain. What mortal lifespan could one grant to someone who had already lived eons with all the blessings and entitlements of the gods? Did she even have time to begin anew?

When she was certain the angels would not be back, Pandora summoned her servant, Dania, who had been huddled behind a palm tree, watching her. "Help me to the guesthouse, Dania. It is time."

Dania offered her shoulder and helped Pandora, her chiton now wet and clinging to her swollen belly, to a bed.

When the pangs of childbirth passed, Pandora looked at her son and was content. "Get word to the bubette," she said. "He must take the child right away. Remind him that things will go well for both of us as long as he keeps his end of the bargain. Then you and I will leave this place. Nothing is over, and they will regret what they have done to me. Even if I do not live to see it, someday my son will avenge this humiliation."

# Chapter Thirty-Three
# Checkmate

Hamelin pushed through the doors of Barnacle Bertie's in a rush. Without a doubt, Bertland had taken refuge with Pandora. After the flyboys put his grandmother in her place, they would come to enforce the transport of Edgar. Hamelin also knew that Luke had not come to help him out of friendship or just to thumb his nose at the flyboys. Timothy's official orders had superseded that: coordinate transport of Bertland's trophy collection—including Edgar—and then Hamelin himself. Luke didn't volunteer that information but, when confronted, didn't deny it, either. Hamelin had elicited from his friend a promise of a brief respite so he could rectify his own situation. Hopefully, Edgar had used his last time on this earth wisely. At this point, transporting him was Hamelin's only opportunity to mollify the punishment Hamelin would receive for creating a mulligan in violation of Section 383 of the soul runners' manual and then lying about it when he had the opportunity to come clean. The sooner Edgar was in the afterlife, the sooner Hamelin could convince the powers that be that he had truly forgotten ever having made Edgar a mulligan. He had sought no personal gain in his dealings with Edgar, only a desire to leave the world a richer place. Surely, God didn't intend for creative gifts such as Edgar's to be squandered.

Hamelin took the steps two at a time, straight upstairs to Edgar's room, and found him slaving away at his desk. "How goes it, Edgar?"

Edgar kept his head down. "Leave. It's taken on a life of its own and I'm almost finished."

"Finished, you say?" Hamelin tried to look over the writer's shoulder and was promptly swatted away.

"Turnips and rutabagas, Russell! *Out* is what I say. I'm at the end, and I can't think with all your confound blathering. Out, out, *out!*"

Hamelin raised his hands in surrender. "If you're almost done, I'm not going to argue with success." He sat in the bedside chair and prayed that Edgar would be swift.

Bertland stood in the doorway of the UPS store and watched Hamelin approach Bertie's. The runner paused a moment on the sidewalk as if he were unsure whether to enter. Or maybe he sensed Bertland's presence. *This way. This way.* Bertland needed but a few minutes of Hamelin's time—a quick meeting of the minds, a swift pact, and a little resultant protection from the feathered bullies about to obliterate his crumbling once-peaceful world.

Bertland's world collapsed a bit more as Hamelin disappeared into the bookstore. Bertland would have to follow him. He had the means to go unnoticed, a natural ability to blend and move undetected through the mortal world. But if the Eighth Street fiasco was any indication, it apparently didn't work well with other immortals. And sending subliminal messages out to Hamelin was like blasting a Bertland homing signal. He drew his essence tightly around himself, quieted his aura, and slipped out the doorway. He didn't like entering a place where the angels might corner him, but desperation had made fools of greater men.

"You are a difficult man to find."

The voice was quiet, controlled, and decidedly trouble.

"You!" Bertland said, whirling around to find the object of his grandmother's sexual desire standing behind him. The demon was either a short hitter or a very selfish lover or, perhaps, both.

"I know how to get him out of there," Bub said. "Get even."

"We're way past getting even. And it's not about him. It's the others."

The bubette struck a match and lit a cigarette. Bertland watched him take a drag and blow out smoke in a long, satisfied *whoosh*. Bertland wondered whether it was all part of the postcoital glow, or merely a mind game of posing and impressing. Bub was a fool if he thought he could stand against an angelic host. For the briefest moment, Bertland fantasized someone kicking this slicky-boy's tuchus.

"Sure it is. If it weren't for him, you wouldn't be in this conundrum. You'd be in Amalfi, sipping nectar with your sister Nedra. What is it you want, Bertland?"

"Peaceful resolution—"

"Come on. *Really* want," Bub said, shaking his head. "Look at me, Pandora's grandson. What is it you truly want?"

Bertland felt his gaze drawn to the bubette's face. "I want Poe's muse back and to be left alone to do my job," he answered in a rush. "And maybe a nice villa in Amalfi. Is that too much to ask? Maybe with a small vineyard." Bertland grimaced. *Where had that come from?*

Bub laughed. It was low and seemed to echo in its own hollowness. "Of course not." He ground his smoke out under his shoe and brushed past Bertland with a sickly smile on his face. He smelled of rotting fish, and his touch burned the skin on Bertland's arm as they made contact. "Come on. To Bertie's, then. I've been dying to try this."

"No. Go on about your business, to grandmother, or wherever else you while away your idle hours. I don't need more trouble or failed parlor tricks."

Bub halted mid step but didn't turn around. "Perhaps you're right. No need to barge in there with an unpolished stunt." Bub turned around with eyes burning like the fires of hell.

Bertland raised his hands in protest. "I'm sorry. Please. Don't waste your time on someone as insignificant as me." He lowered his hands when he realized they were trembling. "Please."

"Very well. I'll take care of this for you, but you do realize it's going to cost you."

Bertland sighed in defeat. "Just get me out of this fix."

They made it no farther than the blue mailbox across the street from Bertie's when Hamelin came out the front door. At once, all three sets of eyes met.

"Unfinished business, Bertland?" Hamelin asked. "And you brought some muscle," he said, zeroing in on Bub. "How lovely—the notion, that is, not you, demon. Come to give it another shot? Just remember, you're on my turf now, bubby-boy."

"I'd really like to finish, if it's all right with you," Bertland said. "Let's wipe the slate clean. Give me the muse and I won't tell anyone what you've been doing with the souls that have been entrusted to you."

"They already know. Bounce *him*," Hamelin said, tipping his head toward the bubette, "and we can start a real dialogue. And make it snappy. The feathered horde is already making a sweep of your grandmother's abode. It's a sanctuary no more."

Bub laughed as he elbowed Bertland aside. "You should have taken your friend Martin with you. Do you want to know what happened after you deserted him? I started at his head and ..."

The bubette stopped as six stern-faced angels suddenly flanked

Hamelin. Their eyes blazed, and Bertland could hear the ruffling of feathers and the tearing of fabric as it lost the battle to contain their erupting wings. Tormenting soul runners might have little downside for the bubette, but surely, he must realize that tangling with even a single angel was insane.

"Go inside, Hamelin," Ezekiel said.

Hamelin stayed put. "No, Ezekiel. Actually, I'd like to see—"

"*Now!*"

Participants in the standoff began moving like chess pieces. Hamelin left the board completely, Bub took a step backward toward Bertland, and the angels all moved forward like pawns establishing a unified front.

"Fickle friend," Bertland whispered. "This was your idea."

Bub ignored the jab. He cocked his head sideways, and a crafty smile creased his face. "Yes, it was," he said. "But now it seems I have a better one. I am wanted elsewhere. Just as I am going to reap what I sowed, you should too." He nodded slightly to his opponents and vanished.

While the bubette had an immediate avenue of escape, Bertland couldn't say the same. What damage had the angels done to Pandora's carefully crafted empire? He closed his eyes and wished himself to the Amalfi coast, but when he opened them again, he was still in the same despicable Maryland backwater, with his persecutors standing before him.

The angel next to the one called Ezekiel—the one with a look of haughty disdain—chuckled. "Don't even think it," he said. "There is nowhere to run and hide now."

"Come with us willingly," Ezekiel said, taking a step closer. "It will go better for you that way."

"Stop!" Bertland said, pointing at him. "I'm protected by agreement—"

"Gone," said the haughty one, also stepping forward. "And your boxes, too."

Bertland looked each of them in the eyes. They were insufferable bullies with no respect for tradition or family. He turned and ran, but they descended on him like a plague of locusts, and he knew that his collecting days were over.

## Chapter Thirty-Four
# Ashes

Hamelin would have liked to see Bertland get his comeuppance, but he valued his friendship with Edgar more. He bounded into Edgar's room, to find him not at his desk, but combing his hair before the mirror over the dresser.

Edgar briefly met his eyes in the mirror before resuming his toilet. He pointed to his writing table with his free hand. "After all these years, there it is. The manuscript is finished, and I'm leaving this in your able hands. I wrote it for you, so you can decide what to do with it. If it sits on your bookshelf until it turns to dust, I won't be caring, now, will I?"

Hamelin shook his head. "No title?" he asked, seeing that the top page was blank.

Edgar rolled his eyes. "I've given that thing my all, and there's nothing left to give. Put any damn title you want on it. Now, do you have the authority to transport me, or have you so muddled up your life that you're a lost soul, too?"

Hamelin chuckled. "A soul is never lost as long as there is hope. I have the authority, although using it will not earn me any applause." He glanced out the window and saw no kerfuffle. He also perceived no movement and no discussion on the street. "They are all gone but will return quickly. If you would like me to be the one, we must do it now."

Edgar spread out his arms in a welcoming manner. "Well, then, sir, have at me."

"Would you like to know where we're going?"

"Not really. Should I lie down, close my eyes?" Edgar asked, blinking furiously.

"It's not necessary," Hamelin said quietly. "And it will be over in a twinkling. If you'd like, why don't you close your eyes and think of the sweetest experience you've ever had? Go out on a good note."

Edgar nodded. "I'm a curmudgeonly old man, Hamelin Russell."

"Yes."

"So if I haven't said it before, thank you. You're not such a bad fellow."

"The pleasure has been all mine."

Their eyes met one last time. Hamelin merely nodded and said, "Now, close your eyes."

Edgar complied and, in the blink of his eyes, left this world for the next.

Hamelin let the manuscript sit for a while—if Ezekiel came now, he would care nothing about Poe's work—and reminisced about his time with the writer. Luke had said he would give Hamelin time to clean up his affairs. It was a generous, inappropriate offer, but Luke had said he could finesse it. Hamelin smiled. Luke had always been the better at handling the politics of things. And what was ten minutes when it took Edgar 170 years to write his magnum opus?

Hamelin had been fond of Edgar in a way that he didn't often experience with his other charges, other than Ryan James, his wife, Marie, and a very few others over the centuries, but most of those were gone now. Virtually everyone from his old life was gone. Oh, how he missed the comfort of the Weigh Station and others of his kind.

Hamelin sat down in Edgar's workspace and picked up the pile of pages on the corner of the desk. They were neatly stacked—edges perfectly aligned as if Edgar had taken some pains getting them straight. What a change from his little bay cottage stuffed to the rafters with needless flotsam and jetsam. He turned over the cover page, set it aside, and began reading. He didn't stop until he had placed the very last page on the overturned stack.

"Oh, Edgar," he murmured, and pushed back from the desk, thinking about all the hoops he had jumped through to get to this point. And then he went at it a second time. He flipped the story back to the first page and started reading again—a story of light and angels and things that watch over you at night. The words mesmerized him, and the story enchanted him with a mood that few mortals could express in words. Edgar's little side trip to the darkest, most tormenting place a mortal could fall into had changed something. Clearly, he had discovered his own heaven on earth. And yet, beautifully, Hamelin was equally sure that it could never compete with the wonders of the new place he now called home.

When he had reviewed the manuscript a second time and it was permanently emblazoned in his memory, Hamelin neatened the stack once more and shoved it aside. As he mulled over what he read, his eyes followed two children racing down the sidewalk ahead of their parents—laughing and pulling on each other to gain an advantage. Their innocence warmed his heart. In spite of all he had been through lately, goodness still abounded in the world. And despite his dark muse, Poe had lightness within him that assured he would spend forever in a land of milk and honey.

When his epic journey with Poe began, Hamelin had saved him so he could complete the great masterpiece he had already begun. But this story was in a completely different vein. It was enlightened; it was brilliant. But if Hamelin published the story, no one would ever believe it came from Poe.

He stayed lost in thought a moment more, then nodded to himself, his decision made. He swept the manuscript into the trash can and set it ablaze with a whispered word. Better for Edgar Allan Poe to at last rest in peace than to invite endless speculation.

When the paper had been reduced to ash, he set out for the Phoenix across the street. He needed a few sweet words and a cold glass of mineral water, served with care and friendship. Luke would track him down soon enough. Luke was nothing if not punctual. When the Weigh Station understood why he had done what he did—and why wouldn't they?—they would send him back here, and he would need a change of pace. Only not the shore this time. Poe had soured him on that. Perhaps the Allegheny Mountains and the Appalachian Trail. An old acquaintance lived there …

Thank you for reading Edgar and the Flyboys. I hope you enjoyed the story. If you have a moment, please consider leaving a quick review on the book's Amazon page.

If you would like to read more about Hamelin Russell, check out Bayside Blues, and Spirit of the Law.

Would you like to know when I release new books?
Here are three ways:

Join my mailing list at:
https://www.louisegordaybooks.com/contact

Like me on Facebook:
https://www.facebook.com/louisegordayauthor

Follow me on Twitter:
https://twitter.com/LouiseGorday

Made in the USA
Middletown, DE
24 August 2021